THE MASTER OF TIDES

Cover artwork, *Cora and the Sand Coin,* by Jamin Still
Edited by Lisa McCoy

ISBN: 978-1-962651-00-4

Library of Congress Control Number: 2023918542

This edition published by Renewed Books
Cedar Rapids, Iowa

Also available in ebook format
First Edition

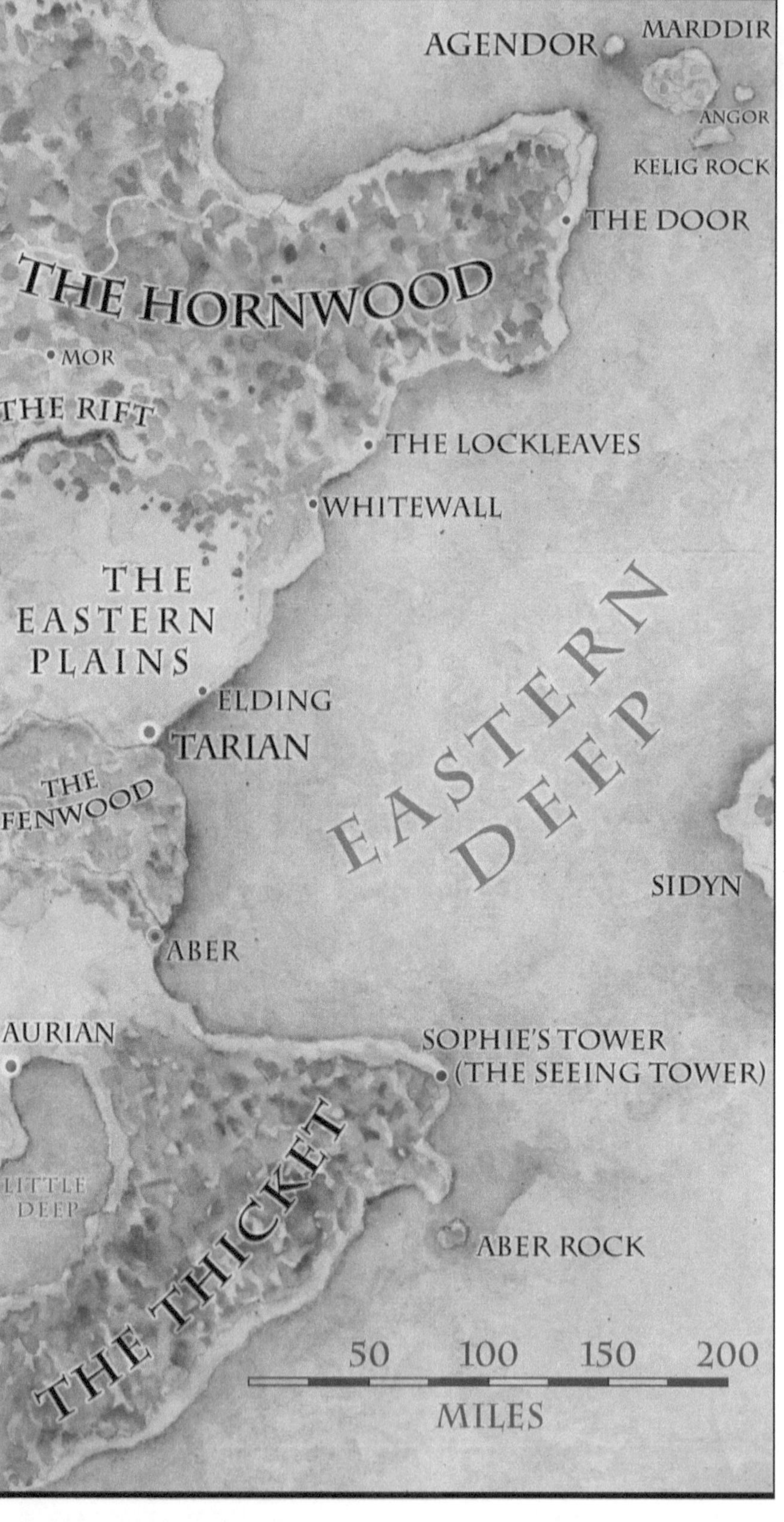

AGENDOR
MARDDIR
ANGOR
KELIG ROCK
THE DOOR
THE HORNWOOD
MOR
THE RIFT
THE LOCKLEAVES
WHITEWALL
THE EASTERN PLAINS
ELDING
TARIAN
THE FENWOOD
EASTERN DEEP
SIDYN
ABER
AURIAN
SOPHIE'S TOWER
(THE SEEING TOWER)
LITTLE DEEP
THE THICKET
ABER ROCK
50 100 150 200
MILES

TALES OF HIBARIA

THE MASTER OF TIDES

BOOK ONE

Jamin Still

RENEWED BOOKS

I

THE MASTER OF TIDES

THE MASTER OF TIDES STOOD on the balcony of his tower that rose from beside the wharf of Tarian. He looked out over the Eastern Deep. In the darkness of night, the sea was sparkling and silent. Calm. So different than what it would be in just a few weeks with the coming of the Turn. The Master sighed. He never looked forward to the Turn. It was beyond exhausting and he was more tired than he had ever been.

A sickle moon rose in the east. It slowly cut through the darkness as it began its march across the sky.

The evening breeze felt cool against the Master's skin. He inhaled deeply. The smells of salt and sand and fish were mingled with the sharp odors of tar and tanneries. These were the smells of the city of Tarian. *His* city.

Far below, Tarian's lights twinkled like fireflies. So many lights. They represented, at least in the Master's mind, the tens of thousands of people that called Tarian home. So many people. *His* people.

There had been many nights such as this. The Master had watched and guarded Tarian for a long time. On countless occasions he had summoned the tides to dash enemy ships against the rocks, to drown those who would attack this place. His was a merciless defense, and calamitous for any who might think to test it. Many had. None had succeeded.

But it was not only marauders that he contended against. It was the sea itself. For three days at the beginning of autumn, at the Turn, the waters of the Deep would advance against Tarian as though a mind controlled them. They advanced and would drown the city were it not for the Master's defense. But during every Turn, the Master stood in his tower and grappled with the tidal surge that strove to destroy the city. During every Turn, he kept the sea at bay until the surge relented and the waters receded.

Under his watch Tarian could not be safer.

The Master of Tides ran his hands over the granite rail of the balcony and found the grooves that fit his fingers. They were grooves worn smooth by days and months and years of gripping the rail as he stood watch.

He had, of course, not always been the Master of Tides. He let his mind drift back. So far back. He could still remember, though dimly, the time before he had been given his power. What had he been? Governor? No, that wasn't it. He had been the leader of Tarian, though, whatever his title, directing the Alliance's Eastern Army against Augrind, the feared Emperor of the Night, in what was later to become known as the Great War. The fight had not been going well. The Western Army had been all but obliterated, and Arosil sacked. Labryn Waite was about to fall. Hope was beginning to wane.

And then they had come.

While the Master had forgotten many details of his past, his memory of the appearance of the Sky Lords was as clear as crystal, sharp as a blade. The three leaders of the Alliance had been gathered in Tarian, in the Grand Council Room. It was late afternoon, and sunlight poured in through the high western windows, making the marble floor glow golden. And then, without preamble or introduction, the doors had opened silently and the twelve Constellations had walked in, noble and shimmering and huge, radiating a wild, untamed power. They had smelled, unmistakably, like stars.

The Constellations had come bearing gifts for the three leaders.

The Master looked down at the Sand Coin that hung around his neck. After a moment, he brushed its gritty, white surface with his finger. The unassuming object contained within it the power of the stars. The Sky Lords had given it to him all those years ago, and nothing had been the same since.

He remembered the rush, the desperation, to understand this new power. To harness it. To use it to turn the tide of the war. Understanding had come slowly. But it *had* come, and not a moment too soon. The Master recalled the attack on Aber, the hundreds of ships that Augrind had marshalled to destroy the city, and how, as the ships had entered Aber's long, narrow harbor, the Master of Tides had become the Master of Tides. He had, in that moment, finally understood the power of the Sand Coin. And with that understanding he had summoned the tides, spoken to them, commanded them. And they had completely and utterly destroyed Augrind's fleet.

The course of the war had turned soon after. The Master's new power, combined with the power now wielded by the leaders of Aurian and Labryn Waite, was enough to assure victory for the Alliance. But Augrind did not go quietly, of course. He fought tooth and nail, destroying much even as he was pushed back. It was then, in desperation, that he had created his shifters, his assassins, and he had sent them in waves. The Master still bore the scars on his shoulder where one of these shifters—one moment a harmless girl, the next a ferocious crag bear— had sunk its teeth into him. It would have killed him had it not been for . . . The Master shook his head. He could not remember.

What he *could* remember was that, in the end, Augrind had been cornered and caught. He had been chained in ice and sleep and imprisoned at the bottom of the Rift, where the Sky Lords had taken it upon themselves to guard him. The armies of the Alliance had hunted down the remainder of Augrind's forces and stamped them out.

The Master had been grateful for the gift from the Sky Lords, unspeakably grateful. The Sand Coin had been the key to changing the outcome of the war in the East. It had saved countless lives. But when the Great War was done, the power of the Sand Coin did not go away. The Constellations did not reappear to claim it. It was still his.

But the Master had not fully understood it for what it was. A gift, yes, but soon he learned it was also a burden beyond imagining.

With the power of the Sand Coin had come the ability to guard Tarian in a way he had been unable to before. At first, the Master had rejoiced. This was the city of his birth, after all, and the place that had formed him, shaped him, made him. He loved its people—their tenacity, their creativity, their optimism. He loved the curves of Tarian's hills, the sounds of its bells, its beautiful buildings, and how Tarian itself almost seemed alive at times. And so it was with joy that the Master had stepped into his expanded power. He stood watch over his city, and Tarian prospered.

Before long, however, the Master noticed that it was increasingly difficult to leave his tower. He was compelled to be here, to stand guard, to watch. The Sand Coin, he came to understand, had become rooted to this place and because the Sand Coin was his, he was rooted here too. And when, over time, the Master realized the Sand Coin also conferred to its owner unnaturally long life . . . A gift, yes, but also a burden almost too heavy to bear.

The Master shook himself out of his reverie and looked up at the moon. The thin crescent was among the stars, among the Constellations. Even now, after all this time, he bore them no ill will. He was not angry about his burden. Their gift had saved Hibaria, and while the Sand Coin had bound him to this place for so many years, who was he to question them? No, he wasn't angry. Just . . . tired.

The shapes of the Bear and the Dragon and the Badger wheeled across the eastern sky. To the north, the Owl and the Wolf and the recently returned Sea Serpent shone, their bright stars twinkling in the inky blackness. To the west were the Raven and the Fish and the Fox. And to the south, the dim, barely discernible stars of the Mountain Cat, the Rabbit, and the Firefly faintly glistened. For it was summer, and these three were guarding Augrind's prison for the season. Soon, in but a matter of weeks, with the coming of autumn, they would emerge from the Rift, to once again take their place in the skies, and the Raven and the Fish and the Fox would descend into the depths. How many times had the Master watched the changing of the guard? Too many times to count, too many times to remember.

As the moon reached its zenith, the Master felt a sudden change within his breast. His power had always ebbed and flowed with the tides, but in the past few years it had moved within him in a different way, in a final way, like a cup being slowly emptied. And now . . . it was as though the last few drops were finally being poured out. He had known his end was coming, but the Master had thought it was still some time off. He felt a draining away, an emptying, a departing. He had known, but he had not prepared. The Master's knees buckled.

Turning, the Master staggered back into the tower. He managed to take a seat at his table. He carefully removed the Sand Coin from around his neck. He sat for a long time, his breaths shallow as the shadows cast by the moonlight slowly moved across the floor. And then, as the clock tower in the Great Square, far below, struck two, he reached for a box the color of driftwood, opened it, and placed the Sand Coin inside. Then he took up a quill and began to write.

Not long before dawn, he finished. He lay down the quill and let out a long sigh, relief mingled with no small amount of weariness. He tried to rise, but his strength was gone. The Master of Tides slid from his chair, collapsed upon the floor, and breathed his last.

For the first time in seven hundred and fourteen years, the city of Tarian was without her defender.

CHAPTER ONE

THE PIKE BURNS

THE SEA ROARED AND HEAVED, *rising up into the raging gale, and then dropping away again with terrifying speed. The valley carved out of the water looked like a mouth opening to swallow the world. Cora screamed as the boat plunged down into the yawning abyss.*

"Hold on!" shouted her father. He gripped the tiller and braced his feet against the ribs of the boat. Cora's mother clung to Hildi, and Hildi held onto Cora. Her father shouted something else, but his words were torn away by the howling wind. Salt spray stung Cora's eyes and filled her mouth, and the lashing rain felt like knives against her skin. And then the boat turned, twisted, and Cora was ripped from her sister's grasp. She flailed, desperately, as she spun through the air. Her fingers brushed Hildi's outstretched hand, but then her shoulder slammed into the gunwale and she caromed away. Cora struck the water, and as the icy sea closed over her, the howling of the storm suddenly ceased.

The currents tore at her with the strength of giants, pulling her away from the boat. She could feel the pulsing of the deep, the heartbeat of the water as it wove itself around her mind, pulling her deeper into the darkness. Her lungs screamed for air. She willed herself to not inhale, but she couldn't hold her breath any longer. She gasped, and the briny sea rushed in and filled her lungs.

Cora awoke with a start, panting and bathed in sweat. The sky through the window was dark and studded with stars. She lay beneath her thin blanket and tried to slow her breathing, tried to slow the racing of her mind.

The Storm had been seven years ago, and in those seven years, Cora had managed to *not* dream about it. She had done everything in her power to forget the details of what had happened that day, and she had largely succeeded. Until now. Somehow, within the last few days, the memories had bubbled up and seeped into her dreams, and Cora had found herself once again surrounded by the waves of black water, tall as mountains. For the past three nights, these nightmares had gripped her. She had seen her family again, lost them again. The memories of the Storm, so long buried, were now fresh as an open wound and Cora could hardly bear it.

There *had* to be a way to forget again.

She rolled out of her narrow bed and rubbed her eyes. She stumbled to the window and looked out over Tarian. The city was wrapped in silence, peaceful in its slumber. Perhaps a walk through those quiet streets would calm her mind.

Cora dressed quickly, tied back her hair, and put on her shoes. She hesitated, then picked up her bracelet from its place on the nightstand, slipped it onto her wrist, and stepped out of her room.

Cora made her way through the echoing halls of the Water Works building, past the bunkrooms of the other workers still fast asleep, down the stone stairs, and out into the city. The night air was unexpectedly cool for late summer, but Cora didn't return for her coat.

The streets were dark with only an occasional pool of yellow light from the highlamps spilling onto the paving stones. At any other time, the darkness would have bothered Cora, even frightened her. Unsavory characters might be roaming the city under cover of darkness, after all, but on this night Cora did not care. Her only concern was ridding herself of her memories.

And so she walked. She started toward the Great Square, weaving through the labyrinthine streets of the Middle Ward, past buildings made of stone and brick and wood and thatch, through shadow and light and into shadow again. As she walked, she quietly said, "*This* is your life now. The Water Works is your life. Protecting the city is your life. These buildings, *this place*, is your life now." The cadence of the words slowly, ever so slowly, pushed back the memories, and Cora's mind began to clear.

As she skirted the square, Cora looked up at the library, at its row of bloodstone columns, rust-colored in the dimness of night, at the shadowy statues of the scholars that flanked the large oak doors. She reached out and ran her finger along one of the columns as she always did when she passed by. Smooth as glass and cold as . . . the icy waters of the Storm. And just like that the memories stirred up by her dream came rushing back.

With a choked sob, Cora kicked a pebble and sent it skittering across the flagstones. Why was this happening now? She had thought the loss was behind her, that she had moved past it. But here she was, awash in fear and longing and sorrow, the intensity of which threatened to undo her. Without knowing where she was going, she ran.

But the memories swirled and filled her mind and she could not escape them.

The Storm had been a vast thing, a horrific thing that had lasted a full week, conjured, it was said, by Imago the Magician, from his far-off island fortress. No one knew why he had called up the Storm. Who could understand the reasoning of magicians? It had happened and it had been devastating.

The Storm had occurred during the height of the serpent hunt, when the fishermen and fisherwomen of the coastal villages were out tracking the sea serpents across the Eastern Deep. Cora remembered the excitement of her parents and the other fisherfolk that year as they sailed their small fleet of boats out into the dark waters of the Deep. It had been a promising year, with more serpents to hunt than normal, and the whole village had come, even those who would normally stay at home.

And then in an instant the sky had turned black, the wind had risen to a scream, and their excitement had turned to terror.

After being swept overboard, Cora had washed ashore, untold miles from home, on the beach outside the city of Tarian. She was alone and barely clinging to life.

The following days were a foggy blur, but when she did recover, Cora found she was in the care of Overseer Thaddeus Blackwood, who was a member of the Council of Tarian. He had gently informed her of the utter devastation wrought by the Storm. Thousands had died. No ships or boats that had been in the Deep during the Storm had made it back to shore. That she had survived was a marvel.

Mr. Blackwood had recently begun a new public works project in Tarian. In his employ at the Water Works were dozens of children and young people, most of them runaways or orphans, who had begun to build the Works in exchange for room and board. Mr. Blackwood had kindly offered Cora a job as well. And because she had lost her family to the Storm, she had accepted.

She had been seven at the time, and had managed to adjust fairly quickly to her new life. She had lost her family, to be sure, but what could she do about it? Nothing. And so Cora the Storm Orphan had gathered the memories of that terrible day, placed them in a corner of her mind, and sealed them off. And then she had begun anew.

The Water Works, she had learned, would be a network of pipes and channels and canals that, when complete, would bolster the city's defenses. The Works would serve to more evenly distribute the waters brought by the Master of Tides when he was protecting Tarian from an attack. For his was a violent and disruptive and indiscriminate defense. The volume of water he moved and the way in which he moved it always dispatched an attacker. But at times it also damaged the docks and some of the buildings around the wharf, not to mention some of Tarian's own ships. Overseer Blackwood's vision for the Water Works was that it would both increase the power of the Master's defense and reduce the damage to Tarian itself. The tides, when called by the Master, would be pulled into the massive array of pipes and reservoirs, which would then focus and redirect them. The Water Works would be the tool that allowed the Master to use the full force of the waters to destroy Tarian's enemies, while minimizing the damage to the waterfront.

Cora had been enamored with the idea of the Water Works from the beginning. She enjoyed seeing the plans slowly become reality. She understood the Works, what it was supposed to do, how the pipes and water gates and traps were supposed to function. Cora understood it all, and while helping to construct the Works, she had also figured out ways to refine it, to vastly improve its efficiency and function. Midway through the construction she had become Works Leader, second only to Mr. Blackwood himself. And in just the last week, she had overseen the Water Works' completion, a full two months ahead of schedule.

Out of breath from her mad dash through the city streets, Cora rounded a corner and stumbled to a stop. Before her was the Master's tower, the Iron Spire. It loomed above the buildings of the Pike, the district that surrounded the wharf. The Spire dwarfed them as it stood guard over the waterfront, a giant finger pointing up into the vastness of the sky. High above the city, at the top of the tower, the Master would be standing, tirelessly watching the sea.

Cora walked over the gritty, green cobble stones that made up the streets on the hill above the harbor, and then began to descend into the Pike. Massive warehouses and merchant houses with high foundations closed in around her like the walls of a canyon, and a chilly breeze brought the smell of salt and fish and tar to her nose. A loose strand of her hair tugged free, red-gold in the light of a highlamp, and Cora tucked it behind her ear. Her footsteps echoed as she moved in and out of shadow, from the yellow light of one highlamp to the next. And then she emerged from the tightly packed buildings, and the harbor opened up before her.

Ships creaked and groaned and seawater slapped against their hulls. Though it was still dark, sailors and merchants were already at work, loading cargo by lantern light and otherwise preparing for the day. Cora stopped beneath an extinguished highlamp, and looked over the wharf.

One of the Works' main outflow pipes was just visible on the south side of the harbor. A system of pulleys and gears was housed beside it in a low, stone building. The machinery had increased the flow of water four-fold, and had been Cora's idea. This place—the docks, where the Water Works focused and enhanced the power of the Master of Tides to defend the city—was now the center of Cora's world. This was her responsibility, her everything. Coming here reminded her of that.

Cora held the lamppost with one hand and gripped the beads of her bracelet with the other. She stared at the harbor, taking deep breaths, sucking the salty air into her lungs.

In the east, the sky began to turn gray.

"Couldn't sleep?"

Cora jumped as a boy sidled up beside her.

"It's not your business, Will," she said. "What are you even doing here?"

Will had been at the Water Works since before she had arrived. He was a little shorter than Cora, but older by several months. He often acted, Cora thought, as though the difference was several years.

"Saw you leave," he said, adjusting the long, hooded cloak he always wore. "A lot of the others have been having nightmares the last few nights. Most of us have, actually. Figured you had one too and wanted to make sure you were alright." Will flashed a smile and leaned against the lamppost.

That the others were also having bad dreams was news to Cora, but she wasn't about to tell that to Will.

"I'm perfectly fine." Cora bit off the words and turned back to the harbor. "I'll see you back at the Works." The boy didn't move.

"I said I'll see you back at—"

"Have you ever thought of making friends?" asked Will. "I'm not saying it would have to be me, but it seems like you could really use a friend. Someone to talk to. All you do is Water Works stuff. And clearly at a time like this," he gestured toward her, "when you're so obviously upset, it would be good to talk to someone. You ever thought of that, Cor?"

Cora had never liked Will. From the moment she had met him, he had acted as though he knew her—casually asking questions he didn't have a right to ask, giving advice that he didn't have a right to give. His ready smile and joking banter were welcomed by all the children, but for Cora, his presumed familiarity had not been earned.

"It's 'Cora'," she said. "And my friendships are of no concern to you."

"They're of no concern to anybody, because you don't have any," said Will with a laugh. "Really, I'm just trying to help you out. I think that since your parents and sis—"

"No!" Cora whipped around and pointed a finger into Will's face. "You don't know anything about what I need." She shook with anger as she stared at him. How dare he think he had a right to tell her what to do? To presume he had a right to say anything about her family?

The boy held up his hands. "Easy, Cor, you don't have to be so defensive. I—"

Suddenly a horn sounded, its note long and deep. Cora felt it in her chest. The sailors straightened and began to shout to one another, hastily tying off lines and scurrying across the decks of the ships. Far out to sea Cora could just make out a red flame. It was a signal from the Eye, Tarian's island watchtower. Red flame meant an attack was coming.

"Well, I guess we'll get to see how good the Works is," said Will.

Cora and Will turned and ran. Up the hill, past the warehouses and shops and inns, across the Great Square, their feet pounded on the stones. Will began to pull ahead. When they reached the university, instead of going through the grounds, Cora turned and cut through an alley, scrambled over a wall, and sprinted through one of the city's parks. She emerged from the trees, just opposite the Water Works building. It was petty, she knew, but Cora hated losing to Will. The boy was still a stone's throw down the street as Cora took the stairs two at a time. Up and up and up she went, past the now empty dormitories, until she reached the Hub. Will arrived a step behind her.

The Hub was the largest room in the Works building, and because it occupied the top floor, it had a commanding view of the city. Large windows looked out to the west, south, and east. The Hub was now full of bleary-eyed workers, with some of the children standing on stools and chairs, resting their elbows on the stone windowsills. There was a buzz of excitement among them as they stared intently toward the sea.

Out of breath, Cora and Will moved toward one of the windows that faced the harbor.

"What's the situation, Finn?" Cora asked. "Are you monitoring the Eye?"

A boy with shaggy hair turned and nodded. "Ships coming. Three of them. I've been watching the Eye, but no flags." Cora joined him and he handed her a spyglass.

First, she pointed it to the island watchtower, but as Finn had said, the watchmen had not hung any flags. So there was no specific message then. Cora swung around and found the ships. They were sailing from the south and east, making straight for the city. At that moment the sun rose and its light revealed billowed red sails with a yellow starburst in the center of each. The markings were unfamiliar to her. As Cora peered through the glass, the ships cut across the harbor mouth. Dozens of fierce looking warriors, weapons glinting in their hands, covered the decks.

"Can't wait to see the Works in action," said a girl named Tria. She glanced over and added, "They have no idea what's about to hit 'em, right, Cora?"

Cora didn't respond. She lowered the glass and waited.

The ships slid across the smooth harbor. Before the Water Works was completed, it was at this point in an attack that the harbor would have turned into a seething cauldron as the Master called the tides.

"Something's wrong," said Will. "Where's the water?"

"Nothing's wrong," replied Cora. "The Works evens everything out, remember? Mr. Blackwood said with the Works we wouldn't even notice the calling of the tides."

"Yeah, all the water gets pulled up the intakes and into the reservoirs, I know," said Will. "But you'd think we'd see *something*."

Cora shrugged. "We'll see plenty when the ships start to break apart and sink. And that'll be any second now." She waited and held her breath. But nothing happened.

And then the marauders were beside the piers, pouring off their ships and running down the docks and into the Pike. Cora kept watching the ships, waiting, hoping, but there was nothing. Her stomach clenched. Something *was* wrong. It was undeniable now. She looked up at the Iron Spire, as though she would be able to see the Master. Then she glanced at the clock and made a mental note of the time.

"Fire!" one of the children shouted. Black smoke came belching out of one of the warehouses, followed by tongues of red and orange flame. And then another building went up in flames, and then another. The distant sounds of bells drifted up to them. And still the tides did not come.

Cora's mind raced. Somehow the Water Works had failed. Instead of giving additional protection to Tarian, the Works had malfunctioned and left the city utterly exposed. And now, for the first time, it was burning.

"Gate reports!" she snapped. "Finn, get me everyone's water gate reports from last night. We'll check them against the model."

Finn scrambled to obey, and one of the children, a girl of about six, began to cry. "Pen, get Rose out of here," said Cora. "Now!"

Finn came running with a stack of papers, and Will joined him and Cora beside a large table that held a model of Tarian. It was a model not just of the city, but also of the entire Water Works—all the canals and pipes and gates. The buildings were removable to access the parts of the Works that were below ground. Cora had built it, skillfully crafting the miniature buildings and waterways to scale.

"I'll get Blackwood. He'll want to know," Will said to Cora.

"No. He'll have heard the horn. He'll be where he needs to be. I need you to mark the model."

"You're the boss, Cor," he said with a grin as he picked up a handful of miniature flags.

Finn read through the reports. "Pike 3. Pike 6. Harbor 4. Glass District 8. Harbor 3 . . ."

Will placed flags beside each gate on the model as Finn read, until they were finished.

"All gates accounted for," muttered Cora. "Finn, is everyone here?"

"Yes. Well, Pen took Rose out into the hall. But apart from them, yes."

"Go get them."

When the girls had rejoined them, Rose still sniffling, Cora said, "Did everyone check your gates last night? Twice? I know you all filled out your reports, but did you make sure your water gates were closed?"

They all nodded.

"But did you check your gates *twice?*" asked Will. His tone was serious, but the corners of his mouth turned up when he caught Cora's eye.

Even in a situation like this, he was trying to make a joke. Annoyed, Cora snapped, "Be quiet, Will. This isn't funny."

She continued addressing the gathered workers. "Did anyone

see anything during your inspections last night, anything out of the ordinary?"

The boys and girls shook their heads.

Cora went back to the window. Smoke corkscrewed into the sky, and gulls circled through the haze, screaming.

It looked like the fires were just in the Pike, maybe into the Glass District, but not beyond. The raiders were loading things onto their ships, boxes and chests and glass objects pilfered from the warehouses and surrounding vessels. Perhaps the City Guard would come, but Cora doubted they would arrive in time. The Guard wasn't used to being needed at the waterfront.

"Rose, I need you to watch the raiders," said Cora. "It looks like they're about to set sail, so let me know when they're back on their ships. Can you do that for me?"

"Okay," said Rose as she wiped at her face.

"Good. Now I need the rest of you to do a thorough inspection," said Cora. "Everyone goes to their assigned section. That's two of you per section. Each of you check and double check every inch of the Works. Look for leaks, breaks, *anything*, and write everything down. Mr. Blackwood, not to mention the Council, will need your reports and I need them to be accurate. And get your gear for repairs. Yes, I know your tools will slow you down, but I want whatever is broken fixed right away. When you're finished, meet back here. Go."

"The raiders are still—" began one of the children.

"They'll be gone by the time you get your things and are out the door. Now go!"

The workers rushed out and Cora went back to the model of the city. She studied the sprawling tangle of miniature pipes, trying to determine the most likely location for the failure. The problem had to be somewhere between the reservoirs and the outflow pipes.

"The raiders are leaving, Cora," said Rose. Cora again looked at the clock and noted the time: 6:04. The attack had lasted just fourteen minutes. She joined Rose and watched as the ships rowed out of the harbor. As they cleared the harbor mouth, the wind filled their sails. Soon they were lost to sight.

Later that morning, Cora stood alone at a window and watched the swirling tendrils of smoke. They twisted high above the city where they were carried away by the wind. Closer to the ground, a thick gray haze all but obscured what was left of the Pike. Occasionally a sea breeze cut through the blanket of drifting smoke, pushing it aside to reveal for a moment the blackened husks of the buildings along the wharf. Scores of people picked through the charred wreckage.

Cora felt hollow, uncertain, disoriented. This was a disaster. There was no other way to think about it. The Water Works, designed to make things better and more efficient, had instead made things worse than they had ever been. And worse still, the initial reports had come back and nothing had been found. There was no broken pipe, no malfunctioning gate, nothing to explain the failure. Not knowing what else to do, Cora had sent everyone out again. By her estimation it would take another four hours before they all returned.

"I wonder where Mr. Blackwood is," she murmured.

"I'm right here," said a voice behind her. Cora turned to see Mr. Blackwood stride through the door. He wore his signature red coat that reached halfway to his knees. He was a big man, thick like the trunk of a tree, with jowls that reminded Cora of a bulldog. His expression was grim. Despite this, he flashed Cora a kindly smile. "I have news. I've just come from Harbor 2. Finn found that the main valve had jammed. A piece of driftwood had lodged itself across the opening."

"I don't understand," said Cora. "He would have found that during the initial inspection this morning."

Mr. Blackwood shrugged. "I agree, but he must have been distracted.

It *has* been a chaotic morning." He set down a sheaf of documents and rubbed his face with both hands. As he picked the papers up again he looked at Cora. His eyes were watery and full of worry. "This isn't good, Cora. This is an inauspicious beginning for the Works, and needless to say the Master will be involved."

"Do you mean he might actually come down from the Spire? And . . . do you think he'll be angry?"

"He *has* to make an appearance. With something like this . . . he will come down. An attack has never succeeded before, but I can't imagine he will let something like this go unaddressed. And yes, I think he'll be angry. Part of the city was sacked, after all, and it was because of the Water Works!" After a moment he added in a reassuring tone, "Don't worry, girl, when I speak with the Master and the Council, I'll take full responsibility for everything."

"That's really kind of you, Mr. Blackwood, but I'm Works Leader. I bear the blame—"

Mr. Blackwood held up a hand. "Stop right there, Cora. Are you at fault? Should you have foreseen that this could have happened? Perhaps, but I should have realized it too, and I didn't. And being the Overseer, the responsibility falls to me. Understood?"

Cora swallowed, looked at the floor, then nodded. "I understand," she muttered. "I just hate that this happened. I should have anticipated it."

"Perhaps." Mr. Blackwood reached down and patted her shoulder. "But you're not perfect, nor can you expect yourself to be. Can you accept that?"

Cora grudgingly nodded. "Yes, Mr. Blackwood."

"Very good!" he said. "Now then. We have to have a plan going forward to address issues like this. Better filters on the intake pipes, perhaps? And we probably need to cover the canals after all. That driftwood was either brought in through the intakes or it fell into one of the canals. Work up a response to show we're addressing this, Cora, as soon as possible. We'll need it for the Council and we'll need it for the Master. He *will* appear, and we have to be ready when he does."

"I'll do it, Mr. Blackwood. But will . . . do you think the Master will decommission the Water Works? Undo everything we've done?"

Mr. Blackwood tapped his lip thoughtfully before replying. "I don't think so, Cora. But it largely depends on our response to this disaster. So write up a draft. Be thorough. I know you will be, girl. It's one of your strengths."

"Of course," said Cora.

"Now then," Mr. Blackwood squinted at the clock on the wall, "I need to gather some things before I head to the Council. There is much to discuss and it will probably go into the evening, so I'll speak with you tomorrow morning. Plenty of time for you to draft a response."

"Yes, Mr. Blackwood."

As the door closed behind him, Cora took a deep breath. "I'm not perfect. I can't expect myself to be," she whispered to herself. It was difficult to say, even harder to believe, but she knew it was true. "I'm not perfect. I'm not perfect. I'm not perfect."

She turned and walked over to the model of the city. Seeing everything laid out before her brought home to Cora the amount of work that needed to be done. She had thought the open canals had adequately been screened, but she must have missed a spot. She would have to go over the whole network again. *I'm not perfect. I can't expect myself to be.*

Cora's eyes followed the tangle of tiny pipes that wove through the Pike and the Glass District. The various pipes made their way to the docks where they converged at Harbor 2.

She was relieved that they had discovered the problem, but at the same time the explanation seemed insufficient.

To begin with, she couldn't believe that Finn had missed a jammed valve in his first inspection that morning. Cora wouldn't have been surprised if someone like Kerry had missed it, or Pen, but *Finn?* It *had* been a chaotic morning, as Mr. Blackwood had said, but she still couldn't see Finn making a blunder like that. It just wasn't like him.

But even if he had, Cora wasn't sure that Harbor 2's valve was large enough to have caused a complete failure of the Water Works. She traced the pipes and canals that fed into Harbor 2 and did some calculations. No, the valve wasn't large enough. The defense would only have been weakened, not shut off completely.

She was missing something. Perhaps there were other points of failure that hadn't been discovered yet. Or . . . She tilted her head and her eyes came to rest on the miniature Iron Spire.

"I wonder . . ." Cora murmured. But then she shook her head. "Impossible."

She glanced at the clock. She should get the report for Mr. Blackwood started. Once the others returned, she could add to it or make necessary changes. If she applied herself, she could be done by sundown.

Cora made her way to her desk, sat down, and began to write.

CHAPTER TWO

INSIDE THE IRON SPIRE

FINN, CAN YOU STAY A moment?" The boy nodded and strode over to Cora's desk. The others filed out of the Hub, their faces tired and covered in filth. Even minutes spent in the Water Works would make you dirty, and they had spent the better part of the day crawling through the pipes and canals.

"Is this about Harbor 2?" Finn asked.

Cora nodded. "Can you explain how you missed the driftwood the first time?"

"Uh-uh. Both Ella and I checked everything separately. Us both missing it the first time . . . Cora, I know it sounds crazy, but I don't think it was there during the first inspection."

Cora rubbed her temples. "Thank you, Finn. You can go."

When she was alone again, Cora began to pace. It was certainly strange that Finn had missed the jammed valve, but that wasn't the issue. No other failures or malfunctions had been discovered in the Works, and so the real problem was that Harbor 2's open valve explained nothing. The Water Works still should have functioned. Maybe the raiders' ships wouldn't have been destroyed, but the Works should have done *something*. But they had done nothing.

"This doesn't make any sense," Cora muttered.

The thought that had flashed through Cora's mind earlier, the one she had dismissed, returned. It was more difficult to brush aside now. She stopped her pacing and stared out the window at the Iron Spire. Both she and Mr. Blackwood had assumed the Water Works had been at fault. But what if the tides had never been called to begin with?

The thought was absurd, not to mention dangerous. To imply the Master of Tides had neglected his duty was as ridiculous as it was treasonous. But then another explanation came to her. What if the Master was *unable* to call the tides. What if he was . . . Suddenly, Cora was filled with fear and dread.

She should tell Mr. Blackwood. But he was with the Council and if Cora interrupted him and it turned out she was wrong, she would make them both look incompetent. "That's the last thing we need, especially right now," she mused. But if she was *right*, Tarian was in terrible danger.

Cora needed proof. And she knew of a way to get it. After a moment of indecision, she retrieved a lantern from a cupboard and her coat from her room, and left the Water Works building.

The sunlight cast long, blue shadows across the city as Cora once again made her way toward the harbor. There was enormous risk in this endeavor, there was no doubt about that, but if Cora was right, it was a risk worth taking. Still, she trembled as she thought about what would happen if she were wrong.

At the docks again, Cora passed by the ruined warehouses. The City Guard was here now, in full force, overseeing the cleanup. The polished armor of the soldiers gleamed, as did the tips of their long, needle-like spears. Merchants and their workers sifted through the charred remains, looking to salvage something, anything. Shipwrights were already making repairs to those ships that had not been completely destroyed. Cora wove her way through the crowd, trying not to breathe the soot, as she made her way toward the Iron Spire.

The Master's Elite surrounded the tower, as they always did, their fists bristling with swords and axes and pikes. They, of course, were sworn to remain at the Iron Spire, to protect the Master of Tides, even if it meant allowing raiders to burn the Pike. Which is exactly what they had done that morning. They stood like statues and only their sea-green cloaks undulated slowly in the breeze, like seaweed on the ocean floor.

Cora did not approach them. Instead, she walked over to a low building opposite the Spire. She inserted a key into the door and, with a twist, she pushed it open and slipped inside.

The dusty building housed an access point to the Works. A large portion of the floor had been removed, revealing an enormous clay pipe. It ran the length of the building and was as wide as Cora was tall. This was Intake Pipe 4, one of the intake pipes that brought seawater from the harbor to a smaller channel farther inland. Cora opened her coat and pulled out the lantern. Once it was lit, she took another key from her pocket and used it to unlock the curved access door that ran along the top of the pipe.

With the handle of the lantern between her teeth, Cora lowered herself into the pipe and pulled the door closed behind her. She locked it from the inside.

The pipe stank of fish and seaweed. There was a runnel of fetid water along its bottom. A green slimy residue covered everything. Holding the lantern high, Cora followed the pipe toward the sea.

This intake pipe, Cora knew, ran directly below the Master's tower, and had been a drainage pipe for the city before it had been repurposed for the Water Works. Beneath the Iron Spire was another access door. Cora had chanced upon it the year before, hidden behind a layer of rust and barnacles, and she was certain she was the only one in the Works who knew about it. Cora came to the door, still somewhat clean from her previous visit, and with some difficulty unlocked it and pushed it open. She pulled herself up out of the pipe and into the Iron Spire.

Cora had been in this little room only once before, but she had never ventured beyond the thick, wooden door that she now faced. She didn't even know if her key would work.

It did. The lock clicked and the door swung silently inward. Cora shuttered the lantern and held her breath. She was fairly certain the Elite only stood guard on the outside of the Spire, but she couldn't be too cautious. If they caught her here, on the inside, she didn't know what they would do. She didn't want to even think about it.

Cora stood at the end of a short hall that was deep in shadow. A muffled silence hung over the place and the air felt . . . alive, like the air during a thunderstorm. The hair on Cora's arms stood on end. Perhaps twenty or thirty steps ahead the hall opened into a room that glowed with orange light. Cora swallowed and crept forward.

Not much was known about the Master of Tides. He had ruled for centuries, ever since the Great War, and the Sand Coin gave him power over the sea. His power allowed him to do battle with the tidal surge that occurred during the Turn, allowed him to call the tides to protect Tarian from those who might do it harm. But beyond that . . . who knew? Could he hear thoughts? Could he see the future? Could he kill you with a gesture of his hand? Cora did not know, which made her current position all the more precarious. But whatever the Master could do, there *was* power here, and it was unsettling to say the least. As she walked, the air seemed to crackle around her, seething with awareness and wordless whispers.

Cora came to the end of the hallway and peered out. She was looking into a massive round room paneled in age-darkened wood. Marble and ironwood statues tall as trees stood in alcoves evenly spaced along the curved wall. The upper bodies and faces of the statues were in shadow, but their feet were illuminated by the light of dozens of oil lamps arranged in the middle of the room. To her left was an ornately carved door, wide enough for six horsemen to ride abreast. The main entrance to the Spire, no doubt. To her right was a stair that spiraled up into darkness. There was, to her relief, no sign of the Master's Elite.

Cora stole across the smooth, stone floor and began to ascend the stair, her footsteps silent on the carpeted slabs of rock. After a minute, she paused to open the lantern.

Around and around, up and up Cora went, and it seemed as though the light of her lantern grew smaller and weaker the higher she climbed. The blocks of granite that made up the walls were the color of night. She reached out and traced a line between two stones, but then quickly withdrew her hand with a gasp. She inspected her hand in the light of the lantern. Her finger, though it bore no mark, tingled as though she had been stung by a jellyfish.

The higher she got, the less sure she became of her plan. What if she was wrong? What would the Master of Tides do? Cora shivered. But on the other hand, what if she was right? What would *she* do?

The minutes passed. Cora stopped to catch her breath. Rest. Climb. Rest. She continued on, her breathing becoming more labored the higher she climbed.

And then she finally came to the top of the stair. A little ahead of her was an open doorway, through which she could see a rectangle of evening sky. A single star glimmered in the deep blue. A gust of wind tore at her coat. Cora saw that if she continued forward, she would step through the doorway onto a balcony that curved away to her right, apparently encircling the outside of the tower. She paused to regain her breath, cocked her head, and listened.

Apart from the mournful sound of the wind, she heard nothing. The air no longer hummed and the whispering had ceased. After a moment, Cora stepped onto the stone balcony and slowly followed it around the tower. The lights of the city twinkled far below and as she continued, the Pike and the harbor came into view. The light from the setting sun allowed Cora to see the full ruin of the Pike, how the shapes of the buildings had changed and their blackened timbers had folded in on themselves.

As she continued along the balcony, an archway appeared in the tower wall ahead. Once again Cora stopped and listened.

She heard nothing but her heart hammering in her chest. With a deep breath, she rounded the corner and stepped inside.

The light from Cora's lantern revealed a room that was spacious and circular, perhaps twenty paces wide, the width of the tower top. In front of her and to the side was a simple table with a stack of blank parchments, some blotting paper, a quill, and an inkpot, along with a chair. Beyond the table Cora could see a fireplace set in the tower wall. No fire burned in it. Beyond the table and chair, situated beside the fireplace, was a small bed. Besides that, the room was empty.

This was not what Cora had expected. This was where the Master of Tides ruled, where he lived; there should be a throne and wall hangings, carpets, lamps, books, comfortable chairs, the trappings of prestige and power. Yet there were none of these things. Only this austere and all but empty room.

As Cora edged around the table, she caught sight of a pile of cloth on the floor beside it. She froze. And then, with a trembling hand, she reached down and gently lifted a corner of the fabric, revealing the face of the protector of Tarian. The Master of Tides appeared terribly frail, all but swallowed by his blue-gray robes. Wrinkles spiderwebbed across his face. His silver hair spilled down to his shoulders, and his right hand lay across his chest. The body smelled faintly of salt and sand. Cora touched the hand and grimaced. It was cold as ice.

She had been right. The Water Works had not malfunctioned. The attack had succeeded because, as unimaginable as it might be, the Master of Tides was dead. And now Tarian was unguarded, vulnerable to attack, vulnerable to invasion. Vulnerable to the tidal surge that was only weeks away. The Council had to be told, and quickly.

As Cora turned to go she noticed a small glimmer beneath the grate in the fireplace. She walked over and bent down, setting the lantern on the floor. Nestled in the ash was a round silver token, like a coin. There was an image of a crow engraved on it, and there was a tiny hole through the metal above the raven's head. As she plucked it from the ashes, her hand brushed against a charred and partially burned paper on the grate. Cora saw that it was a handwritten note and a portion of it was still legible. She tucked the silver token into her pocket and picked up the charred fragment of paper. It read:

. . . now I find that my strength has suddenly faded, my mastery over the waters has waned, and salt is thick in my veins. My power cannot be taken from me, as you know, but it is clear that the time has come to surrender it.

The Sand Coin is in its box. Members of the Council, the choosing of my successor is in your hands. I implore you, choose wisely.

The Coin awaits the new Master of Tides.

The Master had known he was dying. He had known and had written this note, but it had never been delivered.

Cora carefully brought the burned paper back to the Master's table. She was perplexed. This was clearly important. Why would the Master write such a note and then burn it? Cora shuffled through the parchments to see if there was a new letter. Maybe he had smeared the ink on the one she had found in the fire, or misspelled a word, and written it out again. But there was nothing.

Reading through the note a second time, Cora stopped at the mention of the Sand Coin. She looked over the table for a box, and then on the floor, and then around the body of the Master. There was no box. But on the Master's sea-green sleeve there was the edge of a boot print. And it wasn't hers.

Cora's skin prickled. Dread and terror washed over her as she realized what had happened. Someone had been here and whoever it was had burned the Master's note and had stolen the box containing the Sand Coin, the power of the Master of Tides. But who? Who could have done such a thing?

Her hands shook as she took two pieces of blank parchment from the table and placed the burned fragment between them. Then Cora tucked the bundle into her coat pocket. She would take what she had found to Mr. Blackwood. He would know what to do.

Cora stepped out onto the balcony. The sun had gone down and the sky was stained a deep purple and red. The fading light turned everything crimson. Walking quickly, Cora re-entered the tower. She paused and after a moment of indecision she shuttered the lantern and then began her descent.

Down and down through the shadows and prickly stillness, through the whispering air, she went. She descended in darkness, fear gnawing at her insides. The Master of Tides was dead and the Sand Coin had been stolen. It was unthinkable. How could this have happened?

When Cora reached the bottom of the steps, her breathing was ragged. She turned and was halfway to the hall that led to the room with the intake pipe when a gravelly voice said, "Hold fast, intruder! Hold fast or die!"

CHAPTER THREE

THE CELLS

CORA AWOKE TO COMPLETE DARKNESS. She blinked, but it made no difference. As she sat up, her first thought was, *I didn't dream about the Storm.* But even as this realization brought a flood of relief, she remembered where she was, and that relief sluiced away.

Her cell was damp and cold and smelled of decay. Cora could hear the steady dripping of water somewhere close to her, and something scurried across the ground nearby. She hugged her knees to her chest and pressed her back against the stone wall.

When the Master's Elite had grabbed her in the vast room at the bottom of the Spire, there had been a moment—the briefest of moments—when she had considered telling the three guards what she had found. But what if they were the ones who had stolen the Sand Coin? They would have killed her immediately. Instead, she had remained silent and the towering guards had pulled a hood over her face and begun to walk. After a very long time—she wasn't sure how long—they had ended up here.

Cora had shouted and thrashed when the jailer, with the help of the Elite, had put her in the cell, but the jailer had ignored her, locked the door, and walked away. Cora didn't know how long ago that had been, but judging from her growling stomach, she guessed she had slept through most of the night.

Standing slowly, she brushed wet straw from her trousers and edged forward until she bumped into the door. It was heavy and iron studs covered its surface. There was a small barred window near its middle. No handle.

The jailer would come back soon. He would have to. Should she talk to him? Tell him about the Master? She doubted he would believe her. No, Cora would ask the jailer to send for Mr. Blackwood. She would tell him about the Master and he would tell the Council. He might even be able to get her released. But even if he couldn't, the Council would know that the Master was dead, and they would know what to do.

A dim light appeared on the other side of the window. As it grew stronger, Cora heard footsteps. And then the light was right outside her door, shining through the barred window, blinding her. A key turned in the lock. The door opened with a groan.

"Give me five minutes," said the voice of Mr. Blackwood.

"Very good," came the reply, and the jailer shuffled away down the hall.

Cora's eyes began to adjust as Mr. Blackwood entered the cell. She threw herself at him and hugged him tight. "I'm so glad to see you!" she said. "You have to help me!"

He patted her shoulder with one hand and then stooped and set a candlestand on the floor.

"I don't even know what to say, Cora," he began. "I got a message an hour ago that you were here. *Here!* In the Cells! What's this about?"

"Mr. Blackwood, I can explain. It has to do with the Water Works and the Master and the attack. Please, hear me out."

Mr. Blackwood nodded. "Go on."

"Something was wrong, Mr. Blackwood. I know Finn found the

valve open, but that alone wasn't enough to have caused the failure of the entire Water Works. I did the calculations. I know you said to work on a response, but I had a feeling."

"A feeling?" Mr. Blackwood's eyes narrowed. "What kind of feeling?"

Cora took a deep breath and then whispered, "That the Master of Tides was dead."

Mr. Blackwood's face went pale and he quickly looked over his shoulder at the open cell door. "Not a word more, Cora. That kind of talk is dangerous."

"Mr. Blackwood. He *is* dead. I saw his body. And the Sand Coin is missing!"

"You were in the Iron Spire?" Mr. Blackwood's eyes widened.

"Yes."

"And that's where you were caught? By the Master's Elite?"

"Yes."

Mr. Blackwood's eyes flicked back and forth across Cora's face as he absorbed this information. "Did you tell the Elite that the Master is dead? That the Coin is missing?"

"I didn't. I thought maybe they had something to do with it. I was coming to tell you so that you could tell the Council. The Council *has* to know. Tarian is unprotected!"

Mr. Blackwood nodded. "Indeed it is. You were wise to keep it to yourself, Cora. However . . . " He paused. "You realize the position you are in now, don't you?"

"What do you mean?" asked Cora.

"They caught you in the Spire. And the Master is dead and the Sand Coin has been stolen."

The realization of the truth of his words crashed over Cora like a wave.

"Mr. Blackwood, *you* don't think . . . ?"

"Don't be ridiculous, Cora," he said. "You couldn't kill the Master any more than any of us could. And of course I don't think you took the Sand Coin. But *they* will. As soon as they discover the Master is dead and the Sand Coin is missing, they will think you're the one responsible." He rubbed his chin. Finally he muttered, "We have to get you out of here."

"If I try to run, they'll just think I'm guilty," said Cora.

"They're going to think you're guilty regardless. But if you're in here, and the Council thinks you stole the Sand Coin, they could very well execute you."

Cora almost choked. She hadn't thought of that. "What do we do?" she asked.

Mr. Blackwood checked his pocket watch. "Listen. We don't have much time. Take these." He reached into his coat pocket and pulled out a narrow cloth bundle. "I'll arrange a distraction. I'm not sure what yet, but you'll know when you hear it. It will be in the next couple hours. Best get to work right away though," he said, eyeing the door. "Understand?"

Cora took the bundle and nodded as she slipped it into her pocket.

Mr. Blackwood went on. "When you reach the end of the hall, you'll come to a T. Turn right. Left after that and then left again. That will bring you to the guardroom. You should be able to find your way out from there."

Cora nodded again. There was a distant jingle of keys and footfalls echoed in the hall.

"If for whatever reason you're unable to escape today . . . if anyone comes to talk to you," whispered Mr. Blackwood, "do *not* tell them about the Master. Not a word. We don't know who might be involved."

Mr. Blackwood bent down and picked up the candle as the jailer appeared in the doorway. "I'll come see you tomorrow, Cora," said Mr. Blackwood with a smile. "Chin up."

When they had gone and the light had faded and then disappeared, Cora took out the bundle and unwrapped it. She ran her fingers over the set of lock picks. Mr. Blackwood always carried a set, and during the construction of the Works, Cora had carried one as well. The picks were essential for when, inevitably, the keys to the water gates were lost. Cora felt each length of L-shaped metal, pulled out two, and then edged over to the door.

There was no keyhole on this side, of course, but Cora could slide her arm through the barred window and could just reach the keyhole on the outside of the door. Even so, this was going to be difficult. Holding both picks in her right hand, she reached through and awkwardly slid one into the keyhole. Cora moved it around carefully until she felt the lever in the lock. It gave under the pressure, but when she tried to maneuver the other pick into the hole to throw the bolt, the first pick slid to the side and the lever fell back into place. She tried again, but with the same result.

After a half hour or so, Cora gave up in frustration. Her arm was sore, her fingers hurt, and her first attempt had been the closest she had come to unlocking the door. She stood and flexed her fingers. She rubbed her shoulder and slowly worked out the stiffness that had crept into her neck.

"You can do this, Cora," she muttered quietly. "You *have* to do this." She tried again and failed. Again, but this time she dropped one of the picks. It clanged to the floor. Cora held her breath.

She pulled her arm from the window and stood listening for the jailer. Nothing. "This one will have to do," she said as she selected another pick.

At that moment, a bell began to ring. At first Cora thought the jailer had heard the pick fall after all, and was sounding the alarm, but then she heard distant shouts. This must be Mr. Blackwood's distraction.

Relief was followed by panic and then fear; she wouldn't get the door unlocked in time! Cora breathed deeply and slid her arm through the barred window once more. The first pick was in and the lever was up. The second missed the keyhole and slid off the outside of the lock.

Her fingers cramped suddenly and Cora almost dropped both picks. Gritting her teeth, she willed the second pick back to the keyhole. It was in. And with a slow twist of her fingers, she drew back the bolt.

Cora almost whimpered with relief as she pushed open the door. She groped around on the floor until she found the pick that had fallen earlier, and after thrusting it into her pocket, she blindly felt her way down the hall.

There was a faint light ahead, though Cora couldn't see its source, and she ran as quietly as she could toward it. As she neared the end of the corridor, the bell stopped ringing and the shouts subsided. "No, no, no," she whispered. She hoped she wasn't too late.

This was the T juncture that Mr. Blackwood had told her about. She peeked around the corner, but the hall was empty. A solitary torch hung in a bracket on the wall.

Cora crept along, following Mr. Blackwood's directions until she came to the guardroom.

It was, somewhat surprisingly, as unpleasant as the cells. Cora would have thought the jailer and his guards would have made it a more agreeable place, given how much time they had to spend there. But it was as damp and musty as where the prisoners were kept. The one big difference, though, was light. Sunlight filtered in through two barred windows and an open door that stood opposite Cora. Through the doorway she could see a street packed with people.

Between her and the door was a squat, wooden barrel, its staves discolored, its iron bands flaking with rust. It seemed to serve as a table. Around it were several empty chairs. Scattered across the barrel and the floor were playing cards and coins, probably dropped by the guards when the alarm had sounded. Whatever distraction Mr. Blackwood had arranged had apparently pulled them out into the street. How long would they be gone, though? Cora needed to move fast. She stepped into the room.

"It was nothing," came a voice from outside. "Children playing pranks. Thought it would be funny to say we were under attack again."

Cora lunged and ducked behind the barrel as the jailer and a guard entered the room from the street.

"Hilarious. You give them a good beating?"

"The one I caught bit my hand before I could thrash him. The rest scattered like rats. Hope Murun has better luck with the ones he was chasing."

One of the men sighed loudly as he bent to gather the cards. The other righted one of the chairs that had been knocked over. Carefully, slowly, with her back pressed against the barrel, Cora reached out and picked up one of the coins that lay beside her. Then with a flick of her wrist she sent the coin through the doorway that led to the cells. It rang as it struck against the stone.

The jailer swore and the guard drew his sword. They leapt past Cora as they rushed to see what had caused the sound. As they disappeared through the doorway, Cora slipped out onto the street and ran.

A Way Forward

WERE YOU FOLLOWED?" MR. BLACKWOOD and Cora sat in his cavernous office, early afternoon light streaming through the cloudy panes of glass. He held his pipe in one hand and fixed Cora with an intent stare. His forehead was wrinkled in worry.

"I made sure I wasn't. And as soon as I got to the Works, I came straight here. No one has seen me." Cora looked down at her feet and then said, "Thank you, Mr. Blackwood. For helping me. I'm sorry you're involved in this now."

"Look at me, girl." Cora glanced up. "We haven't time for apologies and second-guessing. What's done is done, and I knew what I was doing when I decided to help you escape. The city is in danger, as it hasn't been for a long, long time, and I wouldn't know that if it weren't for you. You and I need to figure out how we're to protect it. Now then. Tell me everything, from the beginning."

Cora thought for a moment, then began. "The jammed valve wasn't enough to shut down the Works. I figured that out pretty quickly. But the Water Works had failed, or so we thought, and so I assumed that another break or leak or malfunction must have occurred and that we would find it as well. When we didn't, I began to wonder if maybe the tides hadn't been called. It seemed unlikely, but the more I thought about it, the more it seemed like the only explanation. I wanted to come tell you, but you were with the Council. To interrupt the Council . . . well, I thought it would be best to have proof first.

"So I decided to see if my suspicions were correct. I know it was a terrible risk, but I decided to go to the Iron Spire to see if the Master was hurt or dead. I let myself in through Intake Pipe 4. Last year I, uh, found a door there that gives access to the Spire." Cora blushed and looked down. "Anyway, I went up the Spire and I found his body." She paused. "And I was going to just leave and come back here and tell you, but then I found part of a note he had written."

"A note?" asked Mr. Blackwood.

"Yes. It was mostly burned, but you can still read some of it." She reached inside her coat and removed the pieces of parchment and laid them on the desk. The burned fragment slid out.

Mr. Blackwood picked up the scrap and read it. He raised his eyebrows. "Interesting. And the Sand Coin was nowhere to be found?"

"I looked for the box, but it was missing. But then I found a boot print. I figured whoever left the print had stolen the Sand Coin and tried to burn the note, though I don't know why they would do that."

Mr. Blackwood rubbed his chin thoughtfully. "Perhaps the portion that was destroyed had something important on it, an instruction from the Master, perhaps."

Cora shrugged. "Maybe. Anyway, when I came down the stair I ran into the Elite. That's how I ended up in the Cells."

Mr. Blackwood was silent a moment, then said, "So, the Master of Tides is dead. Someone has stolen the Sand Coin, no doubt hoping to wield its enormous power. Perhaps Aurian or Labryn Waite is moving against us, but who can say? What we do know is that, for the time being, Tarian does not have a protector. And while we can fortify the docks against marauders—for those same raiders are sure to return after their success yesterday—we still have to contend with the Turn. The tidal surge comes in, what, four and a half weeks?" Mr. Blackwood tapped his pipe stem against his teeth. "That's not much time to find the Sand Coin. In fact, it's too little time. We need to modify the Water Works to do what the Master has done for us for so long."

"I, I disagree, Mr. Blackwood," stammered Cora. "I don't think we *can* modify the Water Works sufficiently. That would be a lot of work to complete in a month, and besides, the Works needs a mind to direct it, especially during the Turn. The surge is so . . . unpredictable and different every year. I think our only hope is to find the Sand Coin and for the Council to choose a new Master. I think it would be a mistake to not look for the Sand Coin."

"Oh!" said Mr. Blackwood. "We will certainly search for it. In the meantime, however, I think it would be prudent to also pursue modifications to the Works."

Cora nodded her head slowly. She supposed it was better to *try* to modify the Works, however insufficient those changes might prove to be, rather than do nothing at all.

There was a sudden knock at the door. Mr. Blackwood motioned to Cora and she scrambled behind his desk.

"Come!"

The door opened and the voice of Mr. Blackwood's steward said, "The City Guard, Overseer. They've demanded to see you. They're . . . here, sir. They refused to wait below."

"Refused?" said Mr. Blackwood sharply.

"Yes, sir. They were quite insistent."

"I see. Send them in."

Cora sat beneath the desk, her chin resting on her knees, holding her breath. She heard the creaking of leather and armor and the jingle of chainmail as several members of the City Guard walked into the room.

"Gentlemen," said Mr. Blackwood stiffly. "What could possibly warrant this interruption?"

"Thaddeus Blackwood, we—" said a rasping voice.

"You can call me Overseer."

"Of course, Overseer Blackwood. This morning a prisoner escaped from the Cells. We'd like to ask you some questions."

"How does this concern me? As I'm sure you're aware, I'm a very busy man with important responsibilities, especially after the events of yesterday morning."

"It concerns you because the prisoner is in your employ. We think it likely that she would come here."

Mr. Blackwood let the statement hang in the air, unanswered. After several moments the silence became uncomfortable. Finally he said, "Are you suggesting that I'm harboring a fugitive?"

"Of course not, Mr. Black—"

"Overseer," Mr. Blackwood said, his voice as cold and hard as iron.

"Of course not, Overseer Blackwood. We simply wanted to let you know that Cora, your Works Leader, escaped the Cells. If you see her or hear from her, please contact the City Guard—"

"I thank you for your visit, gentlemen," interrupted Mr. Blackwood, "but I'm afraid this will have to wait. The Council is convening and I will not be late. Please leave your names with my steward. Now if you'll excuse me."

"Overseer, I must insist—"

"No, Sergeant, *I* must insist. Unless you'd like to accompany me to the Council? No? Then good day."

The members of the City Guard filed out and after the door had closed, Cora exhaled slowly and crawled out from beneath the desk. She rarely saw this side of Mr. Blackwood. It was . . . unnerving.

Mr. Blackwood stood with his back to the closed door, puffing on his pipe. The blue smoke drifted sinuously toward the ceiling.

"The City Guard won't stay away for long," he said. "We should count ourselves fortunate that there has been a breakdown in communication between the Master's Elite and the Guard. If the City Guard had known that you had been caught in the Iron Spire, there is nothing I could say that would prevent them from conducting a thorough search of the Works building. But they will find out, and most likely very soon. And on top of that, when the death of the Master is discovered, you," he pointed at Cora, "will be suspected of stealing the Sand Coin, and if you are found here, I," he pointed at himself, "will be guilty of aiding and abetting you. And, as you know, the penalty for such crimes is death by hanging."

"What do we do, then?" asked Cora.

"We need to hide you," said Mr. Blackwood. He began to pace, his hands clenched behind his back. "Outside of Tarian. I have a sizeable estate near Aber to the south . . . Yes, that's best, I think. We can have you out of the city by evening."

"For how long? I'll need to be here to help you modify the Works! When do you think I'll be able to return?"

Mr. Blackwood bit his lip. "I'm not certain," he mused. "It could be some time. I'm afraid we'll have to manage without you, though. It's just too dangerous. But I *can* keep you apprised of the situation. I have pigeons both here and there, and I often use them to communicate with my steward. You'll have access to them and I'll update you regularly, and you can send me messages too, if necessary." He eyed her a moment, hesitated, and then added, "But if there's an emergency and you need to contact me right away . . ." He crossed the room to his desk and pulled open a drawer. He withdrew two boxes. They were made of honey-colored wood and polished brass and were the size of small books. "Have you ever used a vault?" he asked.

Cora's eyes widened. "Mr. Blackwood, I don't think—"

"That I should entrust you with a vault? Nonsense. You're

responsible, Cora, one of the most responsible people I know, and your safety is important to me. I hope you know that. Take it." He offered her one of the boxes. Tentatively Cora reached out and took it.

"Will I even be able to use it? I haven't been trained, you know."

"Ah! A common misunderstanding. Vaults are made with new magic," said Mr. Blackwood. "That means they can be used by anybody. Their only limitations are that they won't work in places steeped with old magic, not that many such places remain. The Iron Spire, of course, and the older forests of Hibaria. But that won't be an issue for you."

"I don't know," Cora said. "If I break it—"

"You won't. Now, as I said, this is for an emergency only. This particular vault can send once and receive once, so don't use it needlessly. But keep it on your person, just in case. To use it, open it like this," Mr. Blackwood twisted the box he held, "and place the message here. Then close it and press here and here. The box will shake a little and the buttons will put off heat."

"That's it?"

"That's it. And even if you don't send me anything, don't forget to check it for any message that I might send you."

Cora looked in wonder at the small box in her hands and then carefully put it in the inside pocket of her coat.

"I know this is frightening," Mr. Blackwood said. "But you'll be fine. I'll be fine, and Tarian will be fine. We'll find a way through this."

Cora nodded. "How will you tell the Council that the Master is dead? Without raising suspicions, I mean. We can't afford to wait till his body is discov—"

"I'll find a way, Cora. Don't you worry about that. Now then," Mr. Blackwood walked toward the door, "it's time you were off. Gather what you need from the dormitory. The others are still out doing inspections and repairs, so no one will see you. I suggest you use the east door—I know my steward won't be at that end of the building at this hour—

then, as discreetly as you can, make your way down to the docks, to my ship, *The Frosted Crane*. She's at the south pier. Wasn't damaged in the attack, thankfully. I'll meet you at sundown. She's scheduled to sail this evening and you'll be aboard." Mr. Blackwood turned and rubbed his hands together. "Understood?"

Cora suddenly felt numb. A ship. She had not set foot on a ship or a boat since the Storm. Pushing her terror down, Cora managed a nod. She thanked Mr. Blackwood and left his office.

Her steps were heavy as she walked toward the dormitories. Everything had turned out so badly. In going to the Iron Spire, Cora had thought only of keeping Tarian safe and exonerating the Water Works and Mr. Blackwood, not to mention herself. She couldn't have known that the Sand Coin would be stolen and that her presence in the Spire would implicate her and put Mr. Blackwood in a worse position than he had been in before. But that's exactly what had happened and there was no hope of undoing any of it. And now, on top of it all, to keep things from becoming even worse, Cora had to somehow work up the courage to get on a ship and venture out to sea. She wasn't sure she could manage to do that.

The dormitory hall was silent as Cora slipped into her room. Going over to her bed, she fumbled in her pocket for the key to her trunk. She wouldn't need much: a heavier shirt, some extra socks . . . Her fingers closed around what felt like a coin in her pocket, and she drew it out. It was the silver token she had discovered in the Master's tower. She had completely forgotten to show it to Mr. Blackwood.

"Cora! I've been wondering where you were!" said a voice behind her. Cora spun around to see Will standing in the doorway.

"What are you doing back here?" Cora said with alarm. "I thought—"

"I got finished early. I'm pretty good at my job, remember?" He walked over to her. "But really, where have you been? And why do you have a circus token?"

"A what?"

"A circus token," said Will again, pointing at her hand. "From the Wandering Circus. They've been performing here for a few days. I didn't know you went to see them."

"You're sure this came from the Wandering Circus? Look at it closely," Cora said, handing Will the token. "You're positive?"

The boy looked at it and whistled. "Yes, it's theirs and then some. This one has a crow on *both* sides. That means it belongs to someone who works in the circus." He held the token up and showed her. "Cor, how did you get this?"

"I can't tell you that," said Cora. Her mind was racing. This was the clue she needed! If what Will was saying was true, this had been dropped in the Iron Spire by someone from the Wandering Circus. Someone from the circus was responsible for the theft of the Sand Coin. Suddenly Cora felt a spark of hope. There was, perhaps, a way forward. She held out her hand for the token.

Will didn't give it to her. "Can't tell me, huh? Well, how about you tell me where you've been."

"No! It's none of your business. Now give me the circus token!"

He pursed his lips and walked to the window and looked out at the city. "Not till you tell me where you got this."

Cora considered the situation. She owed Will nothing, least of all an explanation. Well, that wasn't exactly true. He had just essentially told her the location of the missing Sand Coin, so she owed him a lot. But it was Will . . .

"I can't tell you where, I just can't," said Cora. "But . . . something important was stolen, and I think whoever dropped that was the thief."

Will considered this and then said, "Was it yours? The thing that was stolen?"

"No, but like I said, it's important."

"How important?"

"Really, really important. I can't tell you anything besides that."

"Important enough to try to get it back?"

Cora narrowed her eyes. "That's my business."

"You know, Cora, I thought about joining the circus a few years ago. I got to know one of the boys in the Wandering Circus. For the past couple years, we've thrown knives together whenever they come to the city. I'm going to see their performance this afternoon."

"What's your point, Will?"

"If you want a real chance at getting this thing back, whatever it is, you would need to join the Wandering Circus. But you'd need an introduction. And that's something only I can provide."

"I can't join the circus. To do that I'd have to have . . . skills. Doing flips or archery or walking on my hands or something. Those performers have probably been doing that since they were small. Really, Will, I don't have time for this. Just give me the token." She held her hand out again.

"Not so fast," said Will. "Two things. First, the Wandering Circus is *only* made up of children and people our age. It's their thing. So you'd fit right in. And second . . . I promise I can get you in, no matter how untalented you say you are."

A circus made up only of young people. Which meant that a child, or at worst, someone her own age had stolen the Sand Coin and was guarding it. If Will really *could* get her in . . . maybe there *was* a way out of this mess. Maybe.

"So what's the catch?" asked Cora.

Will smiled slowly. "You just have to tell me what was stolen."

Cora bit her lip. She hated dealing with Will. For an instant she considered running to Mr. Blackwood to tell him about the circus. But no. He was already neck-deep in trouble because of her, and further involving him would probably only make matters worse. As much as she didn't want to tell Will about the theft of the Sand Coin, it was her only choice.

Besides, with Will's introduction to the circus, Cora could find and return the Sand Coin, and clear Mr. Blackwood's name, not to mention her own. And she wouldn't have to get on that ship . . .

Cora felt guilty leaving Mr. Blackwood without any warning or explanation, but, she reasoned, if she didn't tell him where she was going, he wouldn't have to lie to the Council.

"How can I know you're telling me the truth, Will? How do I know you can actually get me into the circus?"

"You'll have to trust me. But if not," Will tossed her the token and started for the door, "the best of luck to you."

The boy was insufferable. "Fine, I'll tell you," Cora said. "But you can't tell anyone else."

Will smoothly spun around, triumph in his eyes. "Of course. I wouldn't dream of it."

"It was the Sand Coin."

"Serious?" When Cora didn't answer, the grin on Will's face slowly faded. "You're serious."

CHAPTER FIVE

THE WANDERING CIRCUS

THE STREETS OF TARIAN BUSTLED with activity as Cora and Will made their way through the Middle Ward. Shops were hanging yellow and blue flags in preparation for the Week of Memories. It was one of Cora's favorite holidays, an annual festival that commemorated the Great War. There would be gatherings in the squares where the major battles would be reenacted and the history of the conflict recounted.

"Look! They've started to set up their carvings!" said Will. He ran over to a bakery. Through the window Cora could see several waist-high, wooden figures. They were scattered among the baskets of bread on display.

Will pointed at a carving of a human-like creature. "You think Spindles really looked like that? I mean, they were supposed to be *fierce!*"

The creature's fingers were long, and its body was unrealistically thin. "I doubt it," said Cora. "That thing looks pretty weak."

Will had already moved on. He stopped and peered through the window of a leather worker. "This place has a Winged Guardsman from Aurian. A good one too!" He held his hand beside his face to block the sun. "And that's a carving of a shapeshifter, I think. But you'd never know, would you?"

"Let's go, Will. We need to get to the circus. You can look at all these on your way home."

"You're the boss!" Will said, pulling himself away from the window.

It was late afternoon and the sun was hot. They kept to the shade as best they could and soon passed from the Middle Ward into the Upper Ward. They turned down a broad boulevard. It was even more crowded on this street, but they both wove through the throng effortlessly, ducking beneath high-wheeled carts and slipping through the shifting mass of people.

"How many apples you want?" Will called over his shoulder as they turned onto the Needle. Seamstresses and cloth merchants lined the street, but there were some fruit stands as well. He walked over to an apple cart and pulled some coins from a pocket inside his cloak. "Cor?"

"It's 'Cora'. And I'll get my own, thanks."

Will flashed her a smile and shrugged. "Suit yourself."

Cora dug in her bag for some coppers and handed them to the vendor for a pair of summer apples.

"Got everything you'll need in there?" asked Will, pointing at her bag with his chin as they set out again.

"Of course!" Cora tried to sound confident, but failed. She wasn't at all sure that she had brought everything she might need. The small satchel contained some hastily gathered clothes and a blanket, as well as some paper and pen and a bottle of ink. And her money, of course, along with the vault Mr. Blackwood had given her. But had she forgotten something? Cora certainly wasn't going to ask Will his opinion, so she changed the subject.

"Who's this friend of yours? Can he be trusted? I mean, he's not a thief, is he?"

Will bit into one of his apples and chewed slowly. "Good, huh? Crisp. Sweet." When Cora didn't reply he said, "Right. His name is Dane. We met a while back, when the Wandering Circus first came to

Tarian. He's never stolen anything from me, but I suppose I can ask him if he stole the Sand Coin."

Cora quickly looked from side to side, but no one seemed to have heard. Still, she grabbed Will's arm and jerked him to a stop. "This isn't funny!" she hissed. "And you can't mention it where people can hear!"

"Relax, Cor." He brushed her hand away.

"It's 'Cora'," she said through gritted teeth, "and no, I won't relax. This is serious. Now, can your friend be trusted?"

Will looked exasperated. "We're friends, but I hardly ever see him. We throw knives together. That's it. I kind of doubt he's *the* thief, but I don't know." After a pause he added, "But he might know who it is. They're all pretty close. Like a family."

"They're probably *all* in on it," muttered Cora. "The circus is probably just a cover for stealing things."

"I doubt it." Will's tone was dismissive. "Wouldn't be good for business. If they just went around thieving everywhere, they'd eventually get caught and then they couldn't come back. I think it's probably just one of them. A bad apple, you might say." He held up his apple core, pleased with his joke.

Cora ignored it. "They wouldn't get caught if they were really good at thieving."

Will shook his head. "I've seen their performance. It's amazing. They make a lot of money performing, and I can't believe the circus is just a means to an end."

"Fine," Cora said. They walked on in silence for a few minutes. Then she asked, "You're sure you can get me in?"

"I told you I could," Will said with a grin. "Trust me, alright?"

They came to the end of the Needle and turned onto a wide, tree-lined street. It was near the northern edge of the city and ahead Cora could see the city gates. Even though there was a steady stream of people walking through the gates, she could clearly make out members of the City Guard standing on either side of the road. Several lounged in the gatehouse, but three or four of them watched the crowd, occasionally pulling someone aside to ask a question. It was hardly surprising, given it was their job. Still, she stopped, suddenly uneasy. "Wait, Will."

The boy looked at her and then looked ahead at the guards at the gates. "Are they after you, Cor?" His voice was low.

She didn't want to lie so she just said, "We should be fine. There are a lot of people around. I'll just keep my head down." Even so, Cora hastily pulled her hair out of its ponytail and arranged it on her shoulders. It felt odd to have it down. Then she pulled off her coat and stuffed it in her bag. If the City Guard had been given her description, hopefully this was enough to escape their notice.

"Looks nice that way," said Will. "You ever read about the Fire Queen? You could be her. Well, except she didn't have freckles."

"Be quiet, Will."

"I'm not making fun of you. I'm serious. If you had a crown and a spear, you could be her."

Ignoring him, she walked up the street toward the gates. But as she neared them, Will darted past her and ran straight into the nearest guard. The guard grunted in surprise as Will staggered and fell to the ground.

"Watch it, whelp!" growled the guard. Two others came over, and one of them picked Will up by his collar.

"I'm sorry, sir," said Will. "I wasn't paying attention." He made eye contact with Cora and nodded slightly to the side. Cora rolled her eyes, but ducked her head and walked through the gates.

Several minutes later Will joined her.

"That wasn't necessary," Cora said. "I would have been fine."

"Hiding from the guards . . ." Will shook his head in disapproval. "Speaking of trustworthy . . . you're not who I thought you were, Cor." He made a show of looking around before he whispered, "Don't tell me . . . you're a spy from Labryn Waite. No. A shapeshifter. You're not a shifter, are you?"

"Don't be ridiculous, Will."

They joined the stream of people leaving the city, most of whom it was clear were also going to the circus. Clumped in twos and threes, many were talking excitedly about the performance as they made their way up the road.

They crested a hill and there was the circus laid out before them. It was a sprawling collection of wagons and colorful tents, flags, and lanterns. A high rope was strung between two poles and a bright yellow canvas wall surrounded it all. The crowd funneled through a gap in the front. A huge, red banner stretched over the opening. It read:

THE WANDERING CIRCUS
Amazing Acts! Death-Defying Displays! Performing Erdynian!
3 Coppers to See It All!

As Cora and Will drew closer, they could see that two boys were standing beside the entrance, collecting admission. Between the boys sat a massive dog. Its bared teeth were long and yellow and sharp and its eyes were not at all friendly. People handed over coins and the boys dropped them into a heavy looking box and handed them something in return.

"Don't worry, Cor, I'll pay for us," said Will.

"I'm not worried," she replied, "and you won't."

They paid their coppers and the boys gave them tokens. "Keep these with you at all times," said the taller one. He had rust-colored hair and a scar beneath one eye. "You're not safe if you don't."

Cora glanced down at the token. It was the same as the one she had in her pocket, except the image of the crow was only on one side.

Once inside the canvas wall, Will said, "It protects you from the animals. They'll explain at the beginning of the performance. It's also their way of making sure people don't sneak in. They can ask to see your token at any time, and if you don't have one, they'll toss you out."

"How does it protect you? Is it magic?"

"Well it's not a suit of armor. Of course it's magic. It's a charm," said Will.

"You're really unpleasant, you know that?"

Will, unfazed, continued. "The crow on the token, in case you're wondering, is the Erdynian that performs with them. Hard to believe, I know, but it's a real talking bird. I saw it last year and it's pretty amazing."

"I'm sure it is," muttered Cora.

A murmur of anticipation hung in the air as the crowd slowly made its way along a path that wound through tents and animal enclosures. They moved past a fenced-off area filled with horses, then through an area with a variety of cages and pens that housed boars and foxes and badgers. One of the cages, with iron bars that were noticeably thicker than any of the others, contained a bear with shaggy brown fur. It was twice as tall as Cora. It showed her its teeth with a snarl and struck the bars with its claws.

They rounded a corner and passed one of the performers, a pale, thin girl with long, jet-black hair. The girl's hands and wrists were wrapped with narrow strips of cloth that disappeared beneath her sleeves. She was brushing the coat of what looked like a giant weasel, and even though Cora had never before seen a giant weasel, it was the girl's wrappings that held Cora's attention. *She must have been bitten or clawed,* Cora thought with horror.

The crowd kept moving and they came to a large open space cordoned off with rope and fishing nets. The milling throng spread out, and Will led Cora to one end of the ring. The ground here was higher, giving them a clear view of where the performance would take place.

After a while the space around the ring was full. Suddenly, a trumpet rang out and drums thundered.

A wave of young performers entered the ring on horseback. As the galloping horses made a circuit around the ring, the performers stood in their stirrups and then, one by one, they leapt to stand on their saddles, their arms outstretched to either side. The last boy, standing atop an iron-colored horse, casually juggled three balls with one hand while he ate an apple with the other. He looked bored. The crowd cheered.

Cora leaned over and whispered to Will, "You two would probably be best friends." Will raised an eyebrow. "You know, because of the apple."

Will nodded. "No, I understood. That was *almost* funny, Cor. I like that you're trying."

She wanted to knock the smile off his face. But that would only encourage him.

"Ladies and gentlemen!" shouted the boy. He tossed the apple core over his shoulder and let the three balls fall neatly into a bag that hung on his back. "Welcome to the Wandering Circus!" There were more cheers and the boy continued to ride in a circle as he spoke. "Upon entering this fine show, you were given a token." He held up a piece of silver that caught the sunlight. "It is imperative that you keep this with you during the performance. We have gained mastery over the beasts that you will see later, but they remain wild and savage things. We have gained mastery over them, but these animals are not tame." The crowd quieted, unease rippling through it. "But fear not! This token, imbued with power by Rascha the Erdynian, affords you protection. It has power, power to quell the rage of these creatures, and if it is in your possession, you will be safe.

"As a show of our appreciation to you for coming to our performance, it is yours to keep. Now you may say, 'What use would I have for a trinket such as this apart from your circus? I rarely encounter wild beasts.' And I would answer by telling you that this token has other qualities as well. Crafted by an Erdynian, it is a charm against misfortune and a ward against bad dreams. And it blunts the power of bad memories."

Cora looked down at the token in her hand. It seemed unlikely that it could do all the things the boy claimed. But then she remembered waking in the Cells that morning. Last night was the first time she hadn't had a nightmare in several days, and she'd had the token from the Iron Spire in her pocket. Maybe the boy was telling the truth.

She carefully slipped the token into her pocket beside the other and turned her attention back to the boy.

". . . who among us wouldn't benefit from less misfortune? And so, dear patrons, accept this gift from us. Keep it on your person and enjoy the benefits it confers."

The rest of the children had dismounted while the boy spoke, and now began to juggle scarves and colorful balls. They stood on one another's shoulders and leapt and tumbled through hoops, and then through hoops that had been set on fire, and then through hoops ringed with sharp knives. They threw small, disc-shaped targets in the air and shot them with arrows. One girl shot two targets at once, her arrow passing through one and lodging in the other. A boy with hair like straw and crooked teeth threw knives in rapid succession, knocking discs out of the air with ease. Will pointed at him and said, "That's Dane." Cora, along with the rest of the crowd, watched in wonder, clapping and oohing and aahing.

As the performers exited the ring, a fox ran into the ring on its hind legs, pursued by three dogs, also on their hind legs. People roared with laughter. The fox yapped and the dogs barked and nipped at the fox's tail. They made a circuit and were gone again as quickly as they had appeared.

There was more juggling, mostly of knives and lit torches and other dangerous things, and more animal acts. The giant weasel Cora had seen earlier balanced a rabbit on its nose and somehow refrained from eating it. There was a boar race (the boars were ridden by squirrels), and the fox and dogs made another appearance, but this time the fox chased the dogs.

As evening was falling, the great brown bear that had snarled at Cora entered the ring, a boy riding on its back. It was the boy who had made the announcement at the beginning, and he still looked bored despite being on the back of a fierce looking bear. The bear kicked a large ball into the center of the open space and then, trundling over, climbed onto it with ponderous effort. At first the beast simply balanced on the ball, but then with a shifting of its feet, the bear began to slowly roll the ball across the open ground while staying on top of it. All the while the boy sat easily on its back. At one point he yawned. It was all very impressive.

The bear stepped down from the ball and kicked it away with a growl. There was thunderous applause. The boy casually waved, hopped to the ground, and together they walked out of the ring.

A hush fell over the audience as the spectators' attention was drawn to the high rope pole on the far side of the ring. A girl had begun to climb the pegs. Up and up she went until she stood at the top on a small platform. And then she stepped out onto the rope.

Someone in the crowd gasped and people drew back from the nets as a boy led a pack of wolves into the ring. The other animals had seemed tame, despite what the bored boy had claimed, but the wolves were something else. The word "wild" seemed laughably inadequate to describe them. They looked like an avalanche of teeth and claws teetering on the edge of a cliff. The wolves stood taller than the boy, but he appeared unafraid. He calmly motioned to the giant beasts and though they snapped their jaws at him, they followed his direction and spread themselves out along the ground beneath the high rope. They sat on their haunches and began to howl.

Except there was no sound; their howls were silent. The air was suddenly cold, and bits of white and blue swirled up from their open mouths and seemed to gather on the rope above them. Cora thought, *These couldn't be . . .*

"Winter wolves," whispered Will. "Only winter wolves could do that!" For once, he actually seemed surprised by something. He shivered and hugged himself. Cora was speechless.

Above, the girl walked slowly across the now frosty, snow-covered rope. Small chunks of ice dislodged with each step and spun down to the ground. As she drew closer, Cora saw that it was the girl with the bandaged hands.

About three-quarters of the way across, the girl stopped, raised one foot off the rope, and grasped her foot in her hand. Raising her foot could have been part of the act—it probably *was* part of the act—but Cora saw her desperately flick away a piece of ice right before she grabbed her shoe.

"This is ridiculous!" Cora breathed. It was dawning on her that by joining the circus, she too might have to ride a bear or herd winter wolves or maybe even walk across an icy rope, and that she might very well die in the process. Her hands shook and despite the cold radiating from the wolves, Cora began to sweat.

As the girl finished her walk and descended the pole to cheers and applause, it was announced that the final act was the performing Erdynian.

"Just wait," said Will. "Have you ever seen an Erdynian?"

"No, but you might have mentioned it's pretty amazing."

He looked at her, unsure if she was making fun of him. "It is," he finally said.

The sun crept toward the mountaintops to the west and the air grew chill. Children trooped into the ring, many of them carrying lanterns. All the performers were there, and they blew on trumpets or beat on drums and urged everyone to cheer. The audience roared.

At the end of the procession came a milky stag with antlers white as bleached bone. It pulled a small cart. On the back of the cart, on a carved perch, sat an enormous crow.

"Ladies and gentlemen!" shouted a boy. "Behold! Rascha the Erdynian!"

Silence fell. And then the bird spoke. Its voice was clear and it carried across the ring.

"You have, no doubt, heard of Erdynians, though many of you may believe us to be nothing more than a story. But we are real, though indeed there are fewer of us than there once were. We possess knowledge. Wisdom. Power." Several people in the crowd muttered. They certainly *had* heard of the Erdynians, and while impressed, they were also suspicious. These talking creatures were, after all, from Erdyn, the birthplace of Augrind. It was Augrind who had started the Great War and thrown Hibaria and the Islands into chaos.

The crow appeared unruffled by this response and continued to speak. "Allow me to demonstrate this power." The bird peered out at the people, slowly shifting its feet as its gaze swept all around. "You," the bird finally said, cocking its head to one side. "The woman in the front with the red shawl, next to the man in the blue and green striped coat. Yes, you." The woman who had been singled out looked embarrassed and a little nervous.

"You are happy," said the crow. "Despite all that is going on in this city, despite the attack yesterday morning, you are happy."

The woman nodded her head with some hesitation and glanced down at a young boy who stood beside her. The boy pressed himself into the woman and gripped her hand in both of his.

The crow continued. "I'll tell you why. Your son returned to you recently. He was . . . gone for some time, wasn't he?"

She nodded again. A hush fell over the crowd.

"Gone so long that you feared him to be lost. And yet he returned. After having found the Augur Tree."

Cora looked from the crow to the woman and her son, and from their shocked expressions saw that what the bird had said was true.

"As you know," said the crow, "no one knows where the Augur Tree is. But this boy has found it and carries the proof in his pocket."

"H-how can you know what he has?" stammered the woman. The wonder on her face was plain.

"I am Erdynian," croaked the bird. It almost seemed to shrug. Turning its head to survey the rest of the crowd, the crow added, "But lest you doubt I am what I say I am . . . see for yourselves."

There was a stirring in Cora's mind, a feeling as though someone were pressing in from the outside. Her skin tingled and then an image blossomed before her mind's eye. It was a fruit: reddish-orange with streaks of yellow, and it was oval, almost like an egg.

All around she heard gasps and shouts of surprise.

"I see fruit!"

"I see it too!"

"It looks so real I can almost touch it!"

"Boy!" commanded the crow, looking at the woman's son. The boy withdrew one of his hands from his mother's and reached into his pocket. When he pulled it out again, he was holding a piece of reddish-orange fruit.

CHAPTER SIX

Leave-Taking

ORA GASPED. THE BOY WAS holding the same fruit that was just now beginning to fade from her vision.

The people in the crowd murmured in wonder and then began to applaud, slowly at first as though unsure of themselves, but then with increasing enthusiasm. The Erdynian lowered its head as if bowing, basking in the applause. After several minutes of cheering and clapping, the stag turned and pulled the crow's cart out of the ring.

"I told you!" said Will. "Wasn't that incredible? You saw it, right? The fruit?"

"I saw it, Will." Grudgingly, Cora added, "It was impressive. But let's not forget why I'm here. How about you take me to your friend?"

Will led the way through the crowd. They hopped over the rope and made their way toward the center of the ring where they found Dane with two other performers, talking and laughing as they recounted some of their finer moments during the show. Dane caught sight of Will and waved him over.

"Will! It's good to see you. Didn't know if I would this time. Do you remember Felix and Tesh?" He gestured toward the boy and girl he had been talking with.

"Yeah, of course," said Will. "Felix, good to see you. Tesh, I saw that shot. Incredible." It was the girl who had shot two targets with the same arrow. She had brown skin and a mass of dark, curly hair tied up on top of her head. She nodded but didn't smile.

"You up for some throwing?" Will glanced at the sinking sun. "Looks like we have a little time."

"Sorry, but we're packing up and heading out tonight," said Dane.

"Tonight?" asked Will. "Why not in the morning?"

Dane shrugged. "We got here a day late—one of the wagon axles broke—and Anders says we've got to keep moving to make up time. Hopefully we can throw next time we're here."

"Sounds good," said Will. "Listen, this here is Cora. She's a friend of mine and is looking to join the circus—"

"We're full," interrupted Tesh. "Sorry."

Cora didn't think she really sounded very sorry at all.

"Even to take care of some of the animals? She's great with animals, aren't you, Cor?"

"Well, uh," Cora stammered, "I guess—"

Dane shook his head. "We really are full, Will. I mean, you can talk to Anders, but you'll be wasting your time."

"Where can I find him?" asked Will. He didn't seem the least put off by how things were going.

"Striped tent, just past the big feed wagon. But, Will, don't say I didn't warn you," Dane laughed. "Good to see you again. Till next time."

"Next time."

They walked down a row of tents and as soon as they were alone, Cora said, "I thought you said he could get me in!"

"We'll be fine," said Will. "Anders makes the decisions. We'll talk to him."

"Do you know him?"

"No," admitted Will, "but quit worrying. This will work."

Cora stopped and grabbed Will's arm. "You understand what happens if I don't get it back, don't you? This is *important*. Really, really important. I *have* to get into the circus."

Will looked her in the eyes, and after a moment his smile faded and his face grew serious. "I understand," he said.

Cora waited for the joke, but it didn't come. She nodded and muttered, "Good. Thanks."

They passed a wire cage full of squirrels and rabbits, then a large wagon piled with bales of hay, and then came to the striped tent. A red flag fluttered at its peak. Will stopped at the tent's entrance and called out. After a moment, the boy who had looked so bored during the performance emerged. He stood a head taller than Cora and was eating another apple. "What do you want?" he asked Will.

"I take it you're Anders," said Will. "I'm a friend of Dane's. He said you're the person to talk to about joining up."

"We're full," said Anders. "We don't need any help. Which, I believe, Dane would have told you already." The boy looked annoyed and turned to go back into the tent.

Will hesitated a moment and then said, "Wait. You should at least see what you'll be missing out on." He pulled a knife out of his sleeve. Without waiting for a reply from Anders, Will flung the knife. It whipped through the air, the blade flashing as it spun, and stuck in a pole thirty feet away. "Now imagine if she," he nodded toward Cora, "were standing against that pole. Imagine the crowd's reaction to that."

Cora almost choked. "What—?"

"Tempting, isn't it?" said Will to Anders, who was suddenly looking more interested. Will threw a second knife and it stuck in the pole right next to the other one. "I could do this all day."

Anders considered for a moment and then nodded slowly. "Alright," he said, rubbing his chin. "But you can throw knives at anyone. Unless she can do something equally impressive . . ."

"We're together," said Will. "It's both of us or neither of us."

"Neither then."

Will pulled out a third knife and threw it, not breaking eye contact with Anders. Cora watched as it buried itself in the pole between the other two blades. Anders glanced at the pole and pursed his lips. "Fine. But this is how it works: I'll watch you practice, and if I don't like it, you're out. If I do, you get to do a performance. If the performance goes well, you're official, you'll get your tokens and you'll get paid. But if you botch the performance, or any future performance, you're out. If you cause problems, you're out. If I find out I don't like either of you, you're out. Got that?"

"It sounds like you're saying we can't mess up," said Will.

"That's exactly what I'm saying."

Will smiled. "Shouldn't be a problem. I don't make mistakes."

"Good," said Anders. "Now go find Dane again and help him with whatever he needs. We're leaving in a couple hours." With that, Anders disappeared into his tent again.

As soon as Will had retrieved his knives and they were out of sight of Anders' tent, Cora rounded on Will. "What was that?" She was having a hard time not shouting. "Are you *crazy*? You're not going to throw knives at me!"

"Calm down, Cor. You said this was important, right?"

"Well, yes, but—"

"I took that seriously. Want me to go back and say we're not interested now?"

Cora ground her teeth. "No," she said. "But you weren't even supposed to join! You're not a part of this!"

"Two things. One, it became pretty clear you weren't going to get in without me. So I had to join to get you in. I was keeping the promise that I made you. You're welcome, by the way. And two, if you really want to get the Sand Coin back, you can't do it alone. Even though I don't think the whole circus is in on it like you do, whoever *did* steal it is smart and skilled and probably dangerous. You need help. So instead of complaining that I joined, you should thank me."

Cora wanted to punch him. If she *did* need help (and she wasn't convinced that she did), Will was the last person she would choose. "We'll talk about it later," she snapped and walked away, scowling.

When they found Dane again and Will told him the news, the boy was speechless. Finally he said, "I've been trying to get you to join for so long. This is great! So what will the two of you do?"

"Eh, it's not important," said Will, waving away the question. "But Anders said you might need some help packing up?"

"Yeah. I was just about to put the strongbox onto Anders' wagon," Dane said. "Want to give me a hand?" He patted the heavy chest that had been used to collect admission to the circus. "It's not light."

Together Will and Dane heaved the box onto the back of the wagon. It took its place among several other iron-banded boxes and chests. The dog that had guarded the entrance to the circus was now accompanied by two others, and they all sat in the wagon. They growled at Cora when she came close.

"Watch yourself," said Dane with a laugh. "They take their job seriously. And these," he tapped the circus token hanging around his neck, "don't work on them. Neither do the ones you got when you paid admission. The dogs only let me and Tesh and Anders near, so be sure to keep your distance."

"For sure," said Cora. She stepped back, hesitated, then asked, "Are all these chests filled with earnings from performances? That's a lot of money."

"A lot of it is. We've been on the road for a while," said Dane. "But there's other valuable stuff mixed in as well. Belongs to Anders mostly. And there are a couple chests of tokens. We do lots of shows and give out a lot of those. Anyway, why don't you come and help me pack those nets."

He showed them how to roll the fishing nets that served as the barrier during the performance. While they were doing this, Tesh rode up on the bear. She dismounted and the bear began to pull up stakes that had been driven into the ground.

"What are you still doing here?" she asked, frowning at Cora.

"Guess the circus wasn't so full after all," said Cora. "Anders said we could join."

"Unbelievable," muttered Tesh.

"Come on, Tesh," said Dane. "It'll be fine. You know Will is great and I'm sure Cora is too."

The girl just shook her head and went back to directing the bear.

The tents came down quicker than Cora would have guessed. She lost herself in the work of bundling poles and rolling canvas and coiling rope. The high rope poles took a little longer to bring down, but some of the larger animals helped with those, much in the same way that the bear had helped with the stakes. Cora was amazed, but after a while she decided if one could train an animal to run on its hind legs, one could train an animal to do anything.

Now, as the first stars began to appear, as the summer Constellations grew bright in the darkening sky, the circus wagons started to roll north and east along the Eastway. Dane drove one of them, snapping the reins and clucking at the horses, and Cora and Will sat on either side of him on the hard, wooden seat. The wagon creaked and lurched as it bounced over the uneven road.

As they came to the top of a hill, Cora looked back at Tarian. Some of the windows in the taller buildings still shone with lights. Cora thought she could make out the Council Chamber and wondered how Mr. Blackwood's fellow councilors had received the news of the Master's death. She assumed Mr. Blackwood had found a way to tell them without implicating either her or himself. At least now the Council could prepare the city—as best they could—for the larger attack that was sure to come, not to mention the tidal surge that would occur at the Turn.

Cora felt a pang of guilt at having not told Mr. Blackwood where she had gone. He had been nothing but kind to her, and so for her to disappear without a word probably felt like betrayal to Mr. Blackwood. Or, at the very least, like ingratitude on her part. She hoped that wasn't how he felt. But if she could find the Sand Coin and return it, that would make up for everything.

Still, she briefly considered sending him a message with the vault. That she was safe, that she was on the trail of the Sand Coin's thief, that all would be well. She reached into her bag and felt the cool, smooth wood of the vault. But Cora could only use the thing once, and what if there was a real need for it later? It would be best to wait. She withdrew her hand and closed the bag.

The three of them—Cora, Will, and Dane—ate a late supper as they went along, and Cora listened as Will and Dane fell into exchanging stories. It was an easy conversation with plenty of laughter, plenty of give and take. Will was being Will and, in this moment, he wasn't, Cora reluctantly admitted, completely unpleasant to be around, though she had no wish to join in.

She yawned and settled back on the wagon seat, letting the chatter wash over her, and she stared up at the stars. The Bear stalked across the eastern horizon and she could make out the Dragon's tail through the trees a little to the north. It was her sister Hildi who had taught her the Constellations. She had told Cora all their names and all the stories about them that she knew. "They see us," Hildi would say. "They look down and see us. And they don't ever sleep, Cor, and that means you can rest safe."

Cora touched the beads of her bracelet as she looked up at the shape of the Bear. Was it really anything more than just a collection of stars in the sky? Cora wasn't so sure. If the Sky Lords *were* real, they had watched but done nothing to keep her sister and parents safe in the Storm. And that meant that the Constellations weren't to be trusted. They hadn't kept her family safe, and so it was doubtful they would stand guard over her. She had to look after herself.

With a hollow feeling in her stomach, Cora burrowed down deeper into her coat, closed her eyes, and slept.

CHAPTER SEVEN

Mr. Blackwood
Sends a Message

OVERSEER THADDEUS BLACKWOOD stood beside the fire in his study. As he thumbed some tobacco into his pipe, he mulled over the situation he found himself in. Everything had been going so well, but now . . . unease rippled through his mind. Blackwood lit his pipe and lowered himself into his leather chair to think.

There had been signs over the past few years that the Master of Tides was nearing his end—small, seemingly insignificant signs—but they were there for the discerning eye, and Thaddeus Blackwood had a discerning eye. He also had ambitions and aspirations. And so he had proposed to the other members of the Council the construction of the Water Works, a vast project that would, ostensibly, strengthen the Master's tidal defense, focus it, make it more potent. In reality, Blackwood had designed it to ultimately supplant the Master, though of course he kept this to himself. The Master's remoteness and his infrequent interactions with the Council, let alone the people of Tarian, made Blackwood confident he could make the scheme work. At first the members of the Council had balked, raised objections, dragged their feet. But when the Storm had struck . . . any hesitations that had remained within the Council had evaporated.

The Storm had not ravaged the city directly, but everyone had been able to see it furiously churn across the Eastern Deep, a colossal flickering beast on the prowl. It had been a sobering sight. The natural question that many people asked was, "What if the Storm had come for Tarian?" And so a project that promised to better control the surging waters around the city, whether they had been called by the Master of Tides or not, was one that the Council knew must be implemented, and the sooner the better.

During the initial phases of construction, Blackwood had moved tentatively. Perhaps the Master would notice after all and his wrath would descend on Blackwood like a tidal wave. But nothing had happened. Indeed, it seemed that the Master of Tides was completely unaware of the construction of the Works. Emboldened, Overseer Blackwood had continued, bolstered by his workforce of strays and runaways. He had the children weave the Works into the fabric of the city, had them assemble a mind-numbing network of pipes and channels that would provide more of a defense than the Master of Tides ever could. The plan was that when the Master finally died, under Blackwood's guiding hand, Tarian would step from the shadows of the past—a past steeped in old power and arcane magic—and the city would be reborn, defined by its trade and commerce and industry. And Blackwood would lead it.

But before any of this could happen, Blackwood had to deal with the Sand Coin. It was understood, though it had never happened, that when the Master of Tides died the Council would choose a new Master. They would find someone qualified and worthy and bestow on him the Sand Coin and its power. For Blackwood, this would of course ruin everything. He needed the thing gone! He had long ago ruled out taking it for himself, for the power of the Coin exacted a price and changed the one who wore it, and Blackwood wanted neither to pay a price nor be changed. Besides, with the Water Works he didn't need the Master's power. But what to do with the Sand Coin? It had to be removed, hidden, destroyed, *something*, or Blackwood would have a new Master to contend with. But even before he could do that, he had to *get* to the Sand Coin, and that would be no easy thing, even after the Master died.

While Blackwood was grappling with this difficulty, another problem arose. As the Water Works neared completion, he had come to the realization that the Works was too vast a thing, too complex a thing to power once the Master was gone. The wood furnaces Blackwood had built could not possibly be kept burning long enough nor hot enough to make all the machinery run in the way he needed it to. He needed a different fuel.

He needed magefire.

And there was the solution to both his problems. Unpalatable, certainly, but it was a solution nevertheless. And so that spring he had sailed to Agendor.

Blackwood slowly smiled as he recalled the meeting.

He took the chair offered him. It was hard, angular, anything but comfortable, and it put him a little below his host, forcing Blackwood to look up at the man. At the magician. Blackwood was careful to let neither his irritation nor his nervousness show.

"You have come a long way," said Imago, staring impassively at Blackwood. The magician's voice was calm and not unfriendly, but his eyes were hard as flint. He absently adjusted his robes with one hand. The fingers, Blackwood noted, were long and slender, their skin almost translucent. Blackwood shifted uncomfortably before he could stop himself.

"Indeed," Blackwood said, trying to focus on the matter at hand. "As I wrote in my message, I have a proposal that I think will interest you."

"For your sake, I hope you are correct," said Imago.

"I have need of magefire—"

"That sounds more like a request," the magician sneered. He abruptly rose from his chair.

"—for which I will tell you how the Sand Coin can be yours."

Blackwood caught the brief, ever so slight widening of Imago's eyes. For an instant they had looked . . . hungry. But then Imago laughed dismissively, derisively.

"Can you also deliver to me Curyn's Ring? Or the March Wardstone? Perhaps you know the secret to entering the Seeing Tower?"

Blackwood ignored the magician's mockery. "Believe me or do not. But I assure you, if you supply me with magefire, the Sand Coin can be yours by year's end."

"Who are you to make and keep such a promise?"

Blackwood shrugged. "As I said, believe me or do not." When the magician did not reply, Blackwood pushed his chair back and stood.

"Sit, dog!" snarled Imago.

Blackwood once again took his seat but remained silent.

Imago walked to the fire, his back to Blackwood. "Tell me," the magician said, his voice once again even, "how the Sand Coin can be mine."

"The Master of Tides is near death," said Blackwood. "I alone in all of Tarian am aware of this, and will know when he draws his last breath. But even when he is dead, I haven't the resources to enter the Iron Spire to retrieve the Sand Coin—it is too heavily guarded. For one such as yourself, on the other hand, it would, I presume, be a simple matter."

Imago turned and smiled like a cat that had cornered a mouse. "Well," he said, "now that you have divulged your secret, I can dispatch my own spies to inform me when your Master dies. Which means I don't need to give you magefire. In fact, I don't need you at all."

"Ah. I thought you might say that." Blackwood looked down and straightened his waistcoat, taking a moment to polish one of his buttons. "But you do need me." He looked the magician in the eye. "After what you did at Sidyn, you know the three city-states allied against you. Labryn Waite, Aurian, Tarian. And your other designs—yes, I know about your other designs—when they come to fruition, they will push all of the smaller cities and towns into that alliance as well.

"But if you give me what I ask, I can promise that Tarian will no longer stand against you. If you give me what I ask, Tarian will be your ally. Which would be useful in your plans, would it not?"

Imago studied Blackwood, his eyes slightly narrowed. At length he said, "Perhaps it would. How much magefire do you need?"

Now, after all this time, Blackwood's plans had finally begun to unfold. Two weeks ago, his spies, their telescopes trained on the Master's tower, had confirmed that there had been no movement in the Spire for days. He had sent a pigeon to Imago, and the magician had responded that his thief would arrive soon. And the thief *had* arrived and had *managed to steal the Sand Coin without being detected.* Blackwood had received a pigeon telling him the deed had been done and where he could find the magefire.

Everything had been going so well! But then, *on the very next day* the attack had come! It had been wholly unexpected, wholly unlooked for, and Blackwood had been caught on his heels. Attacks this late in the summer were unheard of! He had been making final modifications to his machinery to accommodate the magefire, in secret and alone of course, because even the children he employed were not privy to his real plans. And so the Water Works had failed during the attack. They were not yet ready to function without the Master. Blackwood had thought he had time! And now it was all starting to unravel . . .

The Overseer stood and paced back and forth across the carpeted floor, in and out of moonlight and firelight, puffing furiously on his pipe as he thought.

He had assumed the Master's passing would go unnoticed for weeks, months, perhaps even a year! Blackwood had counted on the magefire-powered Water Works to thwart the tidal surge when it came at the Turn. He had the same expectations for the eventual attacks from Tarian's enemies. He had intended that none of this would be known to the Council until much later. Blackwood would have eventually revealed that his machinery alone had been defending the city. This would demonstrate that Tarian didn't need a Master at all. The transition would have been brought about, just like that.

But the attack had ruined everything. Well, more accurately, Cora had ruined everything. Blackwood had managed to create a plausible explanation for the failure of the Works by planting the piece of driftwood in Harbor 2. That explanation would have stood up to the Council's scrutiny, but Cora had still uncovered the truth.

It was unnerving how quickly she had pieced together what had actually happened. That she had managed to infiltrate the Iron Spire still astounded him. The girl was remarkable! But while Blackwood was relieved she had kept her discovery to herself despite her capture, he knew everything could come crashing down in a moment. One word from her, and his plan would be ruined. So, he had affected her rescue.

It hadn't only been to cover his tracks, though.

Why did it have to be Cora? She was so curious, so intuitive, so intelligent, and he had come to depend on her. He valued her insights. He had come to enjoy working with her. It was more than that, though: Cora was the daughter he had never had. Blackwood saw in her a younger version of himself that had, over time, filled him with affection. With love.

Now all he felt was a dull ache for what he must do.

Blackwood's plan had been to send Cora to his estates south of the Fenwood until all this had passed, until the Sand Coin was farther north, closer to Agendor, but she had failed to appear at the docks.

Blackwood knew she wouldn't go to the Council. But where *would* she go? And why had she fled from him? Did she somehow suspect his involvement in the theft? He had checked the vault paired with the one he had given her, but there was nothing. No message, no explanation for her disappearance. Perhaps he should write to her. But what could he say that would convince her to return? There were too many unanswered questions and they made Blackwood uneasy. Cora was intelligent and resourceful, and he knew she wouldn't just run away. She would want to get to the bottom of the missing Sand Coin, and that just wouldn't do.

Too much was at stake for a misstep now. Blackwood sighed as he stared into the fire. There was no good way to resolve this. There was only one way forward.

He would have to hire a handler.

Blackwood had never used a handler before, had never needed one, but he knew of a man named Hulder who was, Blackwood had been assured, the best handler there was. It was said that Hulder owned seven stalkers and he had never failed a mission.

Reluctantly, Blackwood made his way to his desk. He caught up a quill, dipped it, and scrawled a note, a few words on a bit of parchment. Then he went out onto the balcony. Despite the late hour, the pigeons moved restlessly in their cages. He carefully removed one, then tied the parchment to its leg. For a moment he held the bird, unable to let it go. Finally he murmured, "Forgive me, child." Then Blackwood released the bird into the night sky. Hulder would respond by week's end. And with a stalker involved, Cora would be dead soon after.

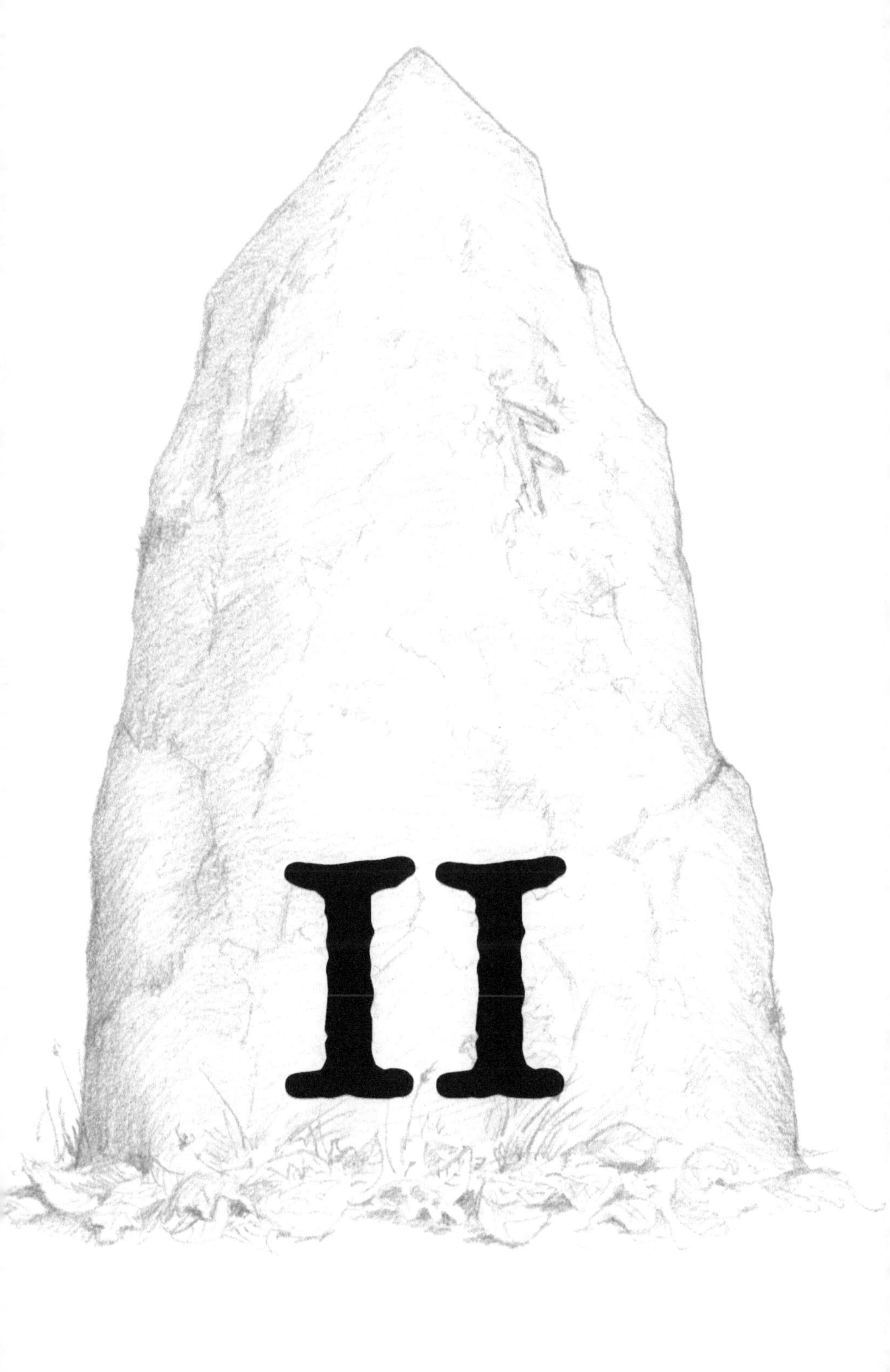

CHAPTER EIGHT

PRACTICE

CORA OPENED HER EYES AND gasped. She sat up, shaking.

"You alright?" asked a voice beside her. It was Dane and he was still driving the wagon and it was still night. Soft moonlight bathed everything in silver. Will was slumped over, wrapped in his cloak, asleep on the other side of Dane.

"I think so," said Cora. Whatever it was she had dreamed was gone. As she worked the stiffness out of her neck, she realized she wasn't even sure if she *had* been dreaming. No, she definitely hadn't been. "That's odd," she muttered.

"What?" asked Dane.

"Oh, nothing. How long before daylight?"

"Couple hours."

Sleep did not return. So Cora sat, looking out at the hills and patches of forest that stretched into the distance on both sides of the Eastway. The trees and folds of land were beautiful in the gray moonlight, but the realization that this was wild country, that it was outside of the protection of Tarian, slowly dawned on Cora.

"How . . . safe are we?" she whispered to Dane as she peered nervously into the darkness.

For a moment the boy looked confused, but then he smiled. "You mean from outlaws or wild animals? We're pretty safe. The dogs will warn us if anyone is near, and most of us can handle knives and bows, and the tokens protect us from animal attacks. And don't forget, we have the Erdynian. Even we don't know all of what Rascha is capable of."

Cora hadn't thought of that, and the knot of worry in her stomach eased. She settled in and watched the landscape slowly change around her until the sky to the east turned the color of pearls.

As the morning light spread across the cold sky, Cora saw the large form of the Erdynian crow floating high above the wagons. Its wings were spread wide, and the feathers looked like ragged sails trailing behind the bird. Its presence had been a source of comfort just hours before, but Cora now realized Will had been at least partly right: Her mission *was* more dangerous than she had anticipated. After seeing the performance the day before, Cora now knew that every member of the Wandering Circus was far more capable than she had initially thought. And she hadn't factored in the Erdynian.

Even so, it wasn't enough to justify enlisting Will's help in the search for the Sand Coin. He was unreliable and impulsive and he would undoubtedly make things worse. Cora just needed to think things through and come up with a plan on her own.

"I'm going to walk for a bit," she said to Dane in a low voice. Will was still asleep beside his friend, his head tipped back against the wagon seat, his hair disheveled, his mouth open. Dane nodded.

Cora jumped down and angled slightly away from the road, until she was a stone's throw away from the wagons. The long grass whispered with her passage. The air was chilly and smelled like the coming autumn.

She didn't have much time to find the Sand Coin. Mr. Blackwood could, as he had said, station soldiers on the docks to fight off the raiders who would probably soon return, but that wasn't really Cora's concern. Her main worry was the tidal surge that was only a few weeks away.

She didn't share Mr. Blackwood's optimism that the Works could be converted in time. And if she was right, the surge would destroy Tarian. She had to have the Coin back to the city by then. If she could get it into the hands of the new Master, hopefully chosen by the Council while she was away, all would be well.

Cora pushed a strand of hair out of her eyes. When Will had told her that the token she had found in the Spire belonged to someone in the circus, her first thought had been to find the person without a token. Finding them would lead her to the Sand Coin. But now that she knew what the tokens were for, Cora realized that whoever had lost their token would have gotten a new one by now. Who in their right mind would risk getting torn apart by winter wolves, or that bear, or the countless other wild animals in the circus, by walking around without the protection of a token?

But now Cora didn't think she needed to know *who* had stolen the Sand Coin at all. It wasn't important. Whatever Will thought, Cora was convinced the whole circus was in on the theft. Whoever had stolen it had almost certainly given it to Anders. He was in charge, after all. And where better to put it than on Anders' wagon that was guarded by the dogs?

Cora paused and shielded her eyes against the light of the rising sun. Up near a bend in the road was the wagon with the circus' earnings, pulled by a team of four horses. The dogs sat in the bed, their tongues hanging from their mouths. Yes, that was where the Sand Coin would be. Now Cora just had to figure out how to get it.

The circus wagons rumbled as they rolled, the long line snaking through the blue-green hills along the Eastway. The road hugged the coastline. There was no stopping that morning, and Cora, Will, and Dane once again ate as they rode, pushing ahead, mile after mile.

"Tell me," said Cora as she licked breadcrumbs from her fingers, "why aren't there any adults in the Wandering Circus?"

"Well," said Dane, "it has to do with how we started. Anders, Felix, Tesh, and I were from a place called Marin. That's a fishing village a ways south of here, past Aber. And our parents were out on the serpent hunt when the Storm came."

"Marin! That was down the coast from where I lived," said Cora. "So you're Storm Orphans too?"

"Yeah," Dane said in a low voice. He flicked the reins and looked away. After a while he went on. "The four of us had been sick. We were mostly better, but our parents decided it would be best if we stayed at home while the rest of the village went out. Everyone went. I mean *all* of them. It was supposed to be a really good year for the snakes and we sent out all of the boats that spring. So after the Storm, out of the whole village, only we were left. We were alone and not sure of what to do. Anders had this idea that we could travel and entertain people. You know, play instruments, perform plays, and people would pay us. Anders is the oldest, and has always had good ideas, so we went with it. It was hard, and it took a while to figure it out, but it's worked."

"Wow," said Cora. "That's . . . extraordinary. But how did you end up becoming a circus? And there are dozens of you now!"

"Well, things changed over time. Anders taught himself to juggle and the crowds really liked that, so we kept pushing in that direction. Tesh and I had hunted with our fathers before the Storm, so we started practicing more with bows and knives. Over time, the Youngers joined and brought different skills with them. And—"

"The Youngers?" asked Cora.

"Yeah. We call anyone who joined later a Younger. Most of them aren't as old as we are. Anyway, about two years ago we met Arburry. Lord Arburry, I suppose I should say. He lives north of here. 'You show promise,' is what he said, and agreed to become our partner. Or benefactor, I guess. He introduced us to the Erdynian and somehow talked it into joining us. He supplied us with the other animals and the tokens to protect us from them, in exchange for a cut of our profits. Victoria—that's the girl who did the high rope walk—joined around the time we met Arburry and she's *really* good with animals. We've done pretty well since then."

"What happened to her hands?" asked Cora.

"You mean the cloth strips?" said Dane. "Not really sure. Maybe someone's asked her, but I doubt she'd tell them. She doesn't talk a whole lot. They're always wrapped, though. Most of us get along with Victoria fine, but she's just kind of strange. Always has been." He shrugged.

The crow's shadow passed over them and with a glance up, Will asked, "What's it like to have an Erdynian around? Do you talk to it much?"

"Not really. Honestly, I thought it would be more interesting when it first joined." Dane looked up and squinted as he watched the crow float high above them. "But it just flies around and sleeps a bunch and does the shows. Which are amazing, don't get me wrong, but apart from that, it doesn't do a whole lot."

"This Lord Arburry," said Cora, "how involved is he in the circus?"

"Well, like I said, he gave us the animals, but he doesn't tell us how to run the show or anything. It's kind of nice. At first, I kind of thought it might be a mistake to partner with him, but he lets us do things our way for the most part. We're actually going to see him now."

"Why's that?"

"The Week of Memories is usually a pretty busy time in most cities and larger towns—the plays about the Great War, the telling of the stories, all that—so during the holiday, less people come to our performances. And with the Week right around the corner, it's a good opportunity to go back, give Arburry his split, then regroup. We'll do a few shows in the villages along the way. They're small enough that we'll get decent attendance, though nothing like we get in the bigger cities. Anyway, after we see Arburry, we'll head to Labryn Waite. We have a series of performances there in a month or so."

"Labryn Waite!" exclaimed Cora. "That's impossible! There's no way we'll get there in a month. We're going in the opposite direction!"

Dane looked at her sideways with a slow grin. "You don't know about the Doors, do you?"

"What doors?" asked Cora.

Dane laughed. "If you manage to stay in the circus long enough, you'll find out."

Try as they might, neither Cora nor Will could get Dane to explain further. The only thing he would say was, "You'll see."

Sometime in the late afternoon, Anders called for a stop. Cora hadn't seen a village since that morning and looking around, she doubted there was anything for miles. "We'll camp over there," Anders said, pointing to a large stretch of grass beside the road. "And even though there won't be a show tonight, we'll get a practice in."

Several of the children groaned. But despite the lack of enthusiasm, the wagons peeled out of line and everyone sprang into action. It was like watching a school of fish or a flock of starlings: A chaotic swarm of children seamlessly came together to unhitch the horses, lift the animal cages off the wagons, then pitch the tents, all within minutes.

As Dane finished setting up a weather-beaten tent, he said to Will, "You'll be in here with me. And Cora, you'll be in with Tesh. Hers is the blue one, down that way." He pointed down the row of tents.

"Is there any other option?" asked Cora.

"Not really." Dane smiled his crooked smile. "You'll get used to her. Really, you just have to get to know her." Cora suspected that getting to know Tesh would only lessen her opinion of the girl, but managed a half-hearted nod. *Besides,* she told herself, *it'll only be a few days. I can put up with her till I find the Sand Coin. Then I'm gone.*

After the tents were up, Dane and Will went to feed the horses.

When Cora started to follow, Dane said, "Help them," and pointed to the rest of the performers as they cleared the practice ground of rocks. Cora made an effort to join them, but the ground was already mostly clear, so she stepped over to a tree and leaned against it to wait for Will and Dane.

"Tired already?" Tesh walked over, giving Cora a disdainful look. "You need a nap?"

Cora's face reddened but she refused to be drawn in.

"Really, I can go get you a blanket. And a cup of milk? Think you'd like that?"

"Leave her alone, Tesh. I asked her to wait here."

Cora turned. Victoria, followed by six or seven badgers, was walking toward them.

"She's helping you?" Tesh's tone was incredulous.

Victoria didn't bother answering, but merely motioned for Cora to follow as she walked past. Without hesitation Cora did.

They made their way to the north side of the practice area. Victoria squatted down and ruffled the fur of two of the badgers. They, followed by the others, immediately began digging.

After a few moments of awkward silence Cora said, "Um, thank you. But why did you do that?"

"Tesh can be spiteful," said Victoria. Her tone was neutral, but her blue-green eyes flashed when she mentioned the curly-haired girl's name.

"Yeah, I noticed. Well . . . I appreciate it. My name is Cora by the way."

"I'm Victoria," said Victoria. She looked at Cora sideways without turning toward her.

Tesh was still watching them so Cora asked, "Do you actually need my help? Honestly, I don't know what to do and could use some direction." The others were beginning to disperse.

Victoria shook her head. "Just the high rope poles need to go up once the badgers are done digging. I'll have the bear do that. Then I'll put up the rope."

Cora glanced down and saw that one of the cloth strips that wound around Victoria's hand had come loose, revealing some markings on the girl's skin. The marks looked like a glistening tattoo of snake scales, all green and blue and silver. "Your, um, wrapping . . ." Cora said.

Victoria looked down and turned even paler than she already was. Something approaching terror flashed across her face as she quickly rewound the cloth to cover the marking. Her eyes flicked up toward Cora when she was done. She looked like a wild animal cornered by a hunter.

Cora was bewildered. But after a moment she gestured toward Victoria's hand and said, "I don't know what those are. Clearly it's important to you that no one sees them. I won't say anything to anybody about them, I promise."

The fear slowly retreated from Victoria's eyes, but they remained guarded. "Thank you," the girl finally said. The silence stretched out before she added, "Tesh is gone now."

It seemed like a dismissal, so Cora thanked Victoria again for saving her from Tesh and left the ring, slipping in among the tents and animal cages.

What a strange interaction. What were those markings and why would Victoria want to keep them hidden? Cora waved away the question. It wasn't her concern. No, she needed to stay focused. Perhaps, now that everything was set up, she could go and find the money wagon and search it if the dogs didn't happen to be around.

She didn't know where she was going, but Cora walked purposefully and had a story ready about how she was getting something for Victoria in case she ran into Tesh again. She wove in and out of the aisles between the tents and had just spotted the money wagon when someone shouted her name. It was Will.

"Where are you going?" he asked as he jogged over to her. "We have to practice! Anders won't like it if we're late."

Practice. Somehow Cora had forgotten. Her stomach turned at the thought of Will throwing knives at her.

"Now? Does it have to be right now? I'm . . ." she trailed off.

"What, going to look for the Sand Coin?"

"You can't keep using its name!" Cora whispered fiercely.

"Right," said Will. "Look, I'll help you later, but we need to go. We *have* to do this practice, and do it well. It's what'll get us in, remember? Otherwise, Anders will leave us behind."

Cora took a deep breath. Will was right. With a sinking feeling, she followed him back toward the ring.

No matter how good Will was, Cora really didn't want him throwing knives at her. He might slip, or the wind might blow the knife just enough off course, or she might not be able to stop herself from moving . . . She desperately tried to think of an excuse she could give to Anders, one he would accept, that would allow her to avoid her part in the performance. But nothing came to her.

Most of the other performers were already gathered, working on their juggling and hoop-jumping, shooting and throwing. Dane was there, twirling a knife in one hand while he talked to Tesh and Felix and Anders. Both high rope poles were up, and Victoria sat on one of the platforms as she secured the rope.

"Alright," said Will. "Go on over and stand against that tree." He pointed to the other side of the ring.

"How about you throw them all first, without me standing there," said Cora. "Just so I can see you're not going to kill me."

"We can't really do that." Will lowered his voice to a whisper and said, "We're supposed to have done this before. You're supposed to be alright with this. And they're all watching."

It was true. Everyone had stopped what they were doing, and their attention was on Cora and Will. Anders moved to the front of the crowd and stood with his arms folded across his chest.

Cora balled her fists and glared at Will, but all she could do was walk toward the tree. It seemed to take a lifetime to cross the ring. When she did, she turned and almost choked. Will was entirely too far away. But Cora took a deep breath, and she heard herself shout, "Ready!" and to her surprise her voice didn't tremble, not even a little.

She wasn't ready at all, Cora realized, as soon as Will threw. She swallowed a scream as the knife streaked through the air and thudded into the trunk just above her head. Someone whistled in appreciation of the throw. The next knife came, and it also struck the tree directly above her. It didn't even look like Will was aiming. Again and again and again, and three more knives *chunked* into the tree and stuck there, quivering.

It was done, and the performers clapped and whistled. Cora sagged against the rough bark. Will raised his eyebrows at her as if to say, "I told you it wouldn't be so bad," and made an elaborate bow to Anders and the rest.

"I don't know, Anders," said Tesh. She was stringing her bow and didn't look up, but her expression looked like she had eaten something sour. "The girl looked like a cornered rabbit. She was terrified. Any other expression would have been better: excited or bored or really *anything* but scared." Several of the others laughed.

Cora narrowed her eyes. "I wasn't—" she began, but Will cut in and said, "Fair point, Tesh. That's something we'll work on. Anders, what did you think?"

"Keep practicing," said the tall boy. "I'll tell you in an hour."

An hour! Cora wasn't sure she could do it. But what choice did she have?

The rest of the performers started to go through their own routines again. Will walked over to her and pulled his knives from the tree. "Think you can act bored?" he asked, looking as though he was trying not to smile.

"This is ridiculous," said Cora. "*She's* ridiculous."

"Don't worry about Tesh. You can't let her get under your skin. You did good, Cor. You just have to loosen up. You can do this."

"It's 'Cora'," she muttered.

"Hey. I mean it," said Will. "You can do this. Trust me."

Cora lost count of the number of times that Will threw the knives. But as the minutes crawled by and he consistently *didn't* hit her, the terror she felt began to recede. She hoped this was reflected on her face. All the while, Anders looked on.

Then, as the light began to fade, Anders held up his hand and declared that practice was over. Cora swallowed as she went to stand beside Will. Everyone gathered around.

All eyes turned to Anders. After a moment, he cleared his throat. "It'll do," he said. "Next performance, you're both on." Behind him, Tesh shook her head and turned away.

Relief flooded through Cora, and Will clapped her on the back and gave a cheer. But the relief was mingled with dread. As much as Cora needed to be in the circus, she didn't want to face the knives again. Which, she realized upon reflection, was just more motivation to find the Sand Coin as quickly as possible.

CHAPTER NINE

Cora Makes a Friend

AFTER SUPPER THAT EVENING, ANDERS said, "We made up a lot of time traveling last night, but we still need an early start if we want to make it to Elding tomorrow. Let's turn in." No one argued—the night and day spent on the wagons, combined with the rigorous practice afterward, had left everyone bone-weary.

Anders suppressed a yawn. "Tesh, Felix, Dane, stay," he said. "We need to talk details about tomorrow."

As the rest wandered off to their tents in twos and threes, Cora smiled to herself. This was her opportunity. She quickly made her way through the camp toward Anders' wagon.

Her excitement was short-lived, however. As she approached the money wagon, she could see that not only were the dogs there, but Rascha was as well. The crow sat atop the strongbox, its feathers gleaming green and purple in the light of a nearby torch. Reluctantly, Cora conceded that her search for the Sand Coin would have to wait.

She found her way to the tent she would be sharing with Tesh. Thankfully, the curly-haired girl was still meeting with Anders and had not yet arrived. Cora quickly slipped off her shoes and wrapped herself in the blanket that lay atop one of the cots. *Tomorrow*, she thought. *I can figure out how to get it tomorrow.* Exhausted, she fell into sleep.

Cora huddled in the boat, soaked to the skin, and strained to hear her father's shouts above the wind. Hildi clung to her arm. Then a wave struck the boat broadside, ripping Cora from her sister's grasp. She spun through the air and was swallowed by darkness.

A cloaked figure slowly took shape before her. The man—if it was a man—wore a long mask that resembled the head of a stag. The mask's antlers, like broken and twisted bones, spread upward and disappeared into the blackness. The man turned toward her and spoke.

"I like yours especially. So full of fear. So full of loss."

Cora tumbled out of her cot. Terror coursed through her. *What had he . . . ?* But even as the question formed in her mind, it was gone, like smoke snatched away by the wind. Why was she awake? She struggled to think, to recall what had just happened, but there was nothing solid—only a vague sense of unease. She simply must have woken up. Maybe one of the animals had made a noise. Cora sat on the ground, listening for a few moments, but all she could hear were night sounds: crickets, a nightingale in the distance, and the hiss of the wind in the grass.

From the cot beside her, Tesh grunted in her sleep. Then her breathing became uneven and ragged, as though she were having a bad dream. But no, that wasn't possible. The tokens prevented nightmares. Cora hadn't had one since she had acquired the token in the Spire, and Tesh certainly couldn't be having one now. Cora shook her head to try to clear her mind of the fogginess that suddenly swirled within it.

After a few minutes, she wiped the sleep from her eyes and stood, disentangling herself from the blanket. She put on her shoes and coat and then slipped out of the tent.

The circus glowed softly in the moonlight, serene in its stillness, a marked contrast with the disquiet that Cora felt. She took a deep breath and started walking.

She walked because she didn't know what else to do. She walked and gripped the beads of Hildi's bracelet in one hand, and allowed her other to brush against the wagons and tents and animal cages as she passed. These were solid things, real things, and as she continued, the unease within her began to dissipate.

Cora left the camp behind and made her way across the Eastway toward a large jumble of boulders she had seen the day before. The rocks, big as boats, were perched on a low hill, surrounded by a stand of pines. She climbed the hill and passed in among the shadowy trees. The boulders were blanketed with pine needles and soft moss and flaking lichen. Cora scrambled up one of them and stood looking out to the east.

Past the dark trunks of the pines was the road and the slumbering circus, and beyond it, the sea.

Usually when she stared at the sea, there was a dull ache, a stirring of bad memories. But now . . . nothing.

"Couldn't sleep?"

Cora whirled around and almost fell off the boulder. Victoria sat cross-legged in the shadow of a tree, not four feet away.

"You startled me," said Cora. "And no, I couldn't sleep. What are you doing here?"

Victoria shrugged. "Thinking."

"I didn't mean to intrude," said Cora, and she turned to go.

Victoria said, "You don't have to. I mean, you can, but you don't have to leave."

It was then that Cora noticed the tear tracks on Victoria's face. She wasn't crying now, but she had been. Cora hesitated a moment, and then sat down beside the girl.

The only sound was that of the wind whispering in the pines. It was a gentle sound, almost like a sigh. Victoria remained quiet.

Eventually, Cora said, "Last week I started having dreams about the Storm. Afterward, I couldn't sleep. The dreams were too real, too raw. I just wanted to sit and cry. I guess what I'm trying to say is, I'm sorry you're . . . hurting."

"Who did you lose in the Storm?" asked Victoria.

"My parents. My sister Hildi."

"I lost my parents too." Victoria's voice was subdued. "And . . . my brother."

"I'm sorry." Cora knew the words were small, but didn't know what else to say.

The wind moaned as it blew through the trees. The bark of a fox drifted up from the encampment.

"Did you see them? In your dreams?" asked Victoria.

Cora nodded and looked down at her hands. "I did. And I hated it. I miss them so much, but I hated seeing them, hated remembering." She reached into her pocket and withdrew one of the circus tokens. "Makes me glad for this," she said.

Victoria sniffed and cleared her throat. "Me too," she muttered.

They sat there in the quiet then, in the shadows of the pines, as the moon and stars wheeled slowly across the sky, marking time.

Eventually, Victoria stood and said, "We'll be leaving soon. I need to feed the animals. Want to help?"

C H A P T E R   T E N

PERFORMANCE

T HEY WERE ON THE ROAD again before the sun had risen. Victoria joined Cora and Will on Dane's wagon. There wasn't a lot of room on the seat, so Victoria sat in the bed, which seemed to suit her fine. She gazed, expressionless, out at the slowly passing hills.

Cora had helped her with the animals that morning, feeding and watering them, but she and Victoria had spoken little, if at all. The silence, both then and now, was less awkward than Cora would have thought. It was, Cora supposed, just a part of who Victoria was.

Cora tried to doze on the wagon, and she managed to drift off to sleep a few times, but it wasn't restful. Around midday she gave up and resigned herself to being tired.

The landscape slowly changed around them. The ground became rockier, and large contours of gray and green stone rose like beasts emerging out of the earth on either side of the road. The grass was coarser, the trees more sparse and wind-swept.

"What's that?" asked Cora as they crested a hill. Below them, and between the road and the sea, was a huge grass-covered mound. It looked like a giant ball that had been mostly buried.

"It's the Bubble. Or the Eastway Bubble, I guess," said Dane. "There are others scattered around the Islands, or at least that's what I've heard. I've only seen this one and the one down near Aurian. It's been here long enough that it's overgrown with grass."

Will raised his eyebrows. "So that's one of Augrind's dreams?" he asked. When Dane nodded, Will let out a low whistle.

Cora had never seen one of Augrind's dreams either, but she remembered the first time she had heard about them. Her father had casually mentioned that Augrind, asleep in his prison in the Rift, dreamt—and those dreams drifted like bubbles through Hibaria and the Islands, sometimes coming to rest where they could be seen. The dreams were filled with horrible things, things only the Emperor of the Night could imagine.

Cora had been terrified until her father had reassured her that the bubbles could not be broken open. Somehow, in a way that he couldn't really explain, the dreams were sealed, inaccessible, and therefore safe. Still, Cora had had nightmares for a week, and her mother had been angry with her father for two.

But now, seeing one of Augrind's dreams for the first time, that fear that she had experienced was only a dull memory. The gargantuan mound was impressive, to be sure, but it did not fill her with terror or dread, and for that Cora was grateful.

In the late afternoon, they came to the town of Elding. As they passed through, Will and Dane greeted the townspeople enthusiastically. Will, not surprisingly, took on the role of showman with ease, standing on the wagon seat and balancing knives on each forefinger as he shouted greetings to the townspeople. He flipped both the knives in the air, caught them, and with a wide grin on his face, pointed at a group of children.

It was odd to think of herself as a performer—or almost a performer—as someone these people would be excited to see. But as much as it made her uncomfortable, Cora knew she needed to act the part. After some hesitation, she waved too, with what she hoped looked like a sincere smile.

"That the best you can do, Cor?" Will said. "You look like you're going to a funeral."

"For the last time, it's 'Cora'," she managed to say while still maintaining a smile and continuing to wave.

"I like 'Cor' better. Has a ring to it. I think you'll come around."

"It doesn't and I won't."

Will only grinned at her.

On the far side of the town, in a field scattered with oak and shagbark trees, Anders whistled and the wagons slowed, then stopped. "We'll set up here," he said. "I'll take Felix and spread word in town that we'll do a performance tonight."

The children guided the wagons off the road and onto the grass beneath the trees, and they began to unpack. Cora joined Victoria in removing some of the smaller cages from the wagons. As Victoria went from cage to cage, she spoke to the animals and scratched their ears and let them lick her hands. Cora followed with food and water.

"You're really happy around them," Cora said. "More than around people."

Victoria looked up at her. "I suppose I am," she said with something like defiance in her eyes. Then in a softer tone she repeated, "I suppose I am."

By the time they were finished with the animals, the tents had been pitched and the canvas wall had been erected. As Victoria installed the high rope poles, Will appeared.

"Ready for tonight?" he asked Cora. "We do this, we're in."

"As ready as I can be." She looked up at the sky. It was beginning to turn pink to the west and overhead was now a rich purple. "Are you sure you can throw in the dark? I mean, I know it won't be pitch dark, but it won't really be light either."

Will winked at her. "You don't need to worry," he said blithely.

Cora did not feel reassured.

As the darkness deepened, the townspeople began to line up at the entrance, curious and excited. It looked as though the entire town had come out to see them.

The circus had hung lanterns and lamps from the trees and tents, and stuck torches in the ground around the ring and along the path leading to it. A gentle breeze, coming in off the sea, rippled the silk flags atop the high rope poles. The stars began to appear, shimmering like scattered diamonds flung across the sky. For the briefest of moments, Cora forgot about the knives and drank in the scene. It was magical.

The townsfolk filed in and filled the space around the ring. Their eager faces were bathed in the yellow torchlight, and their voices were low and full of expectation.

Then the trumpets sounded and the drums began to pound. Cora stood with Will and watched the performers gallop into the ring. Like at the performance in Tarian, they circled and stood on their saddles to the cheers of the audience.

Victoria crouched nearby, next to the cages, and when it was the right time, she sent out the wild animals, gently whispering in their ears. The fox and the dogs, the boars and the rabbits, she spoke to them all, and they leapt to obey her words. When they were finished, the animals would return, nuzzle Victoria's face or hands, and climb back into their cages.

And then she was speaking to the bear, ridden by Anders, and it was loping out into the ring toward the ball.

"We go on after this," whispered Will. "How are you feeling?"

"I'm nervous," Cora said.

"Well, that's better than terrified. I'm sure Tesh would approve."

Cora snorted. "I doubt it." She was still terrified, but she wasn't about to tell that to Will. "I'm nervous about the crowd. All these people watching. I didn't even think about this part of it."

"Don't worry about it," said Will. "You'll be fine. Trust me."

The bear ambled out of the ring, Anders by its side. He pointed at Will and Cora and said, "Don't mess up."

As Cora walked across the open space to the far side, her doubts about Will's ability to throw accurately in the darkness grew. The light from the torches flickered and cast shadows that danced across the ground and across the faces in the cheering crowd. The expressions of the townspeople were clear one moment and then indistinct and half-hidden the next. How was Will going to do this?

Cora turned and stood against one of the high rope poles. The crowd quieted as the people realized what was about to happen. Will had already taken up his position. He looked farther away than he had during practice the day before. Cora stood as still as she could and breathed deeply, in through her nose and out through her mouth. Will spun the knife in his hand and tossed it high in the air. This hadn't been part of their practice! What was he—? And then he caught it and flung it, and the knife buried itself in the pole above her head.

Will did not pause, throwing three more knives in rapid succession. He flipped the last knife in the air, throwing it much higher than he had the first knife, and then caught it and sent it hurtling toward her. It flickered as its edge caught the torchlight, spinning through the light and the shadows. With a thump it struck the pole. The whole thing was over before Cora had a chance to breathe in her third breath. The crowd broke into applause and cheers, and Cora found herself in the middle of the ring, taking a bow with Will.

"What was that?" she demanded out of the side of her mouth.

"My flourishes? Didn't we talk about that? Must have slipped my mind. Anyway," he added, "told you so."

"Told me what?" asked Cora.

"That you'd be fine. And you know what? You looked *really* bored out there. I'd be willing to bet that Tesh wants to be your friend now."

"Be quiet, Will," said Cora, but she couldn't help but smile as they bowed again.

CHAPTER ELEVEN

The Merchant House

AFTER THE PERFORMANCE ENDED AND the
townsfolk had gone home, Cora sat with Will and the other
performers around a crackling fire, eating a late supper. She
had officially made it into the circus and now, finally, she could focus all
her attention on the Sand Coin.

Anders sat talking quietly with Felix and Tesh, and Dane was telling
a story that had the Youngers laughing. The crow perched on a wagon,
all but invisible in the shadows.

Cora took a deep breath and said to Will, "I need a walk. I'll be back
in a bit."

"A 'walk' huh?" Will said in a low voice. "Hold up, I'll come with."

"No—" began Cora, but she was interrupted when Anders stood
and called for silence.

"Congratulations are in order. Our newest members, Will and Cora,
managed to not fail this evening. That's not to say they'll necessarily be
with us for very long."

There was scattered laughter around the fire. Cora forced herself to
join in, though she wasn't sure what was funny.

When the laughter had died down, Anders went on. "To be 'official' is, of course, to be one of us formally," he said. "And these two took their first steps toward that tonight. Their last steps will be taken tonight also."

"What's he talking about?" whispered Cora.

Will shook his head. "I have no idea."

"Will, Cora, to join us, to truly join the Wandering Circus and receive your official tokens, you'll need to pass a final test." Anders paused and seemed to be weighing them. "Go with Felix and Tesh. They'll explain on the way. And good luck to you both."

Cora scrambled to her feet. Will stood more slowly. Felix gestured and they followed him and Tesh out of the firelight and through the maze of wagons and tents.

"What's this about?" asked Will.

Tesh smirked but said nothing.

"No, really," said Cora. "What's going on?"

"You wanted to be a part of this," said Tesh. "Changing your mind?"

"No," said Cora. "I just want to know why we didn't really join the circus when we thought we did. What is this about?"

"You heard Anders. It's your final test."

Leaving the circle of wagons and the glow of the lanterns, Felix led them along a path toward the town. It was late now. The moon was high overhead and its light gilded the long grass. In the distance, Cora could hear the surf on the beach. Somewhere nearby, a nightbird wailed mournfully.

They crossed a field, climbed a low, stone wall, and came to the edge of the town. Most of the houses were dark, though some still had lights in their windows.

"Pretty sure Elding doesn't have a night watch," whispered Felix. "But keep an eye out anyway." Tesh nodded.

"Wh—" Cora began, but Tesh immediately put her hand over Cora's mouth.

"You don't need to talk. But if you do, nothing above a whisper."

Cora pushed Tesh's hand away and glared at her, but remained silent.

They crept along the streets, keeping to the shadows until they were across from a large, stone building. Its windows were covered in iron bars. A wooden sign hung on chains above the door, creaking as it swayed gently in the breeze. In the faint moonlight, Cora could just make out a pair of shears and a bolt of cloth on the sign. It was a merchant house.

Felix glanced up and down the street. Then he leaned in close and whispered, "You'll probably need this." He pulled a shuttered lantern from his coat and handed it to Will.

"Whatever this is, I'm not doing it," hissed Cora.

"You'll do it, trust me," said Tesh in a low voice. "Now listen up. Inside is a stairway that leads to the cellar. You need to get into the strongroom at the bottom of the stairs."

"No way," said Cora. "There's no way we're breaking into a merchant house. We're not thieves!"

"Actually, you are," said Felix as he dug into his pocket. "A few hours ago you took these." He dropped a stack of gold coins into Cora's hand.

She looked at them in confusion.

"I don't understand," she said.

"Not surprising." Tesh smiled sadly and patted her arm. "But here's what you need to know: In the morning, the merchant will go down to the strongroom and discover his missing gold. Immediate suspicion will fall on the circus, because it always does, and he'll come asking questions, and by 'asking questions' I mean he'll show up with a crowd of angry townsfolk, probably armed, definitely angry. You'll both be implicated, and needless to say, it won't go well for you. If you *don't* want that to happen, you'll break in and return the gold. Do that, and you're official."

Cora shook her head in disbelief. "You'd all lie and say we were the thieves?"

"Don't need to," said Tesh. "When you were stealing the gold, you accidentally left your bracelet in the strongroom. You know, the one with jade beads. I assume it's important?" Tesh's smile didn't touch her eyes.

Cora's hand went to her wrist. Hildi's bracelet was gone! Cora felt the color drain from her face. "How did you . . . ?" she began. Then, "How *dare* you? How dare you steal from me?"

Tesh shrugged. "It wasn't strictly personal. You wanted to be a part of the circus. But if it makes you feel any better, we also took Will's sword. It's in the strongroom too."

"Sword? Will doesn't have a sword!" But even as Cora said it, she looked at Will. He had turned pale and the grin that was almost always on his face was gone.

"How much time do we have?" Will asked quietly.

"However much you need," said Felix. "Well, the merchant usually gets an early start. So . . . before he wakes up? You have a lot to do, so I'd get to it."

With a final wave, Tesh and Felix disappeared into the shadows. When they were gone, Will puffed up his cheeks and then slowly exhaled. "Nothing we can't handle, right?" he said.

"You have a *sword? Why?* And where has it been this whole time?" It was the only thing Cora could think to ask.

"Not the time, Cor. Maybe I'll tell you later."

Cora rolled her eyes at his self-important tone. As she thrust the coins into her pocket, she said, "What a mess. How's this even a good final test anyway? This has nothing to do with the circus."

"Actually, it has everything to do with the circus. They want us to perform under pressure, be resourceful, innovative, creative. We can't mess up. The stakes are high. It's perfect. I mean, taking our stuff makes me as angry as it makes you, but you have to see that, right?"

Cora ignored the question and turned her attention to the merchant house. "So how do we get in?"

After a few moments, Will pointed to a window on the upper floor. "There," he said. None of the windows on the second story had bars, and this one appeared to be slightly open.

Cora snorted. "Are you going to fly up there?"

"You'll see. Hold this." Will handed her the lantern, then with a quick glance around, he crossed the street and began to climb the building. It looked impossible, but he gripped the rough stones with his fingertips and wedged the toes of his boots into the gaps between the stones, and up he went, past the barred windows like it was the easiest thing in the world. Seconds later he wriggled through the open window.

Cora shook her head. Who was this boy? As much as he annoyed her, Will was also intriguing. So full of surprises. First the knives, now this, not to mention the sword.

A dog barked somewhere nearby, and Cora edged back into the shadows and held her breath. She strained her ears, but she heard nothing more. She allowed herself to relax, just a little, and settled down to wait.

Cora tried to ignore the anger that bubbled inside her. Anger at Tesh for stealing her bracelet, and anger at herself for allowing it to happen. And now, unless she and Will could manage to break into this strongroom, they would be out of the circus, just like that. She balled up her fists until they hurt.

Cora looked again at the merchant house. Will had been in there for a long time. Where was he? And what would she do if he didn't appear soon?

The door to the merchant house opened, ever so slightly, and Will called to her in a low voice. Cora darted across the street and slipped inside. Will closed the door behind her and locked it again with a turn of the key.

"Where were you?" she whispered.

"I had to come downstairs. Carefully. It's a maze up there and there are a bunch of rooms. I don't think anyone's up there, but you can't be too careful. And I didn't have any light." Will reached for the lantern, but Cora batted his hand away. She adjusted the lantern and soft, yellow light suddenly shone around them.

They were in a spacious storefront. Bolts of cloth lined the walls. Several had been pulled down and were lying on the counter that ran across the back of the room. Various pairs of shears hung on pegs beneath the bolts of cloth. A door behind the counter led farther back into the house. Cora continued to adjust the lantern until it barely gave any light at all.

"There's a stair at the back that goes to the strongroom, I think," said Will. "It's connected to the one I came down."

They lifted the hinged counter flap and went through the doorway. The hall they found themselves in was wide and covered with a length of thick, woven carpet. They silently passed several doors. At the end of the hall was a stairway that led both up and down.

"If we get caught in here . . ." muttered Cora.

"We won't. Come on." Will motioned toward the stair.

With no other choice, Cora descended the dusty, wooden steps. At the bottom, just a few feet ahead of them, was a door made of oak and iron. Will pulled on the handle, but it didn't move.

"Of course it's locked," groaned Cora. She looked around, holding the lantern high.

"Looking for the key? They probably wouldn't hang it up next to the door."

Cora glared at him. "You have a better idea?"

Will shrugged and stooped to examine the lock. "Some of those picks from the Works would be nice. But apart from that—"

"Wait! I *have* picks!" said Cora with excitement. She had forgotten about them. She handed Will the lantern and searched her coat pockets until she found the bundle Mr. Blackwood had given her in the Cells. "Hold the light up."

She went to work on the lock. A few seconds later the door was open and they stepped inside.

The room was small, about the size of the prison cell Cora had occupied only a few days before. The walls were made of stone blocks, big as gravestones, and the ceiling was rough-cut timber. A table and chair stood in the middle of the space, and three large, banded chests lined the wall to their left. One of the chests was open, and its contents gleamed in the lantern light. A short sword stood propped against the wall beside the chest. Its blade was silver and marked with strange characters, and its handle was wrapped in leather. Will walked over and picked it up. After looking it up and down, he carefully slid it over his shoulder, between his coat and his cloak. The handle disappeared in the folds of his hood.

Cora ran her eyes over the table. There was a stack of papers and a ledger and a quill and several bottles of ink. But no bracelet.

"This?" Will reached inside the open chest and withdrew a bracelet with green beads. Cora breathed a sigh of relief as she took it from Will.

"What's so important about it?" he asked.

"Not the time, Will," she said, copying his tone and words from earlier. "Maybe I'll tell you later." She slipped it onto her wrist and drew the string tight, then dug out the gold coins from her pocket and dropped them into the open chest.

"Well, that was easier than I thought it'd be," said Will. "Good thing you had the picks."

Cora had just locked the strongroom door again when the sound of heavy, booted feet came from the floor above them. The footsteps stopped and a man's voice called, "Shaw? Is that you?"

Will extinguished the lantern, plunging them into darkness. Then he grabbed Cora and pulled her toward the stairs.

"What are you doing?" she whispered. "We can't go up there!"

"I know! We're not going *up*, we're getting *behind*," Will said in her ear.

They crouched down and scrambled blindly beside and then behind the wooden steps. Cora's hand brushed through spider webs and came to rest on some rough cloth. The footsteps resumed above them and after a moment, faint, yellow light spilled down the stairway and shone through the gaps in the boards.

"Shaw!" the man shouted. Under his breath he muttered, "It *better* be you if it's anybody."

As the man with the light descended the steps, Cora hastily unfolded the cloth. It was an old, dusty sack. She and Will slipped beneath it.

Immediately, Cora's nose began to itch and her eyes started to water. She was going to sneeze. She wrinkled her nose and bit her lip, hard, willing herself not to. Footsteps crossed the floor, and the door rattled as the man tried the handle. More muttering, and then the man went back up the stairs, leaving them in darkness.

Cora shoved the sack aside and gasped. "That was close," she whispered, wheezing. She coughed into her coat sleeve and wiped her eyes. "I'm guessing that was the merchant who lives upstairs. Now we're stuck here till he goes back to sleep."

"I suppose so." Will drummed his fingers on the darkened lantern. Eventually he said, "Since we have some time, you want to tell me how someone managed to steal the Sand Coin from the Master of Tides?"

"Not really," said Cora.

"If I'm going to help you, I need to—"

"You're not going to help me, Will. I only told you about the Sand Coin because you forced me to. That's all you need to know."

"I'm helping you right now."

"You know what I mean," said Cora. "With finding the Sand Coin."

"Look, Cor. Cora. I'm sorry I made you tell me about the Sand Coin. That probably wasn't right. But I care about Tarian too, and I want to help. Why don't you want me to?"

"I don't trust you, Will. And you're impulsive and reckless and irresponsible."

"How am I those things?"

Cora laughed. "Throwing knives at me comes to mind."

"Above you," corrected Will. "And I did that to get you into the circus! You want to add climbing a building and sneaking in a window to the list? I did that to keep you in the circus. Maybe I'm reckless, but I did those things to help you out."

"Maybe," said Cora. "But there are other examples."

"Like what?"

"I don't know," she muttered.

It was Will's turn to laugh. "Just get over yourself and let me help you. You can't do everything on your own."

"You know what?" said Cora, having difficulty keeping her voice down. "The truth is, I just don't like you, Will. You're abrasive and overconfident and unpleasant."

"Cora, Cora. You're not exactly pleasant yourself, but I don't hold it against you."

"You're a runaway. You treated your family like they were trash," said Cora. The words tumbled out of her mouth before she even knew they were there.

Will was quiet for a moment. Then he said, "That's the root of it, isn't it? All that other stuff bothers you, but that's the thing that *really* bothers you: I willingly threw away what was forcibly taken from you, and you can't get over that."

Cora bit her lip, but said nothing.

Will asked, "Can I tell you something?" When Cora didn't answer, he said, "I was lost in the Fenwood when I was small. The stories about it are true: Inside the forest, I forgot everything about my life before. It was like living in a fog for I don't know how long. But eventually I *did* get out. That's where I got my sword, by the way." Will shifted in the darkness beside her. "My memories came back, and I wish they hadn't because I remembered that I had run into the Fenwood to hide from my father. He used to hit me. For no reason, or no reason that I could understand. And so when I escaped the wood, I didn't go home. I made my way to Tarian and eventually to the Water Works.

"So resent me if you want, and think of me as ungrateful or irresponsible, but our situations were nothing alike. You miss your family? I miss mine too. At least your memories are good ones."

Cora didn't know what to say. She felt ashamed. Her face burned and she was glad for the darkness. Eventually she mumbled, "I'm sorry, Will."

"You couldn't have known. Forget about it," the boy said. After a while he continued. "Look, Cora. I know there are things about me that you don't like. I rub you the wrong way, I make jokes all the time, all that. But you *do* need my help. Getting the Sand Coin back is about Tarian, not about you or me or whether we're friends or not. Just let me help you do this thing."

Cora sighed. "Alright."

"So tell me what happened. How did you even get involved in this?"

Cora told him how her first suspicions had led her to the Iron Spire and how she had discovered the Master's body and that the Sand Coin was missing; how the Master's Elite had captured her and how Mr. Blackwood had helped her escape from the Cells; how he had planned to send her south to hide her from the Council. "He even gave me a vault," she said. "To send him a message in case something happened. Can you believe that?"

"A vault? You're serious? Where is it?"

"I'm serious. It's in my bag, back in the tent. I'm surprised Tesh didn't steal it along with my bracelet."

"She might have, you know. You should check when we get back. Anyway, how big is it?" asked Will.

"As big as a vault is. I don't know."

"Cora, it's a serious question. If it's big enough, we can send the Sand Coin back to Tarian *using the vault.*"

Cora hadn't even considered this. "You're right," she whispered.

"How many days till the Turn?"

"Four weeks exactly."

"So with the vault, we have that whole time to find the Sand Coin. We don't have to factor in the time it would take to travel back to Tarian. This is good news," said Will.

"*If* the Sand Coin fits in the vault. Which it might not. And if it doesn't, we have to leave enough time to get home. We should assume we only have two weeks."

"It'll fit," Will said blithely. "Anyway, what's your plan?"

Cora rubbed her nose. "I'm pretty sure the Sand Coin's on the money wagon. It's guarded all the time, and it makes sense that that's where it would be. So—"

"It's not on the wagon," said Will. "Too obvious."

Cora made an exasperated sound. "I say you can help me and the first thing you do is disagree with me. I can tell this is going to work *really* well."

"I know you're being sarcastic," said Will, "and that's progress for you since you're usually so bad with humor, but I think it *will* work well. Also, I'd like to point out that the actual first thing I did was double the amount of time we have left. So . . ."

"Anyway," Cora continued, ignoring Will's interruption, "I, or *we*, search the wagon, get the Sand Coin, then leave, either returning it to Tarian through the vault or in person."

"I think we need to look other places," said Will. "My guess is that the thief is either Tesh or Felix, especially after what happened tonight. Maybe Anders. We can search their tents and—"

"Will, it's on the wagon. You seriously think Tesh would put the Sand Coin under her pillow?"

"Have you looked?" asked Will.

"No, but it doesn't make sense! The thing is too valuable."

"You're sharing a tent with Tesh, right? I say look for it there before you dismiss the idea. I'll look through Felix's tent. If it's not in either place, we figure out what's next."

Cora ground her teeth. "*I* say we look for it on the wagon. Just because you don't think it's there doesn't mean it's not."

"Fine. We can look for it on the wagon," said Will with a laugh. "But we should look those other places too, Cora."

When the house had been quiet for a long time—Cora guessed over an hour—they slowly made their way up the stair. At the top, Will turned and began to retrace their steps down the hall. It was slow going in the dark, but they didn't want to risk the lantern. They crept along, stopping and holding their breath when the floor creaked beneath them, going on again when the silence held.

They came to the storefront. Patches of pale moonlight shone through the windows and illuminated the room. Will carefully made his way to the front door, but then stopped short.

"Uh-oh," he said. "The key's gone. Merchant must have grabbed it when he heard us earlier. You'll have to use the picks."

Cora, who had gone to the window, shook her head. "There's a light in the building across the way now," she whispered. "And look. Someone's there."

A man peered out the window of the shop across the street and then moved out of view. A moment later the shop door opened and he stepped out. He held a lantern in one hand and a spear in the other. He walked over to a barrel and sat down.

Will grimaced. "No night watch, huh? Well, upstairs it is then. We'll have to climb out."

"I can't do that," said Cora. "There's no way."

"Alright. Well, I've really enjoyed knowing you. When the circus comes through Elding again, I'll come visit you in jail."

"Not funny, Will. But I really can't climb down the building like you."

"We'll figure it out," said Will. "Maybe there's a tree next to one of the windows or something. We have to try."

They retraced their steps to the back of the house and slowly crept up the staircase.

The floor above was a warren of shadowy hallways and darkened doors. They were three steps into the first room when Cora grabbed Will's sleeve. He stopped, and she held a finger to her lips and then pointed. There in the corner, just visible in the pale moonlight, was a pair of sleeping figures on a bed. One coughed and rolled over and then began to quietly snore. Cora and Will slowly backed out of the room. They tiptoed down the hall to the next doorway.

None of the windows in any of the rooms they visited had a tree next to them. Or a drainpipe. Or anything, really, that would make Cora's descent possible.

"Well," Cora said as they looked out a small window at the back of the merchant house. "What now?"

"Look!" Will pointed. A girl had stepped from the shadows of the next building over and was waving at them. A coil of rope hung from one of her shoulders.

"That's Victoria!" whispered Cora.

Will opened the window. He glanced around then hissed, "Cor can't climb down. Can you help?"

Without a word, Victoria ran across the alley, unslung the rope, and threw it up to Will. He quickly tied it around his waist and then braced himself against the wall. "You *can* climb down a rope, can't you?"

Cora gave him a flat stare. "Don't drop me," she said. She edged over the sill and lowered herself, hand over hand, to the ground below. A moment later the rope slithered down beside her. Victoria snatched it up and coiled it as Will proceeded to climb effortlessly down the wall.

Together, the three of them moved like shadows out of the town. Apart from the distant sound of the waves on the beach, the night was quiet.

As they began to cross the field, Cora said, "We couldn't have gotten out without you, Victoria. What were you doing there?"

The girl looked surprised. "Helping you."

"Well, yes," Cora said, "but why?"

Victoria shrugged. "I heard what Tesh and Felix did. They set you up to fail. Usually getting into the circus is hard, but not that hard. Were you able to return the gold?"

"Yes," said Cora. "And get our things. Are . . . are you going to get into trouble for interfering?"

The wagons and tents were still some way off, but Victoria stopped. "They won't know unless you tell them," she said. "You both go on now. I'll come later."

"Thanks, Victoria," said Cora. "Really. Thank you." She squeezed the girl's arm and turned to go, but Victoria grabbed her sleeve.

"You . . ." Victoria hesitated and looked away. "You really should be careful. The Wandering Circus isn't what you think it is. It's dangerous. More dangerous than you know."

"What do you mean?" asked Cora. "Dangerous how?"

Victoria shook her head. "I can't say." She took a deep breath and added, "But you should leave while you can."

Will said, "That's creepily sinister. Want to tell us what you mean, Vic?"

"I can't. I've already said too much," she muttered. "Just . . . just be careful."

Cora and Will exchanged looks. "We will," Cora said slowly. "Thank you."

The girl nodded and Cora and Will set off once more. When they were out of earshot, Cora said, "She's talking about the Sand Coin, Will.

She's trying to warn us that the circus is just a bunch of thieves. Told you everyone is in on it. Or everyone but Victoria, anyway. I wonder why she stays."

"Nowhere else to go," said Will.

"We should bring her with us after we get the Sand Coin."

Will looked over his shoulder. "If she wants to. I'm just not sure that she will."

Before long they were among the wagons and tents and animal cages. Cora gripped Hildi's bracelet tightly and jogged ahead. She went straight to Anders' tent. The hum of a low conversation could be heard, but without pausing, Cora threw back the tent flap and she and Will went in.

Anders, Tesh, and Felix turned, surprise clear on their faces. Tesh recovered first. "You're back!" she said.

"We are. Any more tests for us?" Cora snapped.

"Well, you have to actually complete the one we gave you." Tesh shook her head. "I really thought that bracelet and sword were important to you. I can't believe you'd just pocket the money and walk away—"

"You mean this?" Cora held up the bracelet. Behind her, she heard Will draw his sword. "Now are we official, or what?"

Anders began to clap slowly and broke into a smile, even as Tesh scowled. "Nicely done!" he said.

"More than I expected," said Felix who looked at them with new respect.

Tesh only grunted.

"So we're official?" asked Will.

"Official," said Anders. "Welcome to the Wandering Circus!"

CHAPTER TWELVE

WHITEWALL

ANDERS STEPPED OUT OF THE tent and when he returned, he was holding two circus tokens threaded onto leather loops. He tossed them to Will and Cora. They, in turn, handed over the loose tokens they had received when they paid to see the circus performance in Tarian.

Cora was careful not to give Anders the one she had found in the Iron Spire.

"I wouldn't take these off," said Anders. "You've gone through a lot to join—it would be a pity to lose you to one of the winter wolves. Now get some rest. We'll see you in the morning."

Cora glanced at the money wagon as she and Will exited the tent, but with Anders and Tesh and Felix so close by, not to mention the dogs . . . getting the Sand Coin would have to wait another day. Saying goodnight to Will, she wearily made her way to her tent.

She lit the lantern that hung on the pole outside the tent, grabbed it, and ducked inside. Cora went to her bed and pulled her bag from beneath it. "Well at least there's that," she muttered as she removed the vault and tucked it in her coat. Even with the vault safe, though, it would probably be wise to keep her bag with her at all times. Tesh just couldn't be trusted.

As she took off her shoes, she glanced over at Tesh's cot. After a moment, she walked over and lifted the pillow. Nothing. She patted down the cot but everything was in order. Cora looked around, but there really wasn't anywhere else something could be hidden. "Told you so," she muttered.

Shaking her head, Cora went back to getting ready for bed. As she was pulling back her blankets, Tesh came in. The curly-haired girl didn't say a word. She kicked off her boots and extinguished the lantern while Cora was still taking off her coat.

"Really?" said Cora.

Tesh didn't respond.

Cora sighed, slipped under her blanket, and soon drifted off to sleep.

Early the next morning, as the pale sun rose from the sea, the circus broke camp. Cora and Will climbed sleepily into a wagon with Dane, and Victoria once again joined them. Will looked haggard and couldn't stop yawning.

When Cora asked him why he was so tired, he said, "Didn't sleep much. I had a bad dream."

Victoria looked at him sharply just as Cora said, "I thought the tokens prevented bad dreams." She hadn't slept well herself, though she couldn't say why.

Will shrugged and rubbed his eyes. "Didn't work, I guess. There was this man. A king maybe, I'm not sure. He didn't say anything, but he felt evil. The whole dream felt . . . evil. I can't think of another way to describe it. It sounds ridiculous, but . . ." He looked away, embarrassment plain on his face. "He scared me."

Cora shifted, suddenly uncomfortable. She hesitated and then said,

"I woke up feeling what you just described. Or something similar." She shuddered.

It seemed as though Victoria was about to speak, but before she could, Dane said, "So tell me about the merchant house!"

Will, no doubt glad to change the subject, launched into the story, his flair for the dramatic on full display. Every now and then Cora interjected. When they came to the end, she took over to make sure they left out that Victoria had helped them. When she had finished, Will asked, "So everyone in the circus went through that?"

Dane shrugged. "Yeah, something like that. It shows you can work under pressure, you know?"

Will said, "See Cora? Told you so."

Cora just ignored him.

The circus slowly moved north along the coast, performing in most of the villages and towns they came to. Try as they might, Cora and Will were unable to search the wagon. There was no opportunity—every time they approached it, either Anders or Rascha was nearby, and the dogs never seemed to leave the area around it. Cora grew discouraged and worried. Will was unfazed. He tried to cheer her up and pushed her to look other places.

"I've checked Felix's tent," he said to her one evening. "And six others as well. I even went through Dane's things. It would go faster if you helped out, you know. We'll get it eventually. Did you look through Tesh's stuff?"

Cora nodded. "Wasn't there," she said glumly. "But I suppose it wouldn't hurt to look in some other places too. Let's make a list."

Even with the decision made, it still took some time to follow through on their plans. The circus was constantly on the move, sometimes not stopping to sleep. But when they did stop, there were a thousand things to do, and it was often impossible to slip away to search for the Sand Coin without arousing suspicion.

Despite these frustrations, over the next few days Cora found to her surprise that she was beginning to enjoy life in the circus. It was temporary, she knew, it *had* to be temporary, but she lost herself in the hours spent practicing and performing. Will was still annoying more often than not, but what they did in their performance *was* remarkable and if pressed, Cora would have to admit that it was more thrilling than terrifying now.

After performances, she usually helped Victoria with feeding and caring for the animals. Victoria said nothing more about the danger of the circus, and in fact, they rarely spoke more than a handful of words at all. But despite this, Cora looked forward to their time together. The long stretches of silence while they worked side by side reminded Cora of life with her family, and there was comfort in that.

Almost two weeks passed, and in their spare moments, Cora and Will managed to search every tent but Anders', but with no success.

As the circus approached the village of Whitewall, Cora and Will walked through the knee-high grass together, a little apart from the wagons, discussing their next move.

"So it's either in Anders' tent, or it's on the money wagon," said Cora. "Simple as that. Which was where I said we should search first. And if I recall correctly—and I do—you said that was the last place it would be."

Will ignored the barb, took one last bite from an apple, and tossed the core over his shoulder. Licking his fingers, he said with a smile, "Hopefully we can search both tonight."

Whitewall was the largest village they had seen since Elding, and it huddled atop chalky cliffs that overlooked the sea. The circus set up in a field bordered by beech trees with a clear view of the village.

After their knife-throwing performance, Cora and Will watched as Rascha spoke to the crowd. The crow singled out a fisherman and revealed to everyone that the man had discovered a coin in the mouth of a fish that morning.

Will reached into his shirt and pulled out his circus token. After a moment he removed it from around his neck.

"What are you doing?" hissed Cora.

"Just looking at it. I've been wondering about these things—"

"Put it back on!"

"And not just any coin, mind you," Rascha continued, "a golden royal from Aurian!"

An image of a coin shimmered and appeared before them, and the crowd murmured in wonder.

"Seriously, Will!" whispered Cora. "Quit messing around and put it back on!" She elbowed him hard.

The token fell from his hand, but Will didn't immediately move to retrieve it. Instead, his eyes grew wide.

"What are you—?" began Cora, but Will interrupted her.

"Take yours off. Quick!"

"What?"

"Your token!" he whispered frantically. "And the one from the Spire if you have it on you. Put them on the ground!"

Cora hesitated and looked around. No one was watching them. Reluctantly, she pulled the one from around her neck and the other from her pocket and dropped them onto the grass beside Will's.

As the tokens left her fingers, the image of the golden coin vanished. She jerked back in surprise.

Together, she and Will bent down and retrieved the silver tokens. When Cora straightened, the image of the coin once again hung in the air in front of her.

"Do you see it again?" she asked.

Will nodded.

"What do you think this means?"

Will shook his head. "These things might protect us from the animals like Anders says, but they also give Rascha some sort of power over us. I mean, these are being used to make us see things that aren't there."

Cora slipped the token over her head again, and put the one she had found in the Spire back in her pocket. "I suppose, but seeing Rascha's images is part of the act, and it's pretty harmless."

They looked on as the astounded fisherman, at Rascha's bidding, pulled a golden coin from his pocket and held it aloft to wild applause.

As the crowds drifted away, Will beckoned to Cora. He led her out of the circus enclosure and in among the beech trees, well beyond earshot. The setting sun cast everything in an orange light.

"I don't think we should put them back on," he said, holding up his token. "I think we should throw them away."

"What? Are you crazy?" whispered Cora. "Just because—"

"We don't know what these things do. We *do* know they allow Rascha to plant pictures in our minds, but what else could they be doing? Anything! Doesn't that possibility bother you?"

"I suppose that *remote* possibility bothers me, but *they protect us from the animals,*" Cora said. "I don't want to get mauled by a bear and I doubt you do either, just to keep a bird from occasionally putting pictures in your head. I'm not going to take any chances. Besides, they prevent bad dreams. I haven't had a nightmare since we left Tarian. I'm leaving it on and I think you should too."

Will shook his head in frustration. He held up the token. "It doesn't prevent me having nightmares, Cora. But even if it did, this is terrifying. What are we dealing with here? *Who* are we dealing with? I . . . I can't do it. I won't." He turned and threw the circus token in among the trees.

Cora was stunned. "So are you leaving?"

"Leaving?" Will looked confused. "We don't have the Sand Coin yet. Of course I'm not leaving."

"But the animals!"

"I'll be careful, Cor. But really . . . you should get rid of your token. Both of them."

"I'm not doing it, Will."

Will pursed his lips. "Hope you change your mind," he said. "Anyway, I think the sooner we find the Sand Coin and get out of here, the better."

"Well, yes," said Cora, "I agree, especially now. Even if we found it tonight, we have what, less than two weeks to get it back to Tarian? We're cutting it close."

"Don't forget we can probably send it back through the vault. But even if we can't, the circus has traveled pretty slow and we're really not that far from Tarian," said Will. "If it's just the two of us, we'll have plenty of time to get back."

"*If* we find it soon. You seem to forget that we haven't."

"Well, like you said earlier, it's either on the money wagon or in Anders' tent. And I think tonight we might actually have a chance. Earlier I overheard Dane and Anders talking with Felix about visiting the village after tonight's performance. Apparently, there's an inn there that has really good meat and cabbage pies or something. Sounded gross, but they all seemed excited. I say we go for Anders' tent while they're gone. Who knows, maybe we'll have a chance to check the wagon too."

Cora and Will made their way back to the circus as darkness deepened and settled over the encampment. A chill, damp breeze cut through the air.

Cora shivered. It *was* unsettling that Rascha was using the tokens to make them see images, but to remove it . . . They passed the cages that held the winter wolves. Frost crackled across their faces and their blue eyes glowed in the shadows. Cora shivered again and glanced over at Will. He seemed unconcerned. Well, there was no way *she* was going to take off the circus token, not when animals like this were around. And not when keeping it prevented her from having nightmares.

"Keep an eye out," whispered Will as they wove their way through the camp. But the cold, it seemed, had driven everyone to the fire, if not the inn, and they didn't encounter anyone.

They came to Anders' tent. Its red silk flag snapped in the steady breeze. The money wagon stood beside it, and though the dogs lifted their heads and stared at them, they didn't growl or bark. Cora and Will listened at the tent flap for a moment, then ducked inside.

Will pulled a shuttered lantern from his coat and opened it slightly. In the dim light they looked around.

"Not much to search," said Will. "I'll take the bed. You check under that barrel and in the trunk."

As Cora lifted the trunk's lid, she heard the crunch of footsteps on dead leaves. She grabbed Will's arm and he extinguished the lantern. There was nowhere to hide.

"They might pass," breathed Will. Together, they crouched near the doorway.

The footsteps came closer, but then stopped. It was hard to know for sure, but it seemed that the person was closer to the money wagon than the tent.

"Hide it amongst the valuables," said a voice. "I think it's safer here than with you." The words were spoken quietly, but the voice was high and thin and it carried. It was Rascha. "But first, show it to me again."

Slowly, Cora lifted the tent flap and looked out. The dark form of the crow perched atop a barrel in the wagon bed, its back to Cora. Whoever it was speaking to was hidden on the other side of the wagon. Cora could just see the shape of the figure's legs in the shadows.

"Make it quick, girl," Rascha croaked. After a moment there was a *click* of an opening clasp and the creak of hinges.

"Such power," the bird said in a hungry voice. "The unbridled power of the tides . . . I can feel it, even across all the miles. You've shown the Coin to no one else?"

The response was low and muffled.

"Good," said Rascha. "Now go, before we're seen."

Cora heard another click, and a moment later, footsteps departing. As she strained to see who it was, the crow, with a furious beating of its wings, rose into the night sky. Cora jerked back into the tent and held her breath. But the crow was gone and she was left alone with Will.

They emerged from the tent to find the dogs on edge. They had been silent throughout the exchange between Rascha and the thief, but now they growled and rose to their feet. Cora and Will slowly backed away and lost themselves among the tents and wagons.

"Did you hear that?" asked Cora.

Will nodded. "Who was with Rascha? Did you see who it was?"

"No," said Cora. "It was too dark." She paused and then added, "But I think we both know it was Tesh."

"I'd like to take this opportunity to point out I was right," said Will. "The Sand Coin wasn't on the money wagon. And Tesh had it, which means it was in your tent the whole time." He laughed and ran his hand through his hair.

"Maybe," said Cora defensively. "But when I looked it wasn't."

Will stopped and turned to Cora. With a frown he said, "Rascha said, 'I can feel it, even across all the miles?' What do you think that meant?"

"I don't know." Cora shrugged. She thought a moment and then said, "But the important thing is that we know where the Sand Coin is now. We just have to figure out how to get rid of the dogs."

"I suppose," said Will. "It is an odd thing to say, though." When Cora didn't respond he said, "As far as the dogs go, I have an idea about that. You know where Vic keeps the meat she feeds the winter wolves?"

"Yes."

"Let's grab as much as we can carry and give it to the dogs. With any luck that'll distract them and we'll be on our way home with the Sand Coin within the hour."

An unexpected hesitation came over Cora. The possibility of leaving, really leaving, left her feeling . . . sad. She would miss the circus, she realized. Well, parts of it. She would miss performing, even if it was with Will. And she would miss Victoria. And Cora suspected she wouldn't have a chance to say goodbye. But she nodded, and they walked toward the animal cages.

As they came alongside the feed wagon, Will tugged at Cora's elbow. "Keep walking," he murmured. "There's someone coming."

Cora could hear footsteps running toward them. A moment later Felix appeared from behind one of the tents. He skidded to a stop when he saw them.

"I thought you were in Whitewall eating pies," said Will.

"I was." Felix bent over, resting his hands on his knees. When he had caught his breath, he said, "Storm's coming in off the Deep. You can see it from up there. Anders wants us to pack up and head out."

"What, *now*?" asked Cora.

"Yes. If the storm catches us here, we could be stuck for a long time. These storms are pretty fierce."

As the three of them ran toward the fire to warn the others, Cora and Will's eyes met. They had lost an opportunity that wasn't likely to present itself again soon. And time was running out.

Under threat of a storm, the performers tore down the tents and loaded the cages even quicker than usual. When the last of the barrels and crates had been hoisted onto the wagons, and everything tied down under thick canvas tarps, the circus set out. Packing and loading had taken little more than half an hour.

"I hate storms as much as anyone, but it's not *the* Storm," said Cora as they bumped along. She sat with Dane and Will and Victoria on the wagon seat. "Why the rush?"

Dane looked over his shoulder at the night sky. The stars had been blotted out by thick clouds. "Storms in these parts usually start later in the year. But once they start it's not uncommon for them to last. Usually days, sometimes weeks. We thought we were ahead of the weather, but I guess not this year."

"And we're going to outrun it?" asked Cora.

"Not likely," said Dane. "But the Eastway joins with the Horn Road a few miles to the north, and the Horn is paved with stone. If we can get to that before it rains too much, we're less likely to get stuck. Besides, the farther up the road we are, the weaker the storm will be."

"How long before it starts, do you think?" asked Will.

"Not sure. Soon, though."

The line of wagons, marked by the glowing lanterns each carried, rolled along through the night. The wind was out of the south and it steadily increased as the minutes passed. The smell of rain was now unmistakable. An inn appeared ahead. Despite the late hour, a lantern burned bright beside its red door. The yellow glow of firelight through the windows was warm and inviting. Cora looked at the inn longingly, but they passed it by and it was lost to the darkness behind them.

As the wind rose to a howl, Dane shouted, "Will, there are some oilskin coats behind the seat in a green chest. Get them, will you?"

On the horizon behind them, lightning flickered.

They had just put on the coats when the rain started.

CHAPTER THIRTEEN

THE LOCKLEAVES

THE RAIN CAME IN DRENCHING waves, driven by the swirling gusts of wind that blew in from the Eastern Deep. The trees beside the Eastway were barely visible in the deluge, but Cora could hear their branches as they creaked and rattled and snapped. The howling wind was icy cold, and Cora, Victoria, Will, and Dane huddled together on the wagon seat for warmth.

By the time the sky had lightened to the east, several hours later, the rain was a steady, heavy downpour that had soaked them, despite their oilskin coats. Cora looked over at Victoria. Water dripped onto the girl's face from her sodden hood, and she looked as miserable as Cora felt.

"The Horn Road!" shouted Dane. There was no sign that Cora could see, but the muddy ruts below them suddenly gave way to paving stones. Dane flicked the reins and the wagon picked up speed.

Sometime later, a stand of evergreens appeared ahead, just visible through the gray rain.

"Now that we're on the Horn, we'll probably shelter there, under the lockleaves," said Dane.

A moment later Felix appeared, hunched in his coat as he walked down the line of wagons. He directed them toward the trees.

It took some time, but eventually they managed to get all the wagons in among the evergreens. The trees were much larger than they had appeared at first to Cora. Their tops disappeared into the rainy mist above.

"Get some rest!" Anders shouted as he jumped down from his wagon. "When the rain lets up, we'll head out!"

The spreading branches of the trees came all the way down to the ground and were thick with fine, glossy green needles. As Cora watched, Felix and Tesh held the branches of one of the trees aside, and Anders led the horses along with his wagon beneath them until they had disappeared. Cora and Will exchanged quizzical looks.

"Haven't been under a lockleaf before, have you?" asked Dane with a smile. "Trust me, there's a lot of room and it's dry, even in this." He squinted up at the rain. "I need to go talk to Felix, but feel free to pick a tree. Bring the wagon and horses in." Dane hopped down and threaded his way through the scattered wagons toward Anders' tree.

Cora pushed her dripping hair out of her eyes. She and Will and Victoria climbed down from the seat. Without hesitation, Victoria grasped the harnesses of the horses and pulled them in among the branches of the nearest lockleaf. The wagon followed and appeared to be swallowed by the branches.

With a grin, Will grabbed Cora's hand and said, "Come on."

They passed through thick layers of dark, interwoven branches. The needles were, unexpectedly, soft to the touch. And then they were through. It took a moment for Cora's eyes to adjust to the dimness, but when they had, her mouth fell open. "Wow!" was all she could say. Will whistled.

They stood in a circular space, with the massive bole of the tree in the center. The branches closest to the ground started about twenty feet up the trunk. They stuck out from the tree about fifteen feet before gracefully bending to the ground. The result was a large enclosed space, not unlike a domed tent.

Cora patted the ground. Somehow the soft, brown needles that covered it were not even a little damp. She breathed in deeply through her nose. The air smelled fresh and earthy and sweet.

"Smells better than a tent, for sure," she said as she unbuttoned her coat.

"And it's not nearly as cold in here as outside," said Will.

Victoria unharnessed the horses and she and Cora rubbed them down, gave them feed, and tied them to the trunk of the tree. Then Victoria began gathering dry branches.

"Are you going to start a fire?" asked Will. "Is that safe?"

Victoria didn't answer. She cleared a patch of ground and pushed dead needles into a mound and then carefully arranged the branches she had collected over them. Cora and Will gathered sticks as well and added to her pile. Victoria pulled a flint and striker from her pocket, and a few minutes later she had a little fire burning.

They sat beside it, warming their hands. What little smoke there was drifted up through the branches and out into the storm.

"I'm hungry," said Cora at length. "I'll get food from the wagon."

As she stood, the horses suddenly whinnied and snorted. One of them stamped and jerked at its line.

"Get behind me," said Victoria quietly.

Cora turned, confused, and saw both Will and Victoria standing, staring at something beyond the firelight. Then she saw a hulking shape step from the shadows of the branches that brushed the ground. Cora froze. It was a huge cat, black as pitch. It crouched, ready to spring, all tight skin and corded muscle. Long ugly scars covered its body. A leather collar studded with pieces of bone encircled its neck. The cat blinked and its eyes glowed white in the dim light. From deep within it came a low, rumbling growl, guttural and full of death. Its teeth, like smooth, milky daggers, flashed in the firelight.

"Get behind me," Victoria repeated.

Terrified, Cora scrambled to obey. Will stood fast, his sword suddenly in his hand.

"I said, get behind me!" Victoria spoke the words so emphatically that after a moment's hesitation, Will, too, stepped back.

The creature slowly walked toward Victoria. Its eyes, like glowing moons, swiveled back and forth between Victoria and Cora. Victoria raised her hand, palm out. "No farther," she said. It stopped. A growl still rumbled in its chest and its eyes narrowed. And then Victoria, her face at a level with the beast's, walked toward it until they were nose to nose.

"Peace," she whispered and placed her hand upon the cat's neck. Its growl ceased. Its mouth closed. It sat down.

"What *is* that?" said Cora. "And how . . . ? What *is* that?"

Will licked his lips and said, "Stalker. It's a stalker. Look at the collar."

"That's a *stalker*?" Cora had heard of stalkers before. Their handlers were hired to send the creatures after important targets: barons, generals, Cora had even heard about one sent after a prince. The target rarely survived. What was one doing here? She watched the cat warily. It made the winter wolves look docile. "I don't know what you're doing, Victoria, but that thing's dangerous. We have to . . ."

"It's fine now," said Victoria. And sure enough, the creature lowered itself fully to the ground and began to lick its paws.

Cora was stunned. She sat down slowly.

"It's the token, isn't it?" Cora said suddenly. She pulled it out from beneath her shirt and looked down at the silver circus token.

"The tokens, yes, they're powerful," Victoria muttered. "We would have been dead without them."

Cora glanced at Will and then remembered that he no longer had his token. Yet he hadn't been attacked.

"Vic," said Will. "If that's true, why did you tell us to get behind you?"

"I don't know. I wasn't . . . I wasn't thinking. I just said it."

Will tilted his head and narrowed his eyes. "Yesterday I threw my circus token away. Which means something else protected me just now. I think it was you, Vic."

Victoria threw another stick on the fire. A hunted look passed across her face, the same expression that Cora had seen when she had glimpsed the blue-green markings on the back of Victoria's hand.

When she didn't say anything, Will crouched down beside her. "I'm just trying to understand what happened and why you would credit the tokens with something you did. Also, you being able to . . . do whatever it is you just did is incredible. You're acting like it's not. I don't understand."

"You're right, you don't understand," Victoria said. "And you wouldn't. Why did you get rid of your circus token?"

Will shot a look at Cora and ran a hand through his hair. After a moment he said, "Because during the performance yesterday I dropped it and the image Rascha had conjured, the image of the coin, disappeared. When I picked it up again the picture came back.

"When we joined the circus, we were told the tokens protected us from the animals and took away nightmares and bad memories. Anders said they're charms against misfortune. He didn't mention anything else.

"I started to wonder about the tokens when I had a nightmare a few days ago. That shouldn't have happened. And then yesterday when I realized the token was also being used to make me see things, I grew suspicious of it. I figured it could be doing other things as well, things that I didn't know about, so I got rid of it."

Victoria barely nodded, but remained silent.

"And that brings us to now," said Will. "You said the tokens protected us from that thing," he gestured toward the stalker, "but I don't have one. Which, in my mind, means you protected us. Why lie? Why keep that a secret?"

Victoria looked down at the flames and sighed. At last she said, "You're right, the tokens have no effect on the animals. Not this one," she nodded at the stalker, "nor any in the circus. I keep you safe from them."

"How?" asked Cora.

Victoria shrugged. "I just do. It's a . . . skill, I guess you could say."

Victoria *was* good with animals, and Cora had always thought so, but this was something entirely different.

"You just tell them what to do? And they understand you and obey you?" Cora asked.

"Yes."

"So what are the tokens for, besides making Rascha's act better?" asked Will.

Tears began to leak from Victoria's eyes. "I can't tell you. I wish I could, but I can't. When I warned you the circus isn't what it seems, I meant it. The tokens *do* take away bad dreams, in a way, or at least they should," she said, looking up at Will. "But that's all I can say. Please, you really should leave. Both of you."

Cora glanced at Will, then back at Victoria. "We're not leaving," she said. "Not yet anyway. But when we do, why don't you come with us?"

The girl shook her head. "I can't," she said miserably.

Cora leaned over and put her arm around Victoria's shoulders. "I don't know what this is about, but I'm sorry you're hurting," she whispered.

Victoria smiled through her tears. "Thanks." Then she stood, wiped at her eyes, and walked over to the stalker. She murmured something in its ear as she reached up and removed its collar. The great cat rose and slunk into the shadows. The branches barely whispered with its passing.

Victoria said, "You don't need to worry about it coming back." After a moment she added, "I need to be alone. I'm going to find another tree." Then she, too, was gone.

Cora waited a few moments, and then said, "We're taking her with us, Will. We've got to convince her."

"Maybe." Will sounded doubtful.

After he had gathered some more sticks, he said, "Well, do you want to talk about it? The fact that they sent a stalker after you?"

"Me?" exclaimed Cora. "That's ridiculous—"

"Cora, the Council thinks you have the Sand Coin. They think you stole it."

"But Mr. Blackwood knows I didn't. He wouldn't let them send a stalker after me!"

Will shook his head. "Blackwood can't defend you, not without revealing that he helped you escape. He may have tried to put the Council off, but if they made up their minds, he couldn't have done a thing to stop them. That stalker was meant for you."

Cora's eyes opened wide. She had thought the stalker was a chance encounter, however improbable. But no. It *had* been sent after her. And now that it had failed, the Council would send another. Or a company of soldiers, or an assassin, or . . . the list was terrifyingly endless.

"We have to get the Sand Coin," she said, "and it *has* to be soon, Will. It *has* to be. Who knows what they'll send next? And the Turn is coming and—"

"We'll be fine. We know where it is. We'll get the Coin and use the vault or, worse comes to worst, we'll find a ship. It'll take just a couple days to take the Sand Coin back to Tarian."

Cora hadn't considered a ship. It *would* make for a faster trip, and to Cora's surprise, the thought of sailing no longer filled her with dread. It was the token, she realized. It was taking those memories of the Storm and blurring them, blunting them.

"Maybe you're right," she said. "But even so, we have to get it soon."

Will cocked his head and listened to the rain. There was a rumble of thunder. "If Dane's right, there's a good chance this keeps up. If it does, we'll camp here tonight. We'll get it while everyone is sleeping. Alright?"

"Alright," said Cora.

"Now then. Why don't we get some food and take a nap?"

But the rain stopped by early afternoon. There was a shout, and Cora and Will emerged from their tree to see most of the performers gathered beside the road. The sun was out and the sky above was clear, but to the south, near the horizon, a bank of leaden clouds still churned.

"A break in the weather," said Anders. "Pack up! Let's move while we can. Plan to travel through the night!"

Cora groaned, but Will said, "There's time, Cor. Don't worry, we still have time."

CHAPTER FOURTEEN

A PROPOSAL

THINGS WERE, BLACKWOOD THOUGHT, GOING quite well. And that was surprising, considering.

A week and a day after the attack on the Pike, the Council had still heard nothing from the Master, but they had received a disturbing report from the Master's Elite about a Storm Orphan caught in the Iron Spire the day of the attack, and her escape from the Cells. That it had taken so long for the report to make its way to the Council did not surprise Blackwood one bit; Tarian's government was bloated and inefficient. The report had surprised the rest of the Council though, and they were alarmed, so alarmed that the chief councilor had sent word to the Master, seeking an audience. It was then that his death had been discovered.

The Council had been thrown into turmoil. It was agreed that news of the death of the Master—not to mention the missing Sand Coin— should be kept from the general population, for fear of riots or worse. But within the Council itself, there was no clear consensus on how to proceed. However, behind every idea, every proposal, there was one thing in common: fear.

Now, several days after the discovery of the death of the Master of

Tides, Blackwood sat with the other councilors in the round, vaulted Council Chamber. Candles wavered and guttered in the drafty hall, and cast a feeble light on the other six men and women. Each of their faces was etched with worry.

"Overseer Thaddeus Blackwood, you have the floor." Chief Councilor Wickett bowed her head and sat.

Blackwood stood and walked to the center of the room, turning to face the Council members. "Thank you, Chief Councilor. Ladies and gentlemen," he inclined his head and clasped his hands behind his back, "these past days have been difficult ones. The death of the Master came as a surprise to us all. As citizens of this city, we have come to take his presence, and the security it has afforded us, for granted. And now we find ourselves without a Protector, without a Defender. In but a matter of days or weeks, the raiders who successfully attacked us will return, and they will return in force. In precisely two weeks is the Turn and, as you know, with it comes the tidal surge. What are we to do? How are we to proceed?

"Some of you have proposed that we seek the lost Sand Coin and select the new Master. And I would agree with you, except that to do so is impossible. We have no inkling where the Sand Coin might be and without the Sand Coin, we cannot choose a new Master.

"Now, as some of you have noted, the Works Leader Cora, the Storm Orphan formerly in my employ, *was* found in the Spire on the day of the attack. Naturally, she was imprisoned, but the details of her arrest were not conveyed to me at the time. Nor did she tell me anything when I visited her in the Cells. Had I known that she had been in the Master's tower, things would be very different now. Alas.

"Unfortunately, as we all know, Cora managed to escape and has since disappeared. It is clear she was the thief of the Sand Coin. But despite considerable efforts, Cora remains at large. I hired a stalker—at my own expense, which was not negligible—to track her down. But her trail ended at the docks and, unfortunately, even a stalker cannot track the waves.

"The long and short of it is this: Cora and the Sand Coin could be anywhere. We could scour all of Hibaria and the Islands in search of the girl, but to do so would take considerable time. Time that we do not have.

"And yet," Blackwood went on, "we find ourselves in a position that is far from unfavorable."

The chief councilor frowned and leaned forward. The others exchanged glances. Blackwood continued.

"What was the role of the Master? One." He held up a finger. "To call the tides to defend us against any who would attack our city. Two, to protect us from the annual tidal surge. And three, to mete out justice when we, the Council, could not come to a decision." Blackwood gazed at each of the councilors, his face sober. "The Master of Tides served us well, there is no denying that. But what he did, we now can do.

"Consider the construction of the Water Works over the past few years and their recent completion. With just a few changes that I could carry out in one or two weeks at most, the Works can be as effective in defending Tarian as the Master, against both marauders and the tidal surge. *We* can call the tides. *We* can dash the ships of our enemies to pieces. *We* can keep the sea at bay.

"And because we must, *we* can make the difficult decisions that, until now, we have not. We are not the Master, true, but we have no small amount of wisdom. Together, we can lead Tarian and we can lead her well.

"I do not say these things lightly. Indeed, I say them reluctantly, understanding the enormity of my words and the weight that they carry. These are words that, if accepted and embraced, will mean a great change that will, perhaps, be uncomfortable for some of us. But we are, I needn't remind you, facing a crisis. Not only is the Master dead, but we face an imminent attack and the tidal surge. And as the leaders of this city, this crisis is ours to solve.

"Ladies and gentlemen of the Council, these are my humble views that I believe provide a way for us to move forward. Our city will remain secure. Our prosperity will be assured. I welcome discussion on my proposal."

It was a lot he was asking of the Council, Blackwood knew. And under any other circumstances he would have been ridiculed for what he was putting before them. But the Council was desperate; he could see it on their faces. Even before they started to nod, Blackwood knew that he had them; the Council had no other option. And in accepting his idea, they would, wittingly or not, be accepting his leadership.

The chief councilor surveyed the other five and satisfied there was no dissention, she said, "Overseer Blackwood, if indeed the Water Works can be made to fully defend Tarian, and if you can demonstrate this, we will adopt your proposal. Please, sir, lay out before us the particulars of your plan."

CHAPTER FIFTEEN

The Hornwood

AS THE CIRCUS PREPARED TO depart, Cora, from her seat on the wagon, peered intently at the shadows beneath the lockleaves.

"The stalker's gone," murmured Will. "Quit worrying."

"Maybe there's another," said Cora.

"Trust me, they only sent one. One should have been more than enough to do the job. But here comes Vic, so either way you're fine."

Victoria emerged from the trees and climbed up and sat beside Cora. Her presence was a relief and some of the tension that had been growing within Cora drained away. Moments later Dane joined them, and the line of wagons continued down the road.

They soon entered a largely featureless land, empty of trees and any habitation. It lacked color apart from the pale, yellow grass that continued unabated to the horizon.

"The lockleaves mark the beginning of the Eastern Wild," said Dane. "It's like this for a while now. Just emptiness. We're five, maybe six days from the Door."

"Tell us about the door," said Will. "What's so special about it?"

Dane broke into his crooked smile. "I forgot, you still don't know.

Not just a door. A *Door.* Arburry gave us keys for these Doors that are scattered around Hibaria and the Islands. When we use one key, the Door opens in Labryn Waite, another takes us to the wood outside Arosil, and so on. And one of the keys takes us to Arburry."

"Where does Lord Arburry live?" asked Cora.

"Dunno," said Dane. "Doesn't really matter, though."

"So you can move all over Hibaria and the Islands through a series of Doors." Will ran a hand through his hair. "That's amazing."

"We can get to a lot of places," said Dane. "Not Tarian though, obviously. But the places that *do* have Doors . . . they cut down on our travel time, for sure."

"So it's a straight shot from here to the Door?" asked Will.

Dane flicked the reins and clucked at the horses. "Kind of. Tomorrow we'll cross into the Hornwood for a bit, and then back into the wilderness along the coast. A few days of following the shore, then we get to the Door. It's inland a bit, right at the edge of the Hornwood."

"The Hornwood?" asked Cora, and she had difficulty keeping alarm out of her voice. First a stalker, now the Hornwood. She had heard about the ancient forest that blanketed the land and was so dense that it swallowed light. She had heard stories that said the shadows of the Hornwood were alive, that they moved and breathed and devoured unwary travelers. The Hornwood was one of the last bastions of old magic left in Hibaria. Cora hadn't realized their path would lead through it.

"Not the Hornwood proper," said Dane. "It's just the southern fringe, and then we're out of it again. And the Door, like I said, is right at the forest's edge." He glanced at her and added, "You don't need to worry. We've traveled this way before, and it'll be fine if we stay on the road."

Despite Dane's reassurance, the fear that had settled in the pit of Cora's stomach at the appearance of the stalker only grew as they made their way north.

It began to rain as darkness fell, a cold and swirling rain that once again soaked them to the skin.

"Hope you're comfortable," said Dane with a grin as he pushed his wet hair out of his eyes. "This rain isn't stopping and neither are we."

The following morning, a gray smudge appeared on the horizon ahead of them. Cora watched, bleary-eyed, as the smudge slowly resolved into a tangled mass of towering trees. Looking at the twisted, old trees, cloaked as they were in rain and shadow and mystery, Cora believed the stories she had heard and shivered.

As they entered the wood, a hush fell over the children. What little conversation there had been ceased, and the only sounds that continued were the creaking of the wagon axles and the occasional snort of a horse. Even the patter of the rain fell silent, so complete was the cover of the trees above them. But it was the feeling of the air that held Cora's attention—it seemed to seethe, to prickle against her skin. It was what she had felt in the Iron Spire; the same power that was there was here!

She looked at Will and he managed a smile, but it appeared to be forced. At some point he had drawn his sword, and it now lay across his lap. Cora hugged her bag to her chest. It wasn't a weapon, but it still managed to be a comfort. Dane relit the lantern that hung beside the wagon seat. Up and down the line of wagons, the other drivers did the same.

The wagons wound deeper into the trees, keeping to the paved road, and before long they were rolling and bumping through a half-darkness that reminded Cora of the brooding storm they had just escaped. The pools of lantern light revealed immense, shaggy tree trunks that passed up beyond sight into the darkness above. Strewn around their snake-like roots were moss-covered boulders and drifts of dead, moldering leaves. The damp, prickly air grew noticeably more chill.

"Really, it looks and feels worse than it is," said Dane, but his face mirrored how Cora felt and she did not feel reassured.

Suddenly, the wagons in front of them came to a halt. After a few moments, Felix appeared. "A tree is down across the road. We'll need everyone up there to move it." He continued down the line as Cora, Will, Victoria, and Dane jumped to the ground.

"You don't need your bag, you know," said Dane, looking at Cora. "It'll just get in the way."

She couldn't exactly tell him why she kept it with her at all times now, so Cora just shrugged as she slipped the strap over her shoulder.

"Suit yourself," laughed Dane as they made their way toward the front of the wagons.

Anders, standing on the seat of the lead wagon, directed them. They had just begun to push the tree trunk to the side when a gruff voice rang out.

"Welcome!" it shouted. Everyone looked around, startled. A moment later, a tall figure appeared at the edge of their lantern light, clad in the colors of the forest. The man's face was covered with a dark green scarf. "You may use my road, but you must pay the toll."

Anders crossed his arms. "We've used this road dozens of times. There is no toll."

"Times change," said the man.

"So what's the charge?" asked Anders.

"Why, nothing more than the contents of your wagon, young sir," came the reply.

Anders surveyed the heavy boxes and iron-bound chests and shook his head. "I don't think so," he said. The dogs on the wagon bed growled and bared their teeth at the man.

The man shrugged and raised an arm, and more than two dozen similarly dressed men stepped from the wood. They clutched clubs and staves and several had swords. Three had bows drawn back, arrows trained on Anders. "We're not asking," the first man said.

There was a twang behind Cora and one of the men holding a bow dropped it with a yell, an arrow protruding from his hand. An instant later another twang and another bow went flying. The remaining archer loosed his arrow and Anders leapt from the wagon and rolled, narrowly avoiding it.

Cora glanced behind her and saw Tesh drawing another arrow to her ear. She also saw an outlaw emerging from the shadows of the wood at a run. He was headed straight for Tesh.

"Behind you!" Cora yelled.

Tesh turned, but it was too late. The outlaw swung a club, catching Tesh on the side of her head. She crumpled to the ground.

A few of the children drew knives, and Will had his sword, but more bandits appeared, almost too many to count, all bristling with weapons. A dozen or more rushed at Anders' wagon. They tossed nets over the snarling dogs and began grabbing the chests and boxes.

Above, Rascha was a blur of frenzied, flapping wings. Cora waited for him to use his magic, to do *something*, but he only croaked and screamed down at the outlaws. And then one of them raised his bow and released an arrow. The crow tumbled to the ground, pierced through the heart.

Cora looked around frantically. They had to stop this! One of those boxes contained the Sand Coin!

"The wolves!" shouted Cora. "Release the wolves!"

But it was too late. In mere moments, the wagon was emptied and the outlaws melted back into the trees. Cora crouched down and watched as the men crowded around a large rock. As they placed their hands on the stone, they stepped into its shadow and suddenly vanished. She gasped. No one else from the circus seemed to have noticed.

"Everyone, to me, now!" yelled Anders. He stood looking down at Rascha's lifeless body, shock plain on his face. He shook himself and said, "Dane, Will, you're with me. Bring your knives. And bring a couple horses and a bunch of saddlebags. Tesh, you up for this?"

Tesh had gotten to her feet and was now leaning against a wagon. She nodded and rubbed the lump on her temple with a grimace.

"Good. Victoria, bring the winter wolves. Everyone else, Felix is in charge. Felix, as soon as you've moved the tree, take the Youngers on to the Door. We'll catch up to you." Anders glanced down again at the dead crow and added, "And bring Rascha."

Cora drew a deep breath and cleared her throat. "I saw where the outlaws went. I need to come too."

"I think we can track the outlaws without you," said Anders dismissively. He turned and called out, "Those wolves ready to go, Victoria? Dane? Will? Horses?"

The boys came forward, each leading a horse laden with several saddlebags. Victoria appeared with five winter wolves. She had a bag slung across her body.

"We won't need the horses," she said. "They'll just slow us down."

"We need them to carry the money. In case you didn't realize, we kind of have a lot of it," said Anders. "Alright, let's go."

Victoria gave Anders a flat stare and then bent and whispered to the wolves. They immediately set off, their noses to the ground, following the trail of the outlaws into the trees. Anders and Tesh followed, and Dane and Will brought up the rear with the horses.

The rest of the circus, under the direction of Felix, began to again move the fallen tree. Cora, though, hung back and peered after the search party. They hadn't gone far when they stopped. Cora heard Anders say, "What do you mean, it's gone?"

"It's gone." Victoria sounded shaken. "The trail is just . . . gone."

Cora stepped off the road and through a drift of leaves. "I told you I saw where they went." Eyeing the shadow of the rock, she felt suddenly queasy, but forced herself to continue. "Do you want me to help you follow them or not?"

"Just tell us which way they went," said Anders.

She pointed to the boulder. "There."

Anders looked and then shook his head in disgust. "Victoria, start circling with the wolves. You'll pick up their scent—"

"You won't," said Cora. She stepped past them and stood before the rock. There was an ancient symbol, barely discernible, carved into its surface. The rock's shadow was like a pool of ink and it appeared to swirl in the dimness, despite the lantern that Will held. *Shadows devour travelers in the Hornwood,* she thought. But the Sand Coin was in there . . . She looked at Will, placed her hand on the rock, and stepped into the shadow.

The light of the lantern blinked out, everyone disappeared, and the forest shifted around Cora. The trees twisted and changed, and the fallen leaves whispered and rustled and then were still. Only the prickling of the air remained the same. That and the boulder, barely visible in the dimness, the same symbol etched into it. Cora stood just outside its shadow.

She was on the verge of stepping back into the shadow when Will suddenly appeared and collided with her, and they both went tumbling to the ground. "You were just gone," he said as he helped her up. He looked around, alarm on his face. "What—?"

Victoria and the winter wolves stepped from the shadow, and then Tesh, Anders, and Dane, pulling both horses behind him.

Everyone looked around, eyes wide. "These stones must work like the Doors," said Dane. "We've gone . . . somewhere else."

"But we're still in the Hornwood," said Tesh. "It feels the same. Looks and smells the same too. Still, it would be nice to know where we are."

"It would be nice to know where the outlaws are," said Anders as he drew a long knife from his belt.

Pointing, Victoria said, "The wolves have the scent again." The winter wolves nosed off into the trees, leaving a trail of frost and ice behind them.

With one last look at the stone, Anders said, "Come on." Glancing at Cora he added, "You too."

They moved through the Hornwood like ghosts, silent but for the occasional cracking twig or rustling leaf. Will had extinguished his lantern soon after stepping through the shadow. "They'll see us coming," he had muttered. Now, they crept forward, clumped together in the dimness, their own breath loud in their ears as they strained to see what lay ahead.

Will slipped Cora one of his knives. Looking around at the menacing shadows, Cora wondered if steel could stop what might be lurking in the forest around them. Probably not. Still, she was grateful.

An hour later they came to a hollow. At the bottom, beside an ancient twisted beech tree, was another stone. A different symbol adorned its surface. The trail led into the shadow. Anders turned to Cora and raised an eyebrow at her.

"What? You want me to go first?" When he grinned, Cora said, "The outlaws might be on the other side."

"Better be careful then."

"Fine." Cora glared at him and then tightened her grip on the knife, touched the stone, and stepped into the darkness.

Again, the others disappeared and the forest twisted around her. She stood beside a stone, ankle deep in fallen leaves. There was no sign of the bandits.

She stepped back into the shadow and the others reappeared. "Come on," Cora said. Looking at Anders, she smiled a little too sweetly and added, "You don't have to worry, it's safe."

The outlaws' trail was picked up once more and the winter wolves led the way, their noses to the ground. Occasionally, Dane knelt and examined a faint boot print or a broken fern. "We're close behind," he said at one point. Tesh looked around, an arrow ready on her bow.

When they came to a third stone, Cora didn't even pause. She brushed the faint symbol with her hand and stepped into the shadow.

She froze. There in front of her, within arm's reach, was one of the outlaws. His back was turned toward her and he leaned on his spear. Cora silently backed away and the forest again shifted.

When the others appeared, she whispered, "Guard. He didn't see me, but he's right there."

"How close?" asked Anders.

"Close. Right there, two steps maybe. He's got a spear."

"Tesh, you bring rope?"

"Of course."

"Dane, Will. On the count of three we go through, grab him, and drag him back here."

"He'll shout when you grab him," said Victoria.

Anders muttered something under his breath and then said, "Dane, hit him on the head. Use the butt of your knife. We'll follow and drag him back here."

Dane hefted his knife and disappeared. A moment later Will and Anders followed. They immediately reappeared, pulling the groaning form of the outlaw behind them.

They dragged him well away from the stone and tied him to a tree. When Anders had checked the knots, he squatted down in front of the man. He was just coming to.

"Didn't take us very long to find you," said Anders. "Are we close to your hideout?"

The man didn't say anything. He just glared at them, his face sullen.

"Just to be clear, we don't *need* your help. We have those." Anders gestured toward the winter wolves. "They'll find your friends and the things you stole. They're better than hounds. And silent. And deadly if we want them to be." One of the wolves opened its mouth and turned a glowing eye toward the outlaw. Snow swirled through its teeth and fell softly to the ground.

The outlaw's face grew pale. "It's not far. But if you think it'll be easy, you're in for a surprise."

"We expect it to be at least as difficult as capturing you," said Anders with a nasty smile.

One by one they stepped into the shadow of the stone, touching its gritty surface. On the other side, the same uncomfortable chilly dampness surrounded them, the same murk, the same dim shadows.

"Here's what we're going to do," whispered Anders. He pointed to boot prints in the dirt leading off into the forest. "The trail is obvious. Dane and I will scout ahead until we find the bandits. Then we'll come back and make a plan. Victoria, form a perimeter around the stone with the wolves, a hundred paces or so. If any outlaws approach to use it, take them out. The rest of you, watch for anyone coming through the stone. Tesh, have your bow ready. Got it?"

They all nodded.

"Alright then," said Anders. He spun his long knife in the air and caught it. "Let's go."

In less than an hour, Anders and Dane returned. When they had gathered around the stone, Anders said, "It's not far at all. The bandits are inside a palisade, maybe ten or twelve feet high. It's on an island in a river."

"How many?" asked Tesh.

"Hard to say. Forty or so I think, but it could be a few more. Dane and I were able to climb a tree and see inside part of the camp." Anders leaned down and, using a stick, scratched a rough map of the river and the island and the fort into the dirt. "Our boxes and chests are in the middle next to the fire." He added a number of little squares to the center of the island. "The gate is here, and right outside is a dock and five boats.

"They broke our locks and the chests are open. They're pretty happy with what they found, apparently, judging from the celebration."

"So what's the plan?" asked Will.

"They're eating now, and most are lying around the fire. A few are already asleep." Anders looked up into the gloom. "You can't tell day from night in here, but I think it's safe to say they're bedding down. We wait a couple hours, then use the wolves to freeze us a path across the river. A couple of us will scale the wall. It'll take two of us to open the gate, I think. After that we'll all load everything from the boxes into the saddlebags, put them onto the horses and be off. They'll never know we were there.

"If any of them *are* awake, though, I want Tesh in position here." He scratched a circle in the dirt. "This is the tree we climbed and from it you can see the back part of the enclosure. And back there," he said, tapping the ground, "are barrels of lamp oil. Above the barrels is a lantern. If the outlaws wake up, Tesh, I want you to shoot the lantern and light the barrels. And when those barrels go up, that will create a big enough distraction that we can get our things and get out."

"Wouldn't that take a while? For the lantern to burn through the barrels and light the oil, I mean? Would it even work?" asked Cora.

Anders ignored her. "Any serious questions?" he asked.

Cora opened her mouth but Anders cut her off. "Alright then. Let's rest."

A low birdcall sounded through the dimness. It was Tesh's signal. She had climbed the tree and was now in position. Cora and the others crouched on the bank of the river, hidden in a clump of bushes. They peered across the dark, swirling water at the bandit's island fort.

The fort stood silent. Lanterns, affixed to the top of the log palisade, revealed a wall twice as tall as Anders. The tops of the rough-cut logs were sharpened points.

Will leaned over and whispered in Cora's ear, "Let me guess: Anders wants you to climb the wall. I gotta say, you get all the fun jobs."

Cora shrugged. "I can't help that I'm his favorite."

Will snickered.

"Did I just make you laugh, Will?"

"Huh. I guess you did, Cor. Even a blind squirrel finds a nut once in a while, I suppose."

"Quiet, you two," hissed Anders. Then he raised a hand and Victoria crept forward.

The winter wolves followed her, and she leaned over and spoke to each of them. They lowered their enormous heads to the river and breathed. The water frosted and crackled and hardened. Cora watched as the ice spread across the river toward the island. Victoria stepped out and tested it with her foot. She waved them on.

As Anders and Dane began to cross, Cora tugged at one of the horses and edged it onto the ice. The animal rolled its eyes and tried to pull away. Victoria was there in an instant, soothing the horse and patting its neck. It calmed and a moment later followed Cora onto the frozen river.

The ice groaned as they crossed, but it held, and the wolves continued to breathe, thickening and strengthening it. Soon they were all gathered on the narrow dock facing the gate.

Anders stepped to the wall and braced his back against it. He laced his fingers together and held them at his waist and then nodded to Dane. The boy stepped into Anders' hands and then pushed off, leaping straight up. Dane grabbed hold of the top of the wall and managed to pull himself up and over in one smooth motion. How he avoided snagging his clothes on the sharpened logs was beyond Cora. A moment later his head reappeared and he gave the all-clear signal.

Will took Anders' place and soon Anders was beside Dane on the wall. Then they ducked out of sight.

At that moment, Cora heard a scuffle and a shout from inside the palisade. Then a harsh voice spoke. "I must say, I'm impressed. I wouldn't have thought you would be able to find us. Most don't know the secrets of the shadow stones."

"What, *none* of you were sleeping?" said Anders.

You better shoot that lantern, Tesh, Cora thought as she crept to the gate. Finding a gap between two logs, she peeked through.

It was a small encampment, perhaps the size of the circus ring. A huge tree grew at the far end, sheltering half the island, and several crudely fashioned lean-tos had been built against the inside of the log wall. Glowing lanterns hung from the tree's branches. The leader of the outlaws stood beside a fire that had burned low, and he was surrounded by his henchmen. Two of them held Anders and Dane in vise-like hands.

"When one of my guards didn't report back . . . well, I thought it was prudent to be ready for something like this," said the leader.

There was a whisper and one of the lanterns hanging toward the back of the palisade fell. It struck one of the barrels and its glass broke—and the flame promptly went out.

"You might want to join Will," said Victoria quietly. Cora turned, and Victoria waved impatiently for Cora to move away from the gate. She scrambled over beside Will who was crouched in the shadow of the palisade. The horses were there too, standing on the narrow strip of land between the log wall and the river.

Victoria made a gesture with her hand, and the winter wolves gathered beside her, ran forward, and leapt. One by one the enormous creatures cleared the gate and landed with reverberating thuds inside the encampment.

For a second, there was silence, and then the outlaw fort erupted in shouts and screams. Moments later the gate crashed open and men came pouring out. They skidded across the frozen river and disappeared into the gloom of the forest.

"Now," said Victoria. "Bring the horses." She strode through the gates, and Will and Cora pulled the horses behind them.

Anders pushed himself up from the ground. Blood trickled from a gash on his forehead. "Wolves knocked me down," he grumbled as he shot a glare at Victoria.

Several outlaws, including the leader, had scrambled up the tree. Two of the wolves stood below, their mouths open in silent snarls, sending snow and ice and wind up into the tangle of branches. Victoria spoke a word to the other three wolves and they went to stand at the gate.

"Let's load!" shouted Anders. "Leave the tokens, grab everything else!" He and Dane dumped the contents of the heaviest chest into a saddlebag. Cora stooped and picked up a box. Its lid had been shattered and the light glistened off the silver coins inside.

"In here," said Will, holding open a bag. She poured them in and cast the box aside. The next chest she came to was filled with tokens. But then, out of the corner of her eye, she saw it. On the ground beside the fire was a small, carved box the color of driftwood.

She snatched it up. There was a click and the carved box snapped opened. Cora caught her breath. Inside was a round disc, a little larger than the palm of her hand. It lay on a bed of brown seaweed, its worn leather loop tucked beneath it. A sea flower with five narrow petals was etched into its gritty, bone-white surface.

"Will you look at that," said Will quietly. "Think it'll fit in the vault?"

Cora glanced around as she stuffed the Sand Coin inside her coat pocket. She snapped the carved box closed and dropped it on the ground. "I think so," she said.

"How about that," said Will. "And with plenty of time to spare. What do we have, a couple weeks before the Turn?"

Normally, Cora was annoyed when Will was right, even more so when he pointed it out, but now she only felt relief.

"Yes. I'll send it home as soon as we're out of here," she whispered.

"We ready to move?" called Anders.

Dane finished emptying a chest into one of the saddlebags, and Victoria scooped up the carved box and dropped it in as well.

"Think so," said Dane.

"Then let's go." Anders turned to the outlaw leader in the tree and said, "Sir, it's been a pleasure. Sorry it didn't turn out the way you hoped." He made a mocking bow and waved. The outlaw leader gave him a sour look.

Victoria led them across the ice bridge and once on the riverbank, they made straight for the shadow stone. Tesh emerged from the trees at a jog and joined them. The wolves made a loose circle around them, but even so, everyone was on their guard.

At the stone, Anders pulled them up short.

"We need to go back the same way we came. It's the only way we'll get back to the road. And we need to go fast. The outlaws won't be long in coming after us." He glanced around.

Victoria pulled a saddlebag off one of the horses and heaved it onto a winter wolf.

"What are you doing?" asked Anders.

"The horses can't run through the woods, not without breaking a leg. The wolves can. This is why bringing the horses was a bad idea." She grabbed another bag and put it on a second wolf. When the first horse was unloaded, she leaned toward its ear and said, "I hope you can find our wagons again." Then she slapped its flank.

"Don't be ridiculous!" Anders grabbed at the horse's bridle. "We need to hurry but we don't need to run."

"Really?" said Victoria. "Tell that to them."

They turned to see half a dozen outlaws running toward them from the direction of the river. A moment later, an arrow whistled past Cora's ear and glanced off a tree.

"We need to ride." Victoria gripped the fur of one of the wolves and pulled herself onto its back. "They'll allow it."

Tesh kept the outlaws at bay with her bow as they hastily unloaded the last horse and then clambered onto the backs of the winter wolves. Will pulled Cora up to sit behind him.

"Follow me," said Victoria. As her wolf stepped into the shadow, she leaned down, touched the stone, and disappeared.

CHAPTER SIXTEEN

Escape Through the Hornwood

T HE WINTER WOLVES BOUNDED THROUGH the trees, their paws quiet on the forest floor. Victoria led the way, hunched low on her wolf as it wound in and out of shadow, leaping fallen trees, and ducking under vines and branches. Countless times it appeared that they would slam into a rock or tree, but at the last moment the wolves, without slowing, would veer away and find a way where there was none.

They were cold creatures, and soon Cora's legs were numb. She shivered as she held fast to Will.

After a time, they came to a stream strewn with mossy boulders. Anders called for a halt.

"The outlaws are pursuing," said Victoria. "They know the Hornwood and we don't. This isn't safe. For all we know, there may be other stones that they're using to get ahead of us. We need to go now!"

Anders looked at her, blood crusted above his eye, and tilted his head. "Just to be clear, I'm still in charge," he said. He didn't smile. When Victoria didn't respond, he went on. "Victoria, what you did back on the island was out of line."

"*What?*" said Dane. "She saved us!"

"I had things under control," said Anders, crossing his arms. "We had a plan and for some reason you didn't let it play out, Victoria. Instead, you endangered the winter wolves. Why?"

"The only thing you had was a plan that fell apart almost before it started," Cora said. "The outlaws *weren't* asleep. And when Tesh shot the lantern, it fell and went out. If Victoria hadn't acted, we'd probably all be dead. You're just mad you looked dumb back there."

"I'm telling you, I—"

"I did what needed to be done, Anders." Victoria's eyes flashed. "And I'm not trying to take your position. I just want us to get out of here."

"This isn't finished. We'll talk about it later," was all Anders said as he guided his wolf past Victoria.

They continued on through the murk of the wood. It was a winding, silent run. The wolves kicked up leaves that swirled in their wake. The breath of the creatures trailed behind them like small snowstorms. After a short time, Anders slowed then stopped beside the next shadow stone.

"This one and then one more. I'll—"

An arrow buried itself in his shoulder and nearly knocked Anders to the ground. He grunted in pain as his wolf stumbled into the shadow stone and vanished.

"Vic was right! The outlaws got ahead of us!" shouted Will.

The air hummed and more arrows streaked by. One cut through Will's sleeve, another struck one of the saddlebags. First Victoria, then Dane, then Tesh urged their wolves into the shadow after Anders. Will and Cora brought up the rear.

They stepped through the shadow into chaos. Arrows hurtled in from all sides, whining as they flew past in a blur. Anders lay on the ground. Tesh had dismounted and was crouched beside him, returning fire into the trees. Cora ducked as a spear whistled past.

"We have to move now!" shouted Victoria.

"Anders is in bad shape," said Tesh through gritted teeth. She had a cut across her cheek.

Dane guided his wolf over, reached down, and with Tesh's help, heaved Anders up. Anders was unconscious and his shirt was soaked with blood.

"I think I can hold him here in front of me," said Dane. "For a little while anyway."

Victoria whistled and the two riderless winter wolves came running. Tesh managed to mount one of them even as she sent an arrow toward an outlaw who had just appeared through the trees.

"Go!" Victoria shouted. The wolves surged forward.

Cora leaned down as far as she could, one arm around Will and one gripping the frost-encrusted fur of the wolf. As they burst past an old oak, she caught sight of two outlaws. One raised an axe and hurled it at them, but he hadn't been quick enough. They surged past, and the axe fell harmlessly to the ground behind them.

The shouts of the outlaws quickly faded, but the wolves didn't slow. At Victoria's urging they kept up their ground-eating pace.

Victoria tried to guide them toward the next stone, but twice more they encountered the outlaws.

"It's no use," Victoria said at last. "They've cut us off." With a scowl she wheeled her wolf around. "We'll have to find another way out of the wood."

"Maybe," said Dane, "but right now we have to stop. We have to do something about Anders' shoulder."

They slowed and dismounted in a hollow surrounded by enormous slabs of lichen-covered rock. A trickle of water seeped from the ground between two of the stones and formed a small pool. The wolves immediately started lapping up the water.

Dane sat Anders against a rock and cut away his blood-soaked sleeve. The arrow quivered as Dane held Anders steady. "What do you think?" he asked. "Pull this thing out or leave it?"

Tesh squatted to examine the wound. "The head's poking out the back," she said. "It's a broadhead. Break the shaft off, as close to his shoulder as you can. We'll pull it out the back."

Dane took a deep breath and snapped the arrow. Anders groaned. Then Dane scooped up some water from the pool and poured it on the wound and tried to rinse off what was left of the arrow. "Alright, I'll hold him," he said.

Tesh leaned down and reached behind Anders' shoulder. With a jerk, the broken shaft disappeared. Anders gasped and his eyes opened wide. Blood began to bubble from the wound.

"Um, anyone have something to wrap around this?" asked Dane.

They all looked at one another blankly. Cora frantically rifled through her pockets but there was nothing.

With a look of resignation, Victoria pushed up her left sleeve. The wrapping that wound around her hand continued all the way to her elbow. She quickly began to unwind it. As it came away, the dim light revealed green and blue and silver markings on her skin. The markings, shaped like overlapping serpent scales, glittered and faintly glowed.

"Are those tattoos?" asked Dane. He stared at Victoria, his mouth hanging open.

Victoria handed him the cloth. "Don't worry, it's clean," she said. She unwound the wrapping on her other arm, and Cora could see that it, too, was marked with scales.

"Right." Dane took both strips of cloth and hastily began to wrap them around Anders' wound.

"We all need to drink. Anyone else have a bottle?" asked Tesh as she filled hers. Will held up a water skin. "Fill it," she said. "We don't know when we'll find water again."

When she stood, Tesh looked back the way they had come and said, "We should go. They're probably still following."

"But go where?" asked Will. "We don't know where we are. We

could be anywhere in the Hornwood. The only way to find our way back to the path is to get to the last stone. And to do that would mean we'd have to go back toward the outlaws."

Everyone looked at one another uneasily.

"We need to go east," said Cora. "We'd eventually run into the sea. We could find the wagons after that."

Tesh looked up at the dim light that filtered through the branches above them and then at Cora. Her face was scornful. "Want to tell us which way that is?"

Victoria surprised them all by pointing off to their right. "That way," she said.

Tesh shook her head. "No offense, but you can't know that. I say we keep going the way we were."

"I *do* know that. You need to trust me."

Dane said, "What about going back to the shadow stone? I know it would be difficult, but—"

"The stone is out," said Tesh. "Anders is a wreck and the outlaws will be waiting. You saw how well they defended the shadow stone. They aren't going to suddenly go home. They know that's our only way out."

"Look," said Cora, "why don't we listen to Victoria and—"

Tesh rounded on her. "Why don't you just be quiet? Keep out of this! She doesn't know the way any more than you do! Leave this to someone who's more experienced."

"We need to keep moving," said Victoria as she pulled herself onto one of the wolves. "You should follow me."

She set off without looking back, bearing to the right, and the others, after exchanging quick glances, followed. Tesh scowled and muttered to herself, but guided her wolf after Victoria as well.

Anders sat in front of Dane, slipping in and out of consciousness, and so Cora now had a wolf to herself. They went at an easier pace, but they rarely paused.

After some time, confident that they had outpaced the outlaws, Victoria called for a rest. Everyone, even the wolves, were exhausted.

Dane tended Anders who had awoken when they stopped. "This isn't good," said Dane, looking at Anders' shoulder. "He needs to rest for it to start to heal. He needs to sleep."

"I'll be fine," muttered Anders. He pushed himself into a sitting position, but then fell back. He glared at Victoria and tried to speak, but his words turned into a moan.

"Dane is right," said Tesh. She grimaced when she saw the blood-soaked bandages. "That's not getting any better while you ride." She looked back the way they had come. "But we can't stop long. If they're tracking us, the outlaws will be on us before we know it. We can only rest a little while."

"Anyone have any food?" asked Will. But no one had thought to bring any when they had left the wagons. "So we're lost in the middle of the Hornwood. No food, hardly any water, we're being chased by outlaws, and Anders is seriously wounded. I suppose it could be worse," Will said with a grin. They all looked at one another. Their situation *was* dire, Cora realized.

Perhaps a quarter of an hour later, they set out again. They rode in single file and Victoria chose the path. They picked their way among the silent trees, through drifts of leaves that at times came up to the wolves' shoulders, and over scattered heaps of broken gray stones. At one point, Victoria led them down the middle of a stream for half a mile or so. Regardless of their path, they traveled through a perpetual dimness that seemed to be woven into the fabric of the forest.

Cora noticed, too, that the all-but-imperceptible crackling of the air that she had first sensed upon entering the Hornwood remained. It waxed and waned, but never completely disappeared.

Several hours passed. Cora, like the rest, had lost track of time, but it felt like the onset of night. The cold from the winter wolf had spread from her legs to the rest of her body. She shivered and longed for sleep.

"We have to stop," said Tesh. She guided her wolf over to Dane's and peered down at Anders. He sat slumped in front of Dane, his arms around the wolf's neck. "We'll lose Anders if we don't."

"There's something ahead," said Victoria. "Come on."

Through the trees a stone building came into view. As they approached it, they could see in the dim light that it was a tower. They came to its base and looked up.

"I don't see anyone on the battlements," whispered Dane. High above, a small patch of sky was visible. It was filled with stars.

"And no lights," said Will. "Still, if this is another outlaw fort . . ." He drew his sword and looked around warily.

There was a moment of indecision, but then Victoria said, "Try the door."

CHAPTER SEVENTEEN

THE SIGNAL TOWER

THE WOODEN DOOR OF THE tower was dark with age and marked with images of animals and geometric patterns, carved in the old style. When Will tugged on the iron handle, the door swung open silently. Inside was black as a tomb. Tesh lit the lantern and they crowded around the doorway. The soft light revealed a square room, about twenty paces across. The uneven flagstone floor was bare except for neat stacks of sticks and split wood piled against the facing wall. Above the firewood, a rough, wooden box hung on ropes that were part of a pulley system that extended up through an opening in the ceiling to the floor above. The mortared stone of the walls could be seen where patches of grimy plaster had peeled and flaked away. A ladder ran up one wall and disappeared into a hole in the ceiling.

Victoria stepped inside and cocked her head and listened for a moment. "I think it's empty," she said. "But I'll check to make sure. Stay here. I'll be right back." Before anyone could say anything she scrambled up the ladder and was gone.

"She didn't even take the lantern," muttered Tesh.

Cora looked back the way they had come, half expecting to see outlaws—or something worse—emerge from the gloom. She glanced over at Will, and he gave her a reassuring smile. She couldn't decide whether she was annoyed or encouraged by it.

When Victoria returned she said, "It's empty. But there's food and beds. Come on."

"And be trapped here?" asked Tesh.

"It's a risk," acknowledged Victoria. "But Anders needs rest. You said so yourself."

They crowded inside. After they had lowered Anders to the floor, Victoria guided the wolves back to the door. They began to breathe along its edges.

"What are you doing?" Anders demanded. He had awoken again and was sitting up. His face was pale and his arm hung limply at his side.

"Sealing it," said Victoria. Soon the entire door and doorframe were covered in a thick coat of ice.

Tesh handed Anders her bottle and he drank. "How much do you have left?" she asked Will.

"Mine's half gone. I think that's all we have besides yours."

Tesh made a face.

"There's a rain barrel on the roof," said Victoria. "Anders, are you strong enough to climb? There are beds up near the top."

In answer, Anders got to his feet and slowly made his way to the ladder. "I'll need help," he muttered.

While the others started to climb, Victoria began removing the saddlebags from the wolves. The scale markings on the backs of her hands glistened in the lantern light. Without a word, Cora unfastened a set of saddlebags as well. She wanted to ask about the markings, but she knew they made Victoria uncomfortable. Instead, she held up the bags and asked, "Shall we take them up?"

"No, leave them. They'll be fine here."

Cora tossed them down beside the others. "And the winter wolves?" she said. "We don't have anything to feed them."

Victoria smoothed the fur of one of the wolves. "There's a good supply of dried meat up in the tower. I'll bring some down to them later," she said, stifling a yawn.

They followed the others and as Victoria put her hand on the ladder, she looked at Cora and added, "Thanks for your help. And . . . for being a friend."

Cora grinned. "You're welcome. I mean, of course."

A ghost of a smile flitted across Victoria's face.

The room above was empty except for cobwebs and the ropes that stretched from the hole in the floor to one in the ceiling.

"I think I know what this place is," said Tesh as she looked at the ropes. "Those are for moving firewood, probably all the way to the top of this tower. I've heard that during the Great War, the Sky Lords built signal towers in the Hornwood. Four of them, I think, across the neck of the forest, all the way from the Eastern Deep to the Flints. Augrind's armies destroyed all but one."

They continued to climb through empty room after empty room, stopping in each one to allow Anders to catch his breath. But after a moment or two he urged them on, telling them that he was fine.

In the sixth room they found something very different. A round fireplace was set in the center of the room, with a stone chimney extending up through the ceiling. Surrounding the fireplace were several bunks, and lockers were built into one of the walls.

"Food's in the lockers," said Victoria, "and the rain barrel is on the roof."

Anders sat heavily on one of the beds. He touched his shoulder and made a face.

"Cheese!" said Dane. He had opened one of the lockers and pulled out a wedge. "And honey. And apples and berries and nuts. And there's some dried venison and bread!" He grinned as he dumped an armful of food onto Anders' bed.

Cora hadn't realized how hungry she was. She and the others set about devouring the food. After they had eaten and refilled their water bottles from the rain barrel, Anders pushed the hair out of his eyes and said, "Now that we have a moment . . . there's so, so, *so* much to talk about, wouldn't you say, Victoria?"

Victoria looked at him, her face guarded. He went on. "First you try to take my place, and now it comes out that you're marked." He coughed and his face twisted in pain. "Even if no one else here knows what your scales mean, I do." He drew his long knife and laid it across his knees.

Victoria narrowed her eyes. "I told you already, I'm *not* trying to take over. I don't want your stupid circus. And if you really know what these mean," she held up her arms, "why do you care? They just make your dumb circus more successful!"

"What's with the knife? What are you two talking about?" asked Dane. "What are the scale things?"

"They mean she's practically an animal," Anders said with a sneer. "They're the reason she can talk to animals and they listen. They obey her."

"Leave her alone!" Cora jumped to her feet and balled up her fists. "You'll say anything to make us forget how bad of a leader you are. You hate it that Victoria saved us from the outlaws and now you're trying to turn us against her!"

"You wouldn't say that if you knew what I know," said Anders. "Do you know *why* the animals listen to her? Do you know *why* they obey? Because they have to. She's a shifter." He turned his head and spat.

Everyone looked at Victoria. Her gaze dropped to the floor and her face was a mix of defiance and shame.

"It's true," whispered Dane, and even though he was on the other side of the room he edged away. Cora didn't see Tesh move, but the curly-haired girl was suddenly on her feet, an arrow drawn back on her bow.

Cora swallowed. Victoria, a shifter. A skin-changer. A creature of Augrind. Cora opened her mouth, but she was unable to speak. Victoria looked at her with pleading eyes, but Cora looked away.

"What do we do with her?" asked Dane after a long silence. His voice was thick and unsteady.

"She doesn't go another step with us," said Anders. "She stays here. Probably would prefer that anyway, wouldn't you, shifter? Living in the woods with the animals."

"You seem to forget that she saved us at the outlaw fort," said Will. "She saved *you*. The only reason we know she's . . . what she is, is because she saved your life. You're not bleeding anymore because of her. She could have chosen to let you die and kept her secret hidden, but she didn't. That has to count for something."

"Siding with her, Will? You can stay too." Anders glared at him and coughed again.

"I just don't think you're looking at this clearly. It's not as simple as you're trying to make it," said Will.

"Or it could be that simple, and we could just put her down." Anders glanced at Tesh as he picked up the knife and spun it in his hand. "She'll probably try to kill us in our sleep, anyway. Isn't that right, assassin?"

Victoria shook her head wearily. "I'm not an assassin. I don't want to kill any of you." She looked down at her hands, at the scales, and said, "I'm not even really a shifter. Well, I am, but . . . you wouldn't understand. You couldn't possibly understand."

"I have an idea," said Will. "I say we try to understand."

Anders looked at him and his lip curled in a sneer. "This isn't your call."

"What can it hurt to listen?" said Will. "We'll try to understand. And what I mean by that is, we *don't* kill Vic. Really, guys, if she wanted to kill us, she could have done it a dozen times. A hundred times. Right, Vic?"

Victoria gave Will a confused look. "Um, I suppose," she said.

"See? She could have but she didn't. So let's put away the bow," Will raised his eyebrows at Tesh, "and the knife."

Anders' jaw tightened and he glared at Will, but before he could say anything, Will said, "I'm not trying to take over, Anders. Man, you're insecure. I just think things are moving pretty fast here and killing Vic seems like a hasty—not to mention irreversible—decision. Let's hear her out."

Tesh slowly lowered her bow, but Anders kept a tight grip on his knife. Will shrugged and said, "That'll work for now, I guess. So, Vic. Help us understand."

Victoria shifted uncomfortably and then sat, her back against the stone fireplace. She gave a slight shrug. "Alright," she finally said.

CHAPTER EIGHTEEN

THE SHIFTER

I WAS BORN WITH THESE markings around my wrists,"
Victoria began. "They were just dark loops then. When I was
young, my parents said they would tell me what they meant when
I was older. They always made me cover them, though, and so I knew
they didn't mean anything good." She glanced down at her wrists and
then looked away.

"Besides the markings, I have also always had a connection with
animals, an ability to talk to them and understand them, in a way. And
command them. And like animals, I have an innate sense of direction.
That's how I knew which way was east."

Tesh's sour expression deepened, but she said nothing.

Victoria went on. "I never connected these abilities with the markings,
and in fact I never thought my abilities were abnormal. But that changed
when I was eight. My parents sat me down and told me about the Great
War. I mean, I knew about it in the way that everyone does, that the Sky
Lords and the people of the Islands fought Augrind and that they defeated
him and locked him in the Rift. But they told me more. They told me
about Augrind's followers, those betrayers of the Islands, and how, while
the war was still going on, he gave some of them the ability to shape

shift. These shifters were his assassins and spies, changing form to avoid detection, taking on the appearance of common animals or creatures from Erdyn in order to infiltrate their enemy's ranks.

"Shifting came with a cost, though. Every time a shifter changed its skin, they . . . lost a part of their humanity. My parents told me it was a cost that Augrind's followers were only too willing to pay."

Victoria paused and swallowed. After a few moments she continued. "Then they told me that those given the ability to shift had been marked by Augrind with bands around each wrist. The bands were a part of their skin. I realized what they were saying and I was horrified, and I could tell they were horrified too. My mother started to weep as they told me, and even my father started to cry. I asked them how this could have happened. The war had been hundreds of years ago and I had never met Augrind. I didn't *want* to serve him.

"My father said that it was in our blood. It shamed him to admit it, but we were in the line of one of Augrind's shifters. The markings didn't appear in every generation, he said, but they still appeared occasionally, at random. The last time they had manifested was five generations before. He and my mother had hoped fervently that their children would be spared the curse, and had good reason to think that they would be. But when I was born, I was born marked.

"When they told me this I . . . I didn't know what to do. I didn't *want* to be a shifter. I didn't want to lose who I was as a person. I certainly didn't want to serve Augrind. I feared my connection with animals now that I knew it was related to shifting, but I also feared that what I was, *who* I was, was inescapable."

Everyone sat in rapt silence. Cora felt a mixture of horror and pity. The faces of the others were unreadable.

"So what happened?" asked Will.

"Nothing. Everything. Right after my parents talked to me about the markings, we were out in the boat, my parents and my brother Ori and me. My family is from the Eastern Isles and we were tending to a wounded sea snake. We don't hunt them like everyone else; we shepherd them, I guess you would say. It was toward evening and a storm came up. But not just any storm. *The* Storm. It swallowed us. I don't know how my father did it, but he managed to keep the boat afloat. The wind was screaming and the waves were the worst I've ever seen . . . And then sometime later—I don't know how long—the boat couldn't hold together any longer. It came apart and my parents were sucked under and I grabbed hold of my brother and I don't know what happened. I was thinking about how we were going to die and how I didn't want to die, and then, and then . . . somehow, I was a sea serpent.

"I didn't really have time to understand what had happened and honestly, in the moment I didn't care. I took Ori in my mouth and swam, swam harder and stronger than I imagined possible. We must have outraced the Storm. When I woke up, we were on a rocky beach on an island. I was me again, and Ori was alive. And my arms and hands looked like this."

"They changed after you shifted?" asked Will. Victoria nodded. "And you're . . . less of a person now?"

Tears formed in Victoria's eyes and she hastily scrubbed them away. After a moment she said, "Yes. I'm . . . different than I was."

Anders laughed. "This is ridiculous. Of course you're going to come up with a story like this so we pity you. But a shifter is a shifter. You get no pity from me."

Victoria ignored Anders and took a deep breath before continuing. "A man found me and my brother on the beach. He took us to his house and gave us something to eat and took care of us. But he also recognized the markings for what they were, and he told me that he would expose me as a shifter if I didn't do what he said. When I said I didn't care, he told me he would hurt my brother.

"I didn't want that, of course, so I agreed to work for him. But he imprisoned Ori and said he would only let him go after I had done what he needed."

Cora finally found her voice. "So how'd you get away?" she asked. "How'd you join the circus?"

Victoria looked at her sadly. "I didn't get away. I can't. I still work for him. And now you do too."

"Wait, *what?*" said Dane.

"It's Lord Arburry," said Victoria. "Or you could call him by his real name: Imago."

There was a stunned silence. Cora found it difficult to breathe. Finally, Anders said, "That's utterly preposterous. How could you even suggest—?"

"I'm not *suggesting* it. I know it. And don't forget, he killed my parents in the Storm too. This isn't a joke to me."

Anders shook his head. "So let me get this straight. What you're trying to get us to believe is that we've all been working for *Imago the Magician* for the past two years and never figured that out, that *you've* been working for him for the past, what is it, seven years? You've known this whole time who he is, the man who killed not only all of *our* parents, but *yours* as well . . . and you've never said anything to anyone? You've continued to work for him. That's what you're telling us? That's what you want us to believe?"

Cora felt sick. She turned away from Victoria. It was all too much.

"Yes," said Victoria. "None of you figured it out *because he's a magician!* And I can't leave or do anything because he has my brother. I hate him as much as you do, probably more, but *he has my brother!* And so I work for him. And if I *had* told you, what was I going to say to any of you that wouldn't have resulted in what's going on right now?"

Anders waved his hand dismissively. "The problem is, the story doesn't even make sense. What would a magician want with a circus?

And not just any magician, but Imago? 'I'm Imago and I can do practically anything I want. Oh, I know what I'll do: I'll partner with a *circus.*'"

Tesh snickered.

Victoria threw up her hands. "I knew you wouldn't believe me. But he knows what he's doing. It's the circus tokens. We tell everyone that the tokens keep them safe during the performance and that they're good luck, and that they take away bad dreams, in the hope that most people keep them after they go home. We wear them for the same reason. But they don't protect anyone from the animals at all. I do. No, the tokens make whoever wears one susceptible to Imago's power. And as for taking away bad dreams . . . they don't. The tokens simply mask the nightmares; they keep you from remembering them. Which would be a good thing, I suppose, but at the same time a channel is created between the person who wears it and . . . and Augrind. When you wear a token, your bad dreams strengthen him. This was Imago's plan from the beginning."

Cora's mouth went dry. She looked at Victoria, but Victoria wouldn't meet her gaze.

"The plan didn't work very well at first," continued Victoria. "People didn't keep the tokens after the circus left. Most people don't encounter a lot of wild animals, nor do they have regular nightmares, and it turns out a lot of folks don't care about good luck. So they weren't motivated to keep the tokens.

"Imago realized if his plan was to work, people would have to see the tokens as a solution to a problem they were already experiencing. If, say, everyone who came to the circus had been suffering from terrible nightmares for several days . . . well, a token that prevented nightmares would be a valuable thing, wouldn't it? One that most people would keep."

Anders scoffed. "You're telling us Imago gives people nightmares so they'll keep the circus tokens? He conjured the Storm, but he can't give people nightmares. He's not that strong."

Victoria nodded her head. "You're right, he's not that strong. But Augrind is. Late last year Imago began telling Augrind where and when the circus would be performing. And now, Augrind scatters seeds of nightmares into the town or city the circus will be visiting. He's still bound in the Rift, but he can work freely in the realm of sleep and dreams. Those seeds take root in peoples' minds and turn their dreams into nightmares.

"We tell the people who come to our performances the tokens protect against bad dreams, and since they've been having bad dreams, most now keep the tokens. And those that do forge a link between themselves and Augrind. Every time they dream, he gains real power, substantial power. Do you know how many performances we've done this year alone? Do you know how many people are carrying around our tokens? And every one of them gives Augrind power."

"To do what? What does that even mean?" asked Tesh.

"Imago thinks that if Augrind is strong enough, he'll be able wake up and break free of his prison."

"I don't know." Dane scratched his chin. "All this seems kind of farfetched."

"I think what she's saying is true," said Will.

Anders laughed. "You're kidding me. She can't back any of this up!"

"I wish I was kidding. But there are two things that make me believe her. The first is that, in the days before the circus came to Tarian, a lot of us started having nightmares. One day, out of nowhere, they started." Will glanced at Cora. "The second is that, during a performance, I dropped my token. The image that Rascha was making everyone see suddenly disappeared. When I picked it up again, the vision came back. I don't understand exactly how that's related to Imago, but what it told me was that something strange was going on with the circus. It seems to go along with what Vic is saying. Is Rascha in on this too, Vic?"

Victoria nodded. "Rascha's in on it. Or *was*, I guess I should say. But Rascha wasn't Erdynian. The bird was just Imago's puppet. The magician could see through the bird's eyes and he controlled its movement and speech. Imago worked certain spells through Rascha, and those spells only worked for those with tokens. It was, among other things, Imago's way of keeping an eye on us. An eye on me."

Anders' skeptical expression slowly changed to one of fear with a touch of revulsion, and he reached inside his shirt and removed his token. He tossed it away like it was a poisonous snake. Dane and Tesh did the same. Cora reached for her own, but then stopped, a thought suddenly occurring to her.

"*You* stole it!" The words spilled from her mouth before she could stop them. "You stole the Sand Coin. You stole it for Imago."

Victoria started, her eyes wide. "How do you know about that?"

"Now what are you talking about?" asked Anders. "What's the Sand Coin?"

"It's the power of the Master of Tides. It keeps Tarian safe." Cora stared at Victoria. "Or it did. And now . . . that kind of power will make Imago unstoppable! I . . . I thought I knew you," she said. "I thought we were friends. Is there anything you've *not* lied about?" The words cut like a knife, Cora could see that in Victoria's face, but Cora didn't care. "No, I don't want to know. I don't want to know if there's anything else."

"*He has my brother!*" shouted Victoria. Fresh tears sprang to her eyes and began to run down her cheeks. She hunched down and seemed to fold in on herself. "I have no choice."

Cora felt a thread of pity for Victoria, but pity felt wrong, and she allowed it to be swallowed by her anger and hurt.

Anders coughed and winced. "Well," he said, "I think it's obvious what we have to do."

"What's that?" asked Will.

"We kill her. She's a shifter, and that's enough. But on top of that she's knowingly been working for Imago the Murderer. She deserves to die, twice over."

Tesh nodded, and so did Dane.

"No," said Will.

"No? You'd defend the shifter even now?"

Will nodded. "If Vic had gone to Augrind and said, 'I want to serve you,' and he had turned her into a shifter, I might agree with you. But that's not what happened. One of her ancestors did that, not Vic. The way you're talking about her, you'd think Vic was Augrind's willing minion, using her powers to try to break him free. But she—"

"Victoria *is* trying to break Augrind free!" shouted Anders. "She just admitted it! She's working with Imago and has been using the circus to make Augrind stronger *so that he can break free!*"

"She works for Imago," conceded Will, "but not willingly. She doesn't want to. She's doing it because her brother's life depends on it. We would all do the same thing in her place, and we would hate it, but we would do it. Maybe she deserves to die for that, but if she does, then we all do, too, because we would do the exact same thing to protect our family.

"Besides," he added, "if you kill Vic, we'd have no way to leave the tower. Those winter wolves would tear us apart without her around. But even if that wasn't the case, she's the only one who knows how to get out of the Hornwood."

Will was right, of course, Cora realized. Victoria knew which way to go, and she controlled the wolves. When Anders realized this, he said, "Well, what's to keep her from escaping while we sleep, and leaving us stranded? We should tie her up."

"If Vic wants to hurt us or leave us, she's going to be able to. If we tie her up, she could get out by turning into a bear or something, so that would be pointless. I don't think you understand, Anders; we're at her mercy. But also, we need her."

Anders scowled but didn't argue.

After that there wasn't much more to say. Victoria glanced at Cora again, with a look that begged her to somehow understand, but Cora couldn't meet her gaze. Instead, she walked to the other side of the room and threw herself down on a bunk.

Dane built a fire and the others lay down as well, and all but Will kept well away from Victoria. One by one they drifted off to sleep.

Cora, though, tossed and turned. Her mind was a jumble of clambering thoughts and emotions that threatened to overwhelm her. Finally, she got up and felt her way across the room to the ladder.

She hesitated and then began to climb up. The small square of night sky grew larger and then Cora emerged onto the tower top. She stepped into the chill night.

Stone battlements, gray in the starlight, surrounded her. A large iron basket sat on a raised block in the middle of the tower top. Cora brushed the cold iron with her fingertips and walked to the battlements and looked out.

A sea of treetops stretched into the distance on all sides. Leaves rustled in the night breeze, a quiet murmur drifting through the air like the far-off sounds of waves. And above Cora . . . the stars.

The Sea Serpent took up most of the northwestern sky. Clouds obscured its sinuous tail, but most of its body and its bright, piercing eye shone clear. As a child, it had been Cora's favorite constellation. Now it only made her think of Victoria.

Cora leaned her elbows on the parapet. Why did it have to be like this? Why did the one good thing to happen to her since the Storm— her friendship with Victoria—have to end like this, with Cora learning that Victoria was no friend at all, but instead complicit with the very person who had stolen her family away from her? Victoria worked for Imago and she was a shifter! Anger at Victoria mingled with anger at Will, for defending Victoria, for justifying or ignoring everything she had done. By doing so, Will, too, had abandoned Cora, and now she felt more alone than ever. Tears came, but she scrubbed them furiously from her face.

Cora's jaw clenched and she wished for scales like the Sea Serpent, scales like armor that would keep her from experiencing loss again.

This isn't loss, though, said a small voice inside her. *What happened to your parents was loss. What happened to Hildi was loss. But this—what is happening with Victoria—is not loss. At least,* the voice said, *it doesn't have to be. You can still be her friend.*

Cora shook her head and slapped the cold stone with her palms. How? She would have to ignore that Victoria was doing exactly what Imago had done, and Cora wasn't willing to do that. Imago had taken everything from Cora when he had killed her parents and Hildi in the Storm. Despite this, she had found a new life in Tarian, in the Water Works. But now, because Victoria had stolen the Sand Coin, her new life would be destroyed just as her old life had been.

The wind rose to a howl and whipped at her, sending her hair into her eyes, and it cut through her coat like a scythe. The stars shone down, merciless points of light in an ocean of darkness.

Cora slid down beside the battlements, out of the wind, and pulled her hands into her sleeves. She suddenly ached with how much she missed her family.

"You're not alone, you know," said Will's voice. Cora jumped and a shadowy form climbed from the opening in the floor. "Figured you'd be up here," Will said. He came and sat beside her.

"I don't want to talk to you," Cora said.

"Why?"

"I'm not doing this, Will. You know why. Now leave me alone."

"I'll just say this then, and go. You're taking this whole thing personally, as though Vic set out to deceive you and hurt you. Or you think that her not telling you what she is or who she works for means she wasn't really your friend to begin with. None of that is true, though. You never told her you joined the circus just to find the Sand Coin. That didn't mean you weren't really friends, right?"

"That's different."

Will snorted. "It's not different at all! You had a good reason to keep that from her and she had a good reason to not tell you what she held back. Put yourself in her place. Imagine being her. Just for a minute. Imagine finding out you're a shifter and then being told the only way to save your brother is to use those abilities in the service of the person who killed your parents. Can you imagine how hard that would be? How lonely? How much she must hate herself? And then she meets you and you become friends. Real friends. Of course she's not going to tell you everything. She wouldn't want to lose your friendship. It means too much to her. And for some reason you can't see that."

"Are you done, Will?"

The boy stood. "Can't you see what a horrible position she's in? She stole the Sand Coin and was going to give it to Imago because she loves her brother, not because she doesn't care about you."

"So what, I should give it back?" Cora snapped. "What about Tarian?"

"I don't know," said Will. "But whatever you do, Vic *needs* you, Cora. She needs you as a friend right now."

Will remained for a few moments, waiting for her to respond. When she didn't, he sighed and climbed back down the ladder, leaving Cora alone.

Cora sat for some time, and then reached inside her coat and withdrew the vault. "I'm *not* giving it back to her," she said under her breath. She twisted the box open and dropped the Sand Coin inside. It fit perfectly. Then Cora closed the vault and pressed the brass buttons.

The box did not vibrate. The buttons did not grow warm. Cora pressed them again. Nothing. She re-opened the box. The Sand Coin was still there. Then she recalled what Mr. Blackwood had said about the vault not working in places steeped in old magic. Places like the Iron Spire. Places like the Hornwood.

This was a setback, certainly, but she still had time. Even if it took them a week to get out of the Hornwood, Cora could still get the Sand Coin to Mr. Blackwood by the Turn. She twisted the box shut and tucked it into her coat, and leaned back against the stone parapet. She sat staring at the sky until at last, she fell into a deep sleep.

C H A P T E R   N I N E T E E N

SHADOWS

CORA AWOKE, COLD AND CRAMPED, on the tower top. It was morning. The sky was a dome of colorless cloud. High above, a single bird wheeled in the emptiness. Cora yawned and stretched, grateful for a dreamless sleep.

As she got to her feet, Victoria's revelations about the circus tokens came back to her in a rush, and Cora froze. She had forgotten to throw her tokens away. Her sleep likely *hadn't* been dreamless. Her nightmares had simply been masked and through the tokens, they had been channeled directly to Augrind, somehow making him stronger. Cora fumbled in her pocket and pulled out the token she had found in the Iron Spire. She hurled it over the battlements. But as she reached for the one that hung around her neck, she hesitated.

If she threw it away, the nightmare would be waiting for her when she went to sleep tonight. It would be waiting and she would lose her parents and Hildi to the Storm yet again. Cora's hand trembled. She didn't want to face that, no, *couldn't* face that. It would undo her.

And besides, she reasoned, to survive the Hornwood she needed to be rested and alert. How long would they be here? Three, four more days and nights? Without the token, her nightmares would awaken her and she would be unable to fall asleep again, and her exhaustion would not only endanger her, but everyone else as well.

Too many things depended on the circus token. As Cora thought about it, it just made sense to keep it, at least for a little while longer. She would be helping Augrind, true, but it was a small price to pay to keep her and her friends safe.

Cora felt relief, and after taking a drink of water from the rain barrel and tucking the token beneath her shirt, she descended the ladder into the tower.

Dane was stirring a pot over the fire, but the others still slept.

"She didn't leave," whispered Dane, looking over at Victoria. His tone managed to convey both disappointment and relief.

Cora didn't want to talk about Victoria. Instead, she asked, "How's Anders?" She bit into an apple and stood with her back to the fire.

"A little better. I think it'll be a couple days before he can travel again, though. Makes me nervous."

"About staying here so long you mean?" Cora glanced around. "Yeah, whoever lives here is bound to come back. And who would it be other than outlaws?"

Anders slept most of the day. Tesh examined his wound again and found that it had begun to heal. She switched out the bandages with ones she found in one of the lockers.

Otherwise, the day passed uneventfully. It was nice to not be in a rush for a change, or soaked to the skin by the rain, or cold. Everyone lay on their bunks in the warmth around the fire, and ate from the store of food, or dozed. Tesh counted her arrows and Dane sharpened his knives. Victoria climbed the ladder to the roof and spent most of the day there. For the briefest of moments Cora considered going to talk to her, but then decided against it. What Victoria had done was too much.

Around sunset Will approached Cora. "You send it yet?" he asked.

"No." She would have left it at that, but Cora didn't want Will to think it was indecision on her part, so she added, "The vault doesn't work in the Hornwood. It's made with new magic, and this place is thick with old magic." Will just nodded and thankfully didn't press the matter.

The following morning, Anders awoke, sat up, and said, "It feels better." He flexed his shoulder and winced. "Well, not all the way, but mostly."

"You really should rest another day," said Tesh.

"Maybe, but this doesn't feel safe here. We should go."

Everyone turned toward Victoria. Will said, "What do you think, Vic?"

Without a word, Victoria rose from her bunk and started down the ladder. Anders cleared his throat and said, "Alright. Let's gather everything and go. We should take as much of this food and water as we can carry. And blankets."

The room at the bottom of the tower was frigid, and ankle-deep snow covered the floor. After they pounded on the door to dislodge the ice, they scrambled onto the backs of the winter wolves and Victoria led them out of the tower. Tesh nocked an arrow and said, "Just because we haven't seen the outlaws doesn't mean they didn't follow us. Keep watch."

Anders insisted he was strong enough to ride alone and so Cora found herself paired with Will once more. She hoped he wouldn't bring up Victoria or the Sand Coin. She hoped he wouldn't talk at all, and to her surprise he didn't. He simply pulled her up behind him and moments later they plunged into the murk of the Hornwood.

The wolves wound through the trees in a line. The darkness was oppressive, but it felt unsafe to carry a lighted lantern, so they moved forward blindly, barely able to see the wolf and rider ahead of them. There was a tenseness in the air, and they all rode with weapons out. The sound of the steady padding of the wolves on the leaf-covered ground seemed to grow and fill Cora's ears. Sometimes, when they came to a jumble of rocks or a stretch of ground swept clean of leaves, Cora could hear other sounds of the wood: whispers and creaking groans and the occasional snapping of something in the underbrush. Once, there was a brief flash of light, far to their left, followed by what might have been the scream of an animal.

After some time, Victoria called for a stop. She didn't consult with Anders, but simply whistled and the winter wolves came together in a small open space among the towering tree trunks.

"They need to rest," Victoria said as she slid to the ground. When Anders started to object, she cut him off. "In the Hornwood, I'm in charge. We're not going to keep having this conversation. I'll lead us to the Door, then you can go wherever you want. But until then, you do what I say."

Anders looked furious, but after a moment he dismounted. The others did as well.

"So you know the way to the Door?" asked Will. "I mean, I know you know which way is east, but—"

"I know the way to the Door."

"Is it far?" Cora asked before she remembered she wasn't speaking to Victoria. Victoria continued adjusting the saddlebags on the winter wolves without looking up.

"A few days," she said.

They ate a bite from what they had brought from the signal tower and then they were off again.

Hours later they came to the edge of a wide gorge. A slash of evening sky could be seen overhead. It was the first they had seen of the sky since the tower. It was a dark blue, almost purple, and the stars were just beginning to appear. The opposite wall of the gorge was sheer rock, crumbly and grown over with vines and mosses and small thorny trees. In the fading light they could just make out the bottom. A river wound through a tumble of broken stones and fallen trees.

"We'll camp down there," said Victoria. And then she led them over the edge.

To say the path she chose was not a path was no exaggeration. The wolves leapt from improbable foothold to improbable foothold, finding a way where there was none.

Cora did not scream, but not for lack of fear. It was only because nothing came out when she opened her mouth. She held onto Will, whose heart was hammering as hard as hers, and he wrapped his arms tightly around the wolf's neck.

Finally, they came to the bottom. With shaking hands Dane lit his lantern, and by its light Cora could see that the others had been as scared as she had been. Except for Victoria. She only looked exhausted.

They stood on gravel and pebbles, a stone's throw from the river.

"Camp here?" asked Will. Victoria nodded.

As they lay stretched on the shingle around a small fire, Dane said, "Well the Hornwood hasn't been so bad, has it? I mean, it's dark and creepy, but after the outlaws, I guess I expected worse."

Victoria barked a laugh. "Four different times today we were tracked and would have been attacked if I hadn't bent the creatures to my will and turned them aside. It was worse than you knew."

Anders sat up and worked his shoulder. "Convenient that we never saw or heard anything, wouldn't you say?"

Victoria shrugged. "Do you see or hear anything now?"

Anders' eyes darted back and forth before he could help himself. "Nice try," he muttered.

Victoria caught up a stone and stood. Then she hurled it into the darkness across the river. There was a roar and the sound of snapping tree branches as whatever it was retreated farther downstream. Victoria sat down again.

"The wolves will protect us tonight, but only if you stay within their circle. And we *do* need their protection; there are more of those things," she pointed down the river, "all around."

"What are they?" asked Dane.

"I don't know. Some kind of animal."

They were all shaken, even Tesh, who so often seemed unflappable, even here in the Hornwood. Cora didn't think she would be able to sleep. She edged closer to the fire and huddled under her blanket. Eventually, though, her weariness overcame her.

The next morning they forded the river and as they emerged from the water on the other side, Dane pointed at the ground. Enormous tracks crisscrossed the wet sand, larger by far than those of the winter wolves. Everyone looked at each other and then at Victoria.

"Stay close," she said simply, and then led them up the wall of the gorge.

The forest was less dark than the day before, the trees larger, the canopy of leaves higher. The wolves trotted along, picking their way through the underbrush. Once, a shadowy bird burst from the bushes beside them, and Tesh raised her bow to bring it down.

"Don't," said Victoria. Tesh hesitated but then lowered her bow.

That afternoon the forest changed again. The trees crowded closer together, and the air felt thick and stifling. It was as dark as it had ever been.

Suddenly Victoria gave a shout and the wolves immediately veered to the right. The ground in front of them, the ground they would have been on, shook and began to fall away. Trees leaned in from all sides, groaning and popping and snapping as they crashed into one another and uprooted from the ground.

Victoria yelled again and the wolves surged ahead. The earth was collapsing in an ever-widening circle, threatening to suck them down. The wolves leapt over boulders, and even as they cleared them, the giant rocks fell away and disappeared into the darkness of the opening earth.

To her left, Cora saw a tree branch strike Anders and knock him from his wolf. But as he fell, Victoria was there, and she reached down and somehow, despite her smallness, pulled him onto the back of her mount.

"Go!" Victoria shouted, and the wolves ran faster. Snow and ice exploded from their mouths as they rushed forward. Ahead of them a tree, big around as a tower, and as tall, began to fall.

"Left!" shouted Victoria, and the pack of wolves flowed to the left. The impact of the tree on the forest floor felt like an earthquake and almost knocked them flat, but they managed to keep their seats. They crested a rocky ridge and the wolves soared down the other side.

Victoria didn't let them slow. The ground still shook, though trees were no longer crashing down, but she urged them on through the dimness.

"What *was* that?" shouted Will.

Victoria looked over her shoulder, and in the low light her eyes almost seemed to glow. "I don't know," she said, peering back. "But there's something there now that wasn't before. Something is chasing us."

"Can't you . . . can't you stop it?" asked Cora. She could see fear in Victoria's eyes now.

"No. It's not an animal."

They flew through the trees, and Cora could feel her wolf's sides heaving with the exertion of the run. Will hunched down lower on the wolf's back, and Cora did the same.

Light appeared ahead. The trees thinned and they were suddenly in a clearing. As they hurtled across the sunlit glade, Dane looked back. "The shadows are alive!" he yelled. They turned and saw a swarm of darkness flowing from the forest behind them. The shadows—or whatever they were—remained black, even in the late afternoon sunlight, and were formed into shapes—men on horseback, and men on foot—and they moved with no sound.

A shadow man raised a bow and a streak of blackness tore through the air over their heads.

"Faster!" screamed Victoria, and somehow the wolves ran faster.

They reentered the wood and immediately the wolves angled to the left, presumably guided by Victoria. The ground descended gently before them, and the wolves bounded down the incline. Just ahead, Cora could see a jumble of boulders lying across their path.

"Hold on tight!" said Victoria through gritted teeth, and then her wolf came to the rocks and leapt. Cora hugged Will's middle, and then they, too, were in the air, soaring over a jagged gash of a ravine. They landed on the other side in a spray of dirt and pine needles, and then were off again.

On and on they went, weaving through the towering trees, leaving a swirl of snow and fallen leaves in their wake.

After what felt like an eternity, Dane shouted, "Have we lost them?"

"No," said Victoria, looking back. "They're there."

Anders said, "You can't see in this—"

"I can see," snarled Victoria.

Evening was coming. The dark wood grew darker. The ice from the wolves stung Cora's cheeks, and her hands and legs were long-since numb. *The winter wolves have to be tiring*, she thought. She glanced around at the others and noticed that Anders had one arm around Victoria's waist, but his other hung limply at his side. His face was white. Even if the wolves *could* keep up this pace Anders could not, Cora realized. And if the shadow army still pursued them . . .

Light again appeared before them. The trees simply stopped, and they burst into the open, into a round grassy clearing. It was large, perhaps three or four bowshots across. Tall stones stood in a circle in the center of the space, gilded golden in the setting sun. As they came to the stones, Tesh's wolf stumbled. Tesh was thrown, but she tucked into a ball as she hit the ground, rolled, and came up on her feet.

"Look!" said Will, pointing. Ahead of them, on the other side of the clearing, shadows emerged from the trees. Wheeling around, they watched as more of the creatures stepped into the open, first from the direction they had come, but then from the south and north as well, until they were completely surrounded.

Tesh pulled an arrow from her quiver, Will drew his sword, and the rest of them gripped their knives.

CHAPTER TWENTY

THE BOY

THE ARMY OF SHADOWS STOOD silently and then advanced, slowly tightening the circle around the winter wolves. Their black banners and cloaks fluttered as if in a breeze, but it was a breeze that Cora did not feel, for the air was deathly still.

"Well, I've certainly enjoyed knowing most of you," said Will.

Tesh loosed an arrow, but it went harmlessly through one of the shadows. And then, as one, their pursuers raised their bows.

The sound of a horn rent the air. The dark creatures stopped and turned. There was movement in the shadow throng to the north, and Cora watched as the army swirled and then parted to allow a figure to pass through.

The figure was not a shadow. It was a boy, perhaps her own age, Cora thought. A horn hung at his side, along with a knapsack and a long knife, and he was dressed in greens and browns, a patchwork of cloth and furs and what appeared to be bark and stitched together leaves. He carried a bow and a full quiver of arrows was on his back. He walked across the empty space between them and the shadow men.

His eyes flicked back and forth among them before settling on Victoria.

"You shouldn't be here," he said. "Not in the Hornwood, certainly not in the Ring Glade."

"We are trying to leave." Victoria considered the boy for a moment and then asked, "Do you lead them?" She nodded toward the shadow army.

The boy shook his head. "Not really. But the shadowhunters listen to the horn. Which is fortunate for you."

"Who are you?" asked Cora.

The boy looked at her and Cora wondered if she had been wrong about his age. His eyes were older than the rest of him.

Without another word he turned and began walking back the way he had come. Cora and Will looked at one another and then Victoria nudged her wolf forward. The others followed.

Their shadows stretched out across the browning grass as the sun began to set. As they neared the ranks of shadow men, or the shadowhunters as the boy had called them, he turned and said in a low voice, "Put away your weapons."

Each of them hesitantly obeyed. Tesh was the last to slide her arrow back into her quiver.

The boy stepped into the ranks of the shadowhunters and they moved aside, allowing him to pass. And then the rest of them were among the shadows as well, and the air was cold and, it seemed to Cora, laced with anger and sorrow and foreboding. The shadowhunters and their steeds were pure darkness, more the absence of something than the presence. It was almost, Cora thought, as though these creatures were being seen through holes torn in the air. Or maybe the shadowhunters *were* the holes.

Past seemingly unending ranks they walked. *There must be thousands, no tens of thousands of these things,* thought Cora. *Why are they not attacking us?*

But they did not attack, and then Cora and the others were through. Cora looked over her shoulder to see that the creatures had turned and were watching them. She shuddered.

"We need to go that way," said Victoria, pointing off to their right, to the east.

The boy said nothing, but continued to lead them north. As they reentered the trees, Victoria repeated herself.

"You need to come with me," the boy answered. "Where we're going, it's not far. We can talk there."

He walked lightly, without a sound, flitting in and out of shadow, the horn swinging at his side. They had no choice but to follow.

After some time they came to a part of the forest that was less gloomy. Night had fallen, but they could see the stars through the branches above, something they had not been able to do anywhere else in the Hornwood except at the signal tower. The damp smell of rot that permeated the forest was less here too, Cora noticed.

The boy led them to a stand of beech trees. The towering trunks were smooth and faintly silver in the starlight. One of them, blackened and burned from a lightning strike, had fallen and lay across their path. The boy ducked beneath it and disappeared.

Victoria dismounted and whispered a command to the wolves before she followed. A minute later she called back, "It's a cave. You should come down."

Cora found herself on hands and knees, crawling blindly forward as she followed Will. A thick layer of fallen branches was just overhead, and it shut out light completely.

"Steps," came Will's voice from just ahead. Cora's hands felt smooth stone. "You can stand now," he added.

The stone stairs descended, and from the echoes of their footsteps Cora guessed they were in a tunnel of sorts and had left the wood behind. And then, from below, a light sprang up and she could see again.

She trailed Will down the last few steps and entered a long, low room. The boy had lit two lanterns, and from their light she could see that it was, as Victoria had said, a cave. The walls and floor and ceiling were of reddish stone. There was a pile of skins in the corner, which, Cora realized with slight disgust, was probably the boy's bed. A crude fireplace, carved into the rock, was at the other end of the room, and a section of split tree that served as a table stood next to it.

"Sit where you want," said the boy over his shoulder. "I'll make us some food. Might be a minute."

The others filed in behind Cora. As the boy readied a fire, Anders leaned against the wall and let out a long breath as he slid down to the floor. Dane squatted beside him.

"Nice cave," Will said. "But is it safe? From the shadowhunters?"

As the boy fanned the small fire to life he replied, "They won't come here. And even if they did, you're forgetting the horn."

"Well," said Anders, "we don't really know anything about the horn or how it works."

"I don't understand it all that well myself," said the boy. "But it *does* work. And besides, they won't come to this part of the forest. We're safe here." He took a pot from beside the fireplace and filled it with water from a bucket and then hung it over the flames. "Can you . . . ?" he pointed to a lidded, stone canister beside Cora. She brought it to him. He scooped out some of the contents and stirred them into the pot, then added a handful of leaves from his bag. Small, wild potatoes followed, then what might have been carrots. Lastly, he pulled an entire plucked pigeon from his bag and dropped it into the pot.

"Got anything else in there?" asked Will, nodding toward the bag.

The boy ignored him. "Now then," he said, dusting his hands, "let's talk. What are you doing in the Hornwood? And *how* are you here?"

"That's none of your business," said Anders.

Will cleared his throat. "What he means to say is it's a long story. But the short version is that we were attacked by outlaws and got lost trying to escape them. We don't want to be here and we're trying to leave. And thank you for saving us from the shadowhunters, by the way."

The boy considered this and nodded. "You're welcome. But you haven't answered how you're here. And by that I mean, how have you survived? You're *deep* in the Hornwood. This is an unbelievably dangerous place."

Everyone looked at Victoria. Anders opened his mouth and Cora thought he would tell the boy she was a shifter. But to Cora's surprise Anders did not. Instead he simply said, "We've been fortunate. The wolves we ride have been able to outpace some of the dangers we've encountered, and we found refuge in an old signal tower. There was a supply of food in it—we would be in a bad way without that."

"Glad you found the tower," said the boy. "I keep it stocked. But good fortune isn't enough to keep you alive here." He turned to Victoria with a questioning look.

"I guide them," she said after a short silence. "I have kept the animals of the Hornwood at bay, and I command the wolves to allow us to ride them. It's a skill I was born with." Victoria's voice trembled and she looked away.

"I see," said the boy.

"Who *are* you?" asked Cora.

"My name is Hart," he said, "and the Hornwood is my home."

"Can you . . . command the animals too? Does the horn work on them as well?"

"The horn works on them as well," said Hart.

"Are you an outlaw?" asked Dane.

Hart shook his head and was silent; he seemed to be deciding how much to tell them. Then he took a deep breath and said, "I came here a long time ago. I lost my parents, my entire village, actually, and so I came here to die. But I met someone who helped me . . ." He glanced at the two lanterns that hung from the ceiling. "It's hard to explain what I was going through, and I don't really expect you to understand—"

"We understand, I think," said Will. "We all lost our parents too, one way or another."

The boy raised his eyebrows. "So maybe you do. Anyway, I came here to die, and . . . and the Badger helped me—"

"The Constellation?" Tesh asked. There was a mixture of scorn and incredulity in her voice.

"Yes," said Hart.

"I find it hard to believe," said Anders, "that one of the Sky Lords spoke to you."

"I don't," said Will. "I think he's telling the truth."

Cora didn't know what to think. So she asked, "How did the Badger help you?"

Hart bit his lip and looked at the fire. After a few moments he said, "The Badger helped me grieve what I had lost, and eventually helped me see how my grief was pushing me toward bitterness and anger. How it was reshaping me for the worse. The Badger helped me see a way forward. It took a while. It's taken a while, I guess I should say, because it's not like everything is alright now. My life will never go back to what it was. But I'm not shaped by the sadness now, not in the way I was."

"So why are you still here?" asked Cora.

"Because in the time I've lived here, I've come to recognize that the Hornwood has its own deep sorrow, and it was reshaped by it like I was by mine. The sorrow of this place gave rise to the forest's anger, which made it more susceptible to Augrind's evil. I think that is why the Hornwood is what it is. The animals are wilder here, more vicious. The forest itself is brimming with malice. The shadowhunters are . . . I don't think they've always been shadowhunters. My point is, this place has been reshaped by its sorrow. And I want to help restore it. If *I* can begin to heal, the Hornwood can too."

"How can a forest have sorrow?" asked Dane.

Hart shrugged. "This place is alive, maybe not in the same way you and I are, but it's alive nevertheless, and if you spent enough time here you would know the grief I'm talking about. It's in the earth here, in the trunks and the limbs of the trees, in the water of the rivers and streams."

"What do you mean when you say you want to restore it?" asked Cora. "Do you really think you can drive out all the evil creatures here, somehow get rid of the shadowhunters?"

"Oh! I guess I wasn't clear," said the boy. "There *are* some evil creatures here, to be sure, some of Augrind's minions, but not many. *Those* need to be gotten rid of, and I do that when I can. But most of the Hornwood is not that. As I said, the shadowhunters weren't always the way they are, and neither were most of the animals. They've been warped and changed. Twisted. I want to help restore them, not eliminate them."

"And the horn is a part of that," said Victoria.

Hart picked up the horn and looked at it. It was the length of his forearm, and in the lantern light Cora could see that its entire surface was intricately carved with leaves and vines and woven designs. It was yellowed with age.

"It's a part, but it's not all. What you saw out there," Hart nodded toward the doorway, "was good, of course. I was able to use it to stop the shadowhunters from attacking you. And at other times I've used it to bend other forces in the Hornwood to my will. But I can't help but think that I'm supposed to do more than that. I want the creatures of the Hornwood to *want* to do certain things, not to *have* to do certain things. And so I sound the horn only when I must."

"So if the horn is only a part of what you're doing here, what's the rest?" asked Will.

"I think understanding the sorrow of this place is essential to its restoration. And I think I've finally discovered what the Hornwood has lost and where that sorrow comes from. It's the Augur Tree. It used to be here and I . . . I think I need to bring it back. If I can do that, I think the wood will begin to heal and remember what it has forgotten."

"Well finding the Augur Tree should be easy," said Anders sarcastically. "Look, Hart, this is certainly . . . interesting. And I think it's great that you want to make the Hornwood a better place, and not overuse your horn and all that, but practically speaking, we're in a bit of a bind. Unless those shadowhunters are gone in the morning, and stay gone, we're not going to make it out of here. So do you think you could guide us out?"

Hart rubbed his chin. "I can," he said slowly, "but it will be a few days. Maybe a week. I leave tomorrow on business that can't wait."

"Business? You have some sad trees that need comforting or something?" quipped Anders.

"Something like that," said Hart with a small smile. "You all can stay here until I return. And then I can take you back south. Or north if you prefer."

"We need to go east," said Victoria.

"The Hornwood in that direction is impassible." Hart rose and returned to the pot, stirring the contents with a wooden spoon. "There are countless ravines east of here, deeper than you can imagine."

"It has to be east," said Victoria. "There has to be a way."

Hart studied them for a few moments. "There is a way," he conceded, "but you won't like it."

"Why?" asked Victoria.

"Do you know of the shadow stones?"

"We do," said Anders. "We've used some of them."

If Hart was surprised, he didn't show it. He said, "It's only by using the stones that you can get to the eastern edge of the Hornwood. But it's a dangerous path, and I'm reluctant to take you on it."

"More dangerous than the rest of the Hornwood?" asked Tesh with a laugh.

Hart nodded. "That path makes the rest of the wood look safe. I told you there aren't many of Augrind's creatures in the Hornwood, and that's true; there are only a few that roam free here. But there *is* a part of the wood, sealed off and only reached by the shadow stones, that is filled with his minions. Thousands of them. Crows. Darkboars. Jackals. Even Spindles."

Cora and Will's eyes met. All she could think of was that ridiculous wooden carving they had seen in Tarian before they joined the circus. She never would have thought they might see a real Spindle, but now. . .

"Unfortunately," Hart continued, "that's the only path to the east. If you take it, your chances of survival are low. But if you insist, I'll guide you along it."

"If it's so dangerous, why would you be willing to take us?" asked Will.

"Normally I wouldn't. But it just so happens that's the path I'm traveling tomorrow."

CHAPTER TWENTY-ONE

AUGRIND'S DREAM

WE'LL GO WITH YOU," SAID Victoria with barely any hesitation. "When do we leave?"

Everyone looked at one another. Cora didn't even want to imagine such a path and judging from the others' faces, she doubted she was alone in this. *First a stalker, then shadowhunters, now Spindles!* She wondered if they could possibly be as bad as the stories said.

"Early," said Hart. "But you need to know something first. This . . . place we'll be going isn't normal. It's . . . a dream. And to be more specific, it's one of Augrind's dreams."

There was an uncertain silence. Then Cora asked, "Like one of the Bubbles? I didn't think it was possible to get inside them."

"Yes, it's one of the Bubbles. One lodged here a long time ago. And you're right, normally this wouldn't be a concern; Augrind's dreams are usually contained, inaccessible. But because the dream happened to enclose two shadow stones, it *is* accessible. And because it happened to enclose the only two shadow stones that allow for travel from this part of the Hornwood to the eastern part . . . well, if you want to get there from here, that's our path. And, I should say, it *is* as bad as it sounds. Or maybe worse. To travel through Augrind's dream means we'll be going through Augrind's imagination. That means that the creatures we encounter there, while they can attack and injure and kill us . . . we can't kill them. The rules are different there. The dream, I don't know, somehow rebuilds his creatures, revives them as soon as they're wounded."

"If we can get in, can his creatures get out?" asked Will.

"I don't think so. They exist only in his dream."

"What about your horn?" Cora asked. "Does it work there?"

"No," said Hart. "I tried it once. All it did was bring every creature within earshot, and I couldn't command any of them. I barely escaped."

"Wonderful," said Anders darkly. "It sounds to me like you're leading us to certain death."

Hart glanced at him. "It's dangerous, but it's not *certain* death. I went through the dream twice before. I think I can lead us through again, if you do as I say."

"Sounds pretty certain to me," muttered Anders. "I say we go back south."

"I go with Hart," said Victoria. "The rest of you can do what you want."

After a few moments of silence Will said, "Well, I guess we're going with you then."

"You think you can speak for me?" said Anders.

"Think about it," said Will. "The only way we're getting out of the Hornwood is with either Hart or Victoria. If they die in the dream, as you're so certain they will, and we stay here . . . we're stuck here with no way to escape. So we die too, probably at the hands of those shadowhunters. But if they survive, and Hart comes back for us, we might as well have gone with them to begin with. So we might as well go with them and hope we all make it."

Cora wished there was another way, but what Will said made sense. The others saw this too and seemed to accept it, though reluctantly.

There wasn't much more to be said after that. Hart served up the stew, and it was, to Cora's surprise, quite good. After they had eaten, they arranged themselves on the uneven floor around the fire. After a day of riding the winter wolves and barely surviving the Hornwood, Hart's cave, though not exactly comfortable, was a welcome refuge.

Cora lay with one arm under her head and stared at the fire. The reddish-orange flames danced and waved and the burning wood smelled sweet.

"We'll leave first thing in the morning," said Hart. "The stone is about an hour from here. And if all goes well, we'll be in the eastern Hornwood by tomorrow afternoon."

He extinguished the lanterns and they all settled down to sleep. Will lay on a deerskin to Cora's left and was soon breathing deeply. He had spoken to her several times since the night he had found her on the top of the signal tower, but to Cora's surprise he hadn't pushed her to talk to Victoria again. For some reason this annoyed her. Glancing at Victoria, Cora could see, by the dim light of the fire, that she was still awake but lost in thought, staring at the ceiling. Victoria was, Cora realized, utterly exhausted. *And why wouldn't she be?* thought Cora. *She's only spent the last few days guiding us and saving us and helping us, despite how we've treated her.* Cora felt a pang of shame, of embarrassment at how she had abandoned her friend.

But she's a shifter. And she works for Imago, a voice in her head replied fiercely. *The person who killed Mother and Father. And Hildi. And she'd be willing to let Tarian be destroyed too.*

Deep down Cora knew this wasn't why she was angry, not really. But she clung to it as desperately as she clung to Hildi's bracelet, and closed her eyes and fell into sleep.

They woke to the smell of porridge. Hart was preparing bowls for them. Will brought out the berries they had taken from the signal tower, and sprinkled them into each bowl. They ate quickly with little conversation and when they had finished, they gathered their things. The mood was somber. It was clear that no one was looking forward to traveling the dream. Hart slung his quiver and bow onto his back, along with his other gear, and the horn over his shoulder, and then silently led them up the stairs.

He eyed the wolves and said to Victoria, "They'll be no good in the dream, you know. Whatever control you have over them will be gone there." Cora's heart sank. Without the wolves what chance did they have? Victoria only nodded. She unbuckled one of the saddlebags and retrieved the driftwood-colored box and tucked it into her bag. Then she removed the saddlebags from the winter wolves and whispered in their ears. They bounded off into the gloom.

"We can't just leave the money," protested Anders.

Victoria pursed her lips. "You can carry it if you want."

Anders made a face, but left the saddlebags where Victoria had dropped them.

The path they took wound through stands of giant oak and shagbark. Brambles choked the space between the trees, but Hart seemed to effortlessly find a way through and around, and rarely did he have to pause or backtrack.

The oak gave way to ash and other trees that Cora didn't recognize, and large mossy boulders leaned over their path, casting dark shadows on the drifts of leaves.

As they wound through the rocks, Will turned to her and said, "I want you to know that I'm glad you let me do this with you, Cora. Look for the Sand Coin I mean, and be your friend. Thanks."

"Sure," she mumbled.

"I just wanted you to know that, in case we don't make it through the dream," Will said. "I'd hate it if I never told you that."

Not long after, they came to the lip of a hollow. They crested it and began to descend. The trees were packed closely together, and the air was stifling and still. The leaves kicked up by their feet smelled of damp decay.

Hart stopped beside a blackened, half-buried rock covered in pale lichen. The rock's shadow looked like ink, like night itself. Like the other shadow stones, this one had a symbol carved on its face, barely visible beneath the lichen. Everyone crowded in around Hart.

"Remember," Hart said, "what we do in Augrind's dream has little effect on his creatures. So fighting will accomplish nothing except drawing more of them to us. Our best chance lies in sneaking through and remaining silent."

"What about light?" Anders asked. "I'm assuming if it's Augrind's dream, it'll be blacker than death there."

"We won't need it. When I came here before I marked the trail with stardust. It will both light our way and protect us somewhat from Augrind's creatures. They hate it and will stay away unless we do something stupid." Hart rubbed his chin. "Now then. When I came here before, it was seven hours from stone to stone, so we have a journey in front of us. Remember, whatever happens, remain silent. Not a word."

"Anything else?" asked Victoria.

Hart shook his head. "Ready?" At their nods, he touched the stone and stepped into its shadow.

Before, Cora had thought that there was only one kind of darkness, a darkness that prevented one from seeing. Where they now stood, though, was dark in a different way, in a way that was deeply unsettling, if not terrifying. This darkness *did* make it difficult to see, but worse, it pressed in and seemed to seep through her coat and through her skin and into her mind. She could smell it and taste it, and it was not pleasant.

Cora looked up, and far above, barely discernible through the branches of the trees, was a dark, red-tinged sky. The forest sounds that she had become accustomed to—birdcalls, the whispering of the wind in the leaves, the humming and chirping of insects—were absent in this place. She realized that any sound they made would be deafening in this stillness.

Hart pointed to the ground. A scattering of blue-white dust snaked off into the undergrowth, faintly illuminating the trail and the surrounding vegetation. It cast their faces and the trees in a pale, ghostly light.

Hart set out. Victoria signaled for Anders to follow, then Dane, then Tesh. She gestured for Cora to go next, followed by Will, and Victoria brought up the rear.

Cora walked with the knife Will had given her clutched in her hand, despite what Hart had said. Weapons might not be a good idea to use in Augrind's dream, but it still felt safer to have one on the ready than to not.

The trees along their path were broken things, strangled by vines and poisonous looking growths. More often than not the bark of the trees was split open, and sap oozed like blood from hideous wounds.

Hart set a steady pace. They wound through the forest, crossed silent, sluggish streams, and picked their way over the boulder-strewn ground. The smell of rot was all but overpowering in this place, drifting up from where their feet kicked the damp, fallen leaves. Cora almost wretched more than once.

As they walked, Cora became aware that the token around her neck had grown bitingly cold. The metal, nestled in the hollow of her throat, felt like ice. She reached beneath her collar and moved the token between her shirt and her coat so that it no longer rested against her skin.

They came to a ridge where the trees had been flattened, as though by a massive blast of wind. It was the first time they had seen the sky unobstructed by branches. It was cloudless and the color of dying coals.

As they crossed the open space, clambering over the fallen trees or wriggling beneath them, a cry rent the air. They froze. It was the first sound they had heard in the dream. Cora looked up and squinted. Four black shapes drifted high overhead, barely visible against the dark red sky. The shapes appeared to be birds, but they were the largest birds Cora had ever seen. And they were skeleton-thin.

Crows, she thought. *If this is Augrind's dream, those are Crows!*

Without a word they continued on, and soon were beneath the cover of the trees once again. Cora held her breath, waiting for any indication that they had been seen by the Crows, that they were being pursued, but none came.

Hours passed. Cora's legs ached, but any thought of rest in this place was unimaginable. The fear of the dream drove them on. Twice more they heard the shriek of a Crow and once they heard hideous laughter echoing through the trees. When the laughter finally stopped, Cora felt a sharp pain inside her ear. She reached up and gently touched her earlobe. Her fingers came away wet with blood. The blood appeared purple in the glow of the stardust.

In a panic she whipped around, but Will held a finger to his lips and Victoria moved up to put a reassuring hand on her shoulder. Blood trickled from their ears too. *Almost there,* Will mouthed. *Stay calm.*

And then, abruptly, the trail of stardust ended. At first Cora thought they had come to the shadow stone, but as Hart cast about, his eyes bent toward the ground, it became clear that the trail had somehow been erased.

Without hesitation, Hart pulled something from his pocket. It was a bottle and it glowed bright in the darkness. *More stardust,* Cora thought. *Fortunate for us.* Then the boy retrieved a creased piece of paper from his coat. When he unfolded it, the light from the bottle illuminated an old map. Hart studied it a moment and then set out.

Every few steps Hart dropped some of the stardust on the ground behind him, reestablishing the trail that had been lost. It was slow going, but he seemed confident in their direction and this gave Cora some hope.

As they crossed a dry streambed, the piercing wail of a Crow shattered the silence. Even through her shirt Cora could feel the coldness of the circus token intensify. She glanced up, and through the branches of the trees she saw two of the creatures wheeling in the sky. One of the Crows banked and flew in their direction. It gained speed and then disappeared as it merged with the darkness of the forest off to their left.

Hart motioned them to the ground. They crouched, backs against a fallen tree, and waited. Cora strained her eyes, desperately trying to locate the Crow. Fear coursed through her. And then beside her, Tesh coolly nocked an arrow, drew it back, and released.

The body of the Crow slammed into the ground beside them, Tesh's arrow embedded in its skull.

Hart held up the bottle to examine the bird. "I told you using weapons was a bad idea," he breathed. "We need to run."

"Won't that draw attention?" asked Anders.

"We already have. Anywhere else that Crow would be dead. But not here. I *told* you this. Things are about to get bad." The Crow twitched, opened an eye, and screamed.

They turned and ran. And then the trees to their right exploded.

Cora and the others were thrown to the ground as a hail of splinters and broken rock raked them from the side. A cloven hoof crashed into the earth where they had been standing. The hoof was huge, easily as big as a wagon, and its scarred surface glinted like obsidian. What Cora could see of the creature's leg was a mass of coarse, shaggy hair matted with brambles and mud. Darkness dripped from it. The beast shifted its weight and the hoof sank deeper into the ground. And then the creature roared.

The sound was deafening, like a thunderous waterfall, like a hundred cities collapsing, like the howling of the Storm.

Hart staggered to his feet and hurled the bottle of stardust at the monster. The bottle, like a glowing, white-hot meteor, arced through the air and struck the beast on the flank. There was a flash of blinding light as the bottle shattered. The monster roared again, this time in pain, and turned and fled, obliterating everything in its path. Branches and bark and broken pieces of tree fell down around Cora as the creature sped away. And then, as the last leaves drifted down, there was silence once again. It had all happened in less than a minute.

Cora barely suppressed a groan as she stood. The others brushed themselves off and got to their feet as well. Their faces showed what Cora felt: shock that they were somehow still alive. Cora looked behind them. The Crow that Tesh had shot had been crushed beneath a fallen tree. Its wings still thrashed, but it made no sound. Without a word, Hart waved for them to follow and they limped after him.

They tried to run but had to settle for a hobbling trot. Hart studied his map, but kept looking anxiously up at the sky. Through the branches of the trees Cora could see more Crows gathering high above. Soon there were a dozen, and then twenty, and then there were too many to count. Their long, thin cries echoed through the dream. What were they waiting for?

"How much farther?" panted Anders.

The red sky flickered, going dark for an instant, and then appeared again, as though a flash of black lightning had flared across it. As one, the skeletal birds turned and dove toward them.

Hart called over his shoulder, "It's just ahead!" but his words could hardly be heard over the chorus of screams of the approaching Crows.

Tesh turned and shot an arrow right past Cora's ear.

"What are you—?" Cora began, but then something heavy slammed into her back, accompanied by a horrific stench. Cora's knees buckled and she fell to the ground.

"Saving your life," snarled Tesh. "You're welcome."

Will heaved the Crow's body off her and pulled Cora to her feet.

"Hurry!" shouted Hart. "The stone! The stone!" A broken branch spun past Cora and clipped the back of Will's head. He dropped to the ground, but Cora kept hold of his hand and they both stumbled toward Hart's voice. Ahead of her Anders, Dane, then Tesh suddenly vanished. A howling wind whipped at Cora's hair. Hart, standing beside the stone, reached out, grabbed Cora's hand, and dragged her and Will into the darkness.

CHAPTER TWENTY-TWO

RETURN TO THE DREAM

THE LIGHT SHIFTED AND THE oppressive weight of the darkness of Augrind's dream suddenly vanished. They tumbled over one another and lay panting on the ground. The air Cora sucked in through her mouth tasted so fresh, so clean. Beside her, Will groaned and tentatively touched the back of his head. *He's lucky to be alive*, Cora thought. The tree branch that had struck him had been as big around as his leg, but it had been a glancing blow. Even so, he couldn't get to his feet.

Cora coughed and sat up, wincing when she noticed a long splinter of wood sticking out of her forearm. With a grimace she pulled it free and flicked it away from her.

The others were in worse shape. Every one of them was pin cushioned with needle-like slivers of broken tree, and they all had cuts and scratches on their faces and necks and hands. Hart's arm looked broken, and he had a long gash that ran across his forehead. It looked as though Anders and Tesh had been raked by Crows' talons, and one of Dane's eyes was swollen shut. And . . .

"Where's Victoria?" Cora twisted around, but Victoria wasn't there.

"When did you see her last?" asked Hart. Everyone stared at him blankly.

Cora's mind spun as she thought back. "Right before the trail disappeared," she said. "And right after we heard the laughter." She shuddered as she remembered, and reached up and touched the dried blood on her ear.

"She must have been injured during the attack," said Hart.

Cora was aware of the vault then, in her coat pocket, pressing against her side. It still contained the Sand Coin. She had what she had come for. She could, in a matter of minutes, walk to the edge of the Hornwood and send the Sand Coin back to Tarian, and all would be well.

As she reached for the vault, Cora felt Hildi's bracelet shift against her wrist. She looked down at the jade beads and suddenly recalled when her sister had given her the bracelet, *why* she had given it to her. And Cora knew in that moment that, despite everything she had told herself, she had to go back. Victoria *was* her friend. If she walked away from Victoria and sent the Sand Coin to Tarian, all *wouldn't* be well. True, Victoria was a shifter, and she did work for Imago, but it wasn't as simple as Cora had tried to make it. And Cora couldn't leave her behind, not like this.

Cora cleared her throat and said, "We . . . we have to go back for her. She won't be far."

"Are you crazy?" said Anders. "Look at us. We can't do anything in this state. We barely made it out ourselves. Besides, you know what's waiting on the other side. It's pointless."

"She would go back for one of us," said Cora. "Even if it meant putting herself in danger." Anders looked away. Cora glanced down at her shaking hands. "You're right, though; you're all too hurt to go. But I'm not."

"Cora," said Hart quietly. "There's next to no chance you'll be able to rescue her alone, if she's even still alive. The Crows might be gone by now, but they might not be. Even if they are, you won't know which way to go."

"So give me the map," said Cora. "Tell me what to look for. I have to try. She's . . . my friend."

The boy studied her a moment, then stood and pulled the crumpled map from his pocket. He hobbled over to her and showed her the map. The paper was covered in small symbols and lines. "It's detailed, and that makes it hard to read in this light. When you step back into the dream, you'll be here." Hart pointed to the right side of the map, to a black square. "And here is the streambed where we were attacked."

"Alright," said Cora. "That's kind of straight forward."

"These," said Hart, tracing his finger over a series of triangles, "represent landmarks next to the path. Mostly they're trees, but this one is a rock. And this one is that hollowed out stump. Do you remember it?"

Cora didn't.

"Keep checking the landmarks. It shouldn't take long for you to get back to where the path was last marked. You'll be able to see the stardust some distance away." Hart paused and then asked, "Cora, are you sure about this?"

She looked him in the eye and nodded.

"Try to be quiet. And be quick."

Cora took a step toward the shadow stone.

"Wait," said Will. "I'm coming with you." But when he tried to get to his feet, his legs gave out. He struck the ground in frustration.

"It's alright, Will," said Cora as she patted his shoulder. "I know you would if you could. I'll see you in a bit."

"Good luck," said Hart just as Will said, "Be careful. And don't forget the way back."

Cora's heart pounded as she stepped back into Augrind's dream. She half-expected to be torn apart by Crows immediately or smashed to a pulp by the stone-hoofed monster. But she stood alone among the trees, wrapped in the overpowering darkness of the place. She held her breath and listened. Off to her right something large, something heavy walked ponderously away through the underbrush. Above, she could hear the receding cries of innumerable Crows. She waited a minute more without moving. Then, reasonably sure that her arrival had gone unmarked, she withdrew the map and held it up in what little light there was.

It wasn't enough. Cora could barely make out the black square, let alone the shapes that showed the direction of the path. She debated going back for a lantern but dismissed the idea almost immediately. If she held a light, Augrind's creatures would be on her before she had gone three steps.

Cora tried to ignore the fear that bubbled inside her, tried to shut out the whispering voice that told her this was a foolish thing to do. Instead, she ever-so-carefully circled away from the shadow stone, looking for footprints. Finally, after what felt like an hour, she found some, almost indiscernible in the darkness. *Tesh's*, she thought, though she couldn't be sure. She set out in the direction they seemed to come from.

Five steps, ten steps, fifteen. The ground was covered in wet leaves and bore no trace of their passing. Had she guessed wrong? Cora hesitated, then continued. She was about to turn around when she glimpsed something half-hidden in the shadow of a rock. She stooped and picked it up. It was one of Dane's knives. With relief, she went on.

Past broken branches, torn up trees, and every once in a while a footprint, Cora slowly made her way back along the path. Sometimes the signs of their passage were close together, but more often than not they were far apart, and more than once Cora was sure she had gone wrong. Panic would begin to rise within her, but she ruthlessly pushed it down. *I can't give up. I have to find her.* And she would continue until she happened upon the next sign.

When the stardust first appeared through the trees, Cora thought she was imagining it. But when she blinked, the faint glow remained. As she drew near to where the trail of dust ended, the full scope of the stone-hoofed creature's destruction came into view. The pale light revealed a circle of trees shorn off a few feet from the ground, their shattered trunks lying atop one another like scattered sticks. Cora moved in among them, careful not to step on the brittle branches that crisscrossed the damp earth.

A faint sound, quiet as a whisper, issued from somewhere ahead. Cora felt a surge of hope. She crept forward, cautiously feeling among the tangled branches. She came to where she thought she had been thrown when they were first attacked. The sound was less faint now. She stood and peered into the shadows just ahead of her.

There was a quick flurry of movement and Cora recoiled and almost screamed. But then she saw it was the wing of the Crow that Tesh had shot, the Crow that had been flattened beneath a fallen tree. The creature still moved, still fought to free itself, its wings carving out troughs in the wet forest soil.

With a shudder, Cora angled away from the Crow. She scooped up a handful of the stardust and held it in her palm like a candle.

The minutes stretched out. It was a painstaking search, made slower by the necessity for silence. Cora lifted branches when she had to, carefully pushed aside the broken chunks of trees, and sifted through mounds of damp leaves in an ever-widening circle. The knees of her trousers became sodden, covered in the filth of the dream, and the sleeves of her coat were darkened with putrid mud. The faint rhythmic thrashing of the Crow's wings did not cease, and became to Cora like the ticking of a clock that threatened to strike the hour at any moment.

Cora's face was damp with sweat. Her fear was mingled with doubt now. What if Victoria wasn't here after all? What if, instead of being injured, she had left them on purpose? This was Augrind's dream after all, and she was a creature of Augrind. But no. Victoria could have abandoned them countless times in the Hornwood, and she had not. She had proved herself a friend, time after time, even when everyone, including Cora, had rejected her. No, Victoria *had* to be here. *I can't give up,* Cora told herself.

The circus token radiated cold through her shirt. Somewhere in the distance something bellowed. It echoed through the dream.

Cora redoubled her efforts, frantically widening her search, increasingly heedless of the noise she made. And then she found her.

Victoria lay in the shadow of a boulder, all but covered by a rotting strip of bark. Cora pushed the bark aside. Her friend's eyes were closed, and she had a knot the size of a goose's egg on her temple. But, to Cora's relief, she still breathed.

When Cora pulled Victoria into a sitting position, the girl's eyelids fluttered open and her body went tense. She immediately reached for her bag but relaxed when she realized it still hung from her shoulder. Cora put a finger to her lips and after a moment Victoria nodded.

With difficulty they stood and made their way to the circle of broken trees. Victoria was unsteady on her feet, and she leaned heavily on Cora's shoulder.

Again, there was a bellowing roar. It was closer now. Cora could feel a slight tremor in the earth.

Victoria looked around, a questioning look on her face. "The others?" she whispered in Cora's ear.

They made it out already, mouthed Cora. She scraped together another handful of stardust from the ground and pulled out the map. It took her a moment, but she was able to identify the symbols that she thought represented a large boulder and a leaning tree that stood opposite them. The path led that way. She pointed and they set out.

With each passing second, the shaking of the ground grew more noticeable. "We have to hurry," whispered Victoria, looking over her shoulder.

They had to be getting closer to the stone, but they could just as easily pass it if they made a wrong turn. Cora tried to compare the map to the surrounding landscape, but it was impossible to do as they limped along. She stopped and bent over the map.

"Cora, come on!" hissed Victoria.

Cora looked up, then back down at the map. Nothing that surrounded them corresponded with the symbols on the parchment. She checked again, turning this way, then that. "I don't know where we are!" she finally whispered.

Hoof beats were audible now, pounding on the path somewhere behind them. Whoever—or whatever—it was would be upon them in moments. Victoria wheeled around to face their pursuer.

The clear note of a horn cut through the air, coming from somewhere off to their left.

"It's Hart!" said Cora. "Follow the horn!"

It sounded again, and Cora and Victoria scrambled through the undergrowth toward it, tripping over vines and fallen branches. The hoof beats, too, changed course.

"I see him!" panted Cora.

Pulling Victoria after her, Cora slammed into a tree, but glanced off it and kept her footing. Hart, a shadow among shadows, spotted them and waved his arms wildly.

"Look out!" screamed Victoria.

A beast snorted in the darkness beside them and Victoria jerked Cora down just in time. A massive, glistening black blade swept through the air where her head had been.

Cora rolled, came up on her feet beside Victoria, and together they ran.

A raspy voice snarled and yelled a command, and Cora felt the ground quake. She and Victoria stumbled, regained their balance, and leapt toward the shadow that had just swallowed Hart.

But even as Cora's hand touched the stone and she sank into the shadow, something grasped hold of her coat and didn't let go.

CHAPTER TWENTY-THREE

Through the Door

AS THE DARKNESS FELL AWAY and they crashed to the ground, Cora twisted around, trying to free herself from whatever clung to her coat. She stopped struggling when she saw with horror what it was.

A pale, thin-fingered hand gripped her collar. But the hand was two, no, three times longer than it should have been. As she watched, the hand's arm emerged from the shadow, a slender, sinewy thing, sleeved in black chainmail that drank the light. And then, incrementally, the rest of the figure came through. It was tall, too tall, with black armor that looked like scraped bone and a billowing rag of a cloak. An ebony blade hung from the figure's belt. A helm fashioned to resemble the skull of a deer covered its long, thin face. It was, without a doubt, a Spindle.

"Let go!" Cora screamed, and she tried again to pull away, but the hand was like a vise. Hart shouted and an arrow—probably Tesh's—struck the armored figure, but the shaft bounced away harmlessly.

The Spindle's other hand was still within the shadow, pulling on something as yet unseen. And then a bridled snout slowly appeared and resolved into a huge creature covered in coarse hair and mud, with tusks like broken tree trunks. It was like watching a rat emerge from an impossibly small hole, except it wasn't a rat. It was a boar and it was as big as a house.

And then Will was beside Cora and he swung his sword. The blade cut into the exposed wrist and the Spindle snarled and released Cora. She scrambled away on all fours.

"Stand clear!" shouted Victoria. The boar shook its head and pawed the ground and charged. But instead of attacking them, it slammed into the back of its rider, driving one of its tusks into the Spindle's back. The creature screamed in agony and together it and the boar toppled to the ground like a pair of felled trees. The impact shook the forest.

"Go!" said Victoria. Her voice was strained and a vein stood out on her forehead. "I don't know how long I can command it! The Door is that way! It's not far!" She pointed off to her right with a shaking hand.

Cora and the others ignored her. Hart put the horn to his lips and sounded a blast. Dane and Will and Anders drew their knives and hurled them at the Spindle as it grappled with its mount on the forest floor. Tesh took aim and this time her arrows found their marks in the joints of the Spindle's armor.

But the only wounds that seemed to be affecting their enemy were those being inflicted upon it by the boar. The creature tore at its master, savaging the Spindle's chest and arms with its tusks and teeth and hooves. The Spindle bled freely, but still it struggled against the beast. And then the Spindle found its sword.

"Run!" shouted Victoria. The Spindle's hand closed around the hilt of its weapon. Slowly the blade inched out of its scabbard. When it was clear, the Spindle gave two swift thrusts and the boar was dead.

They ran.

As they sped through the trees Anders withdrew a silver chain from beneath his shirt. On it was two keys. "How far?" he gasped.

Victoria glanced over her shoulder. "Too far, I think."

They leapt a stream and scrambled up an incline. Cora's breaths were ragged and a pain was forming in her side.

Hart again sounded the horn. The note hung in the air, clear and commanding.

"I don't think your horn works on Spindles," said Anders.

"It's coming!" called Dane. They could all hear it now, crashing through the underbrush behind them.

A fallen tree lay across the ground just ahead. Without pausing they slid beneath, regained their feet, and sped on.

"This way!" Victoria turned and they raced down a gully choked with ivy and nettles and drifts of leaves.

There was a whistling whine and the Spindle was suddenly there, bloody but whole, standing in front of them. Cora and the others skidded to a stop. The figure's long, pale fingers flexed as it adjusted its grip on its sword hilt. It laughed and raised its weapon.

A silent swarm of darkness burst from the trees and engulfed the creature.

"Shadowhunters!" gasped Cora. They had answered Hart's call. The shadowhunters were a blur of swords and axes and spears, and though they themselves made no sound, their weapons crackled like lightning when they struck the Spindle.

Victoria's eyes darted back and forth. "It's not enough. They're no match for this thing. Come on!"

They ran again.

The trees began to thin and Cora could taste salt in the air. They must be near the edge of the Hornwood. Her side burned like fire and she gripped it with one hand as she fought to keep up with the others.

"Anders!" shouted Victoria. "It's straight on! Two hundred paces!"

Anders surged ahead, his long legs eating up the ground, one of the keys clutched in his right hand.

The Door appeared out of the gloom, an enormous wooden thing banded in iron that looked like it belonged in a castle. But it stood alone, surrounded and supported only by a stone frame. Anders slammed into it with a grunt, but he managed to insert the key into the lock. He twisted it and pushed the Door open and stepped inside. When he looked back he screamed, "RUN!"

Dane was in the lead and a heartbeat later he darted through the Door. Then Tesh and Hart and Will. As Victoria slipped through, Cora heard the whistling whine of the Spindle behind her.

She willed herself to run faster.

"Duck, Cor, duck!"

The Door was beginning to close. Cora dove for the opening and heard the whisper of the Spindle's blade as it sliced the air where she would have been. She tumbled across the narrowing threshold and landed in a heap. With yells, the others threw all their weight against the Door. It swung toward the doorframe but then stopped.

"Push harder!" shouted Anders. Cora could still hear the whine of the Spindle, and through the crack of the Door she could see the creature's knee pressed up against the frame. The opening began to widen. She scrambled to her feet, and snatching Will's sword from his hand, Cora stabbed the Spindle with all her strength. It hissed, but did not move. Cora stabbed its knee again and did not stop until, with a bellow, the Spindle finally pulled away.

For an instant Cora saw the creature, tall and lean and dark as a nightmare, staring at her through the crack. And then the Door slammed shut.

CHAPTER TWENTY-FOUR

An Unwelcome Visitor

BLACKWOOD STOOD ON THE WHARF with the rest of the Council and looked out at the water. A single ship floated in the middle of the bay. He wiped the sweat from his upper lip. Now was the moment of truth. His years of planning had come down to this. Blackwood raised his hand.

The waters did not move. Neither did the ship. One of the councilors coughed nervously.

"It doesn't appear that your—" began the chief councilor, but she stopped when, with a popping groan, the ship abruptly listed to starboard. They could all see the frothing bubbles on the water now, concentrated around the vessel. The sound of cracking timbers echoed across the bay and even Blackwood was stunned when, a moment later, the ship broke in half and slid beneath the surface.

He masked his surprise, though, and raised his other hand and made a fist. He knew that however successful he might be at destroying a ship, it would count for nothing if he could not demonstrate the full scope of the Water Works' power.

"Attend to the tidal marker now, if you will," Blackwood said.

The members of the Council shifted their gaze to the stone pillar that rose from the water beside the second pier. They let out a collective gasp as the level of the water in the bay began to drop. In less than a minute it was down a full fathom.

"Impossible!" said the chief councilor. "The volume of water you are moving is—"

"Staggering? Unbelievable? Astounding?" Blackwood allowed himself a small smile. "Indeed it is. And the machinery is only operating at quarter capacity."

"I must admit, I had my doubts, Overseer," the chief councilor said. "Fortunately for all of us, I was wrong. We owe you a debt."

That evening found Blackwood back in his study in the Water Works building. He eased himself into his chair and lit his pipe. A day to celebrate, to be sure, and none too soon; the Turn was only three days away, and with it, the tidal surge. But now, thanks to Blackwood, Tarian was ready for any threat. Yes, it was a day to celebrate, but it was also time he considered his next move.

Leading the Council had always been in the back of Blackwood's mind, but now he wondered why his sights had been set so low. There were too many constraints within the structure of the Council. Well, one constraint, really: the necessity for consensus to move forward with anything. Which meant that *everything* took a very long time. He shook his head. It really wouldn't do . . .

"Thaddeus Blackwood, we need to talk," said a voice that sounded like gravel. Blackwood sprang to his feet and whipped around. A man he did not recognize stepped from the shadows behind Blackwood's desk and came and stood before him.

"How did you get in here?" Blackwood demanded.

The grizzled man did not answer, but instead looked Blackwood up and down like a wolf eyeing its prey. A scar ran down the side of the man's face and when he reached up and scratched his jaw, Blackwood saw that three of his fingers were gone. It was all Blackwood could do to not shrink back.

"It's not important how I'm here," said the man. "It's important *why* I'm here. I'm here because my stalker is missing and I want answers."

Blackwood felt the blood drain from his face.

"Hulder?"

The man gave a nod that was almost imperceptible.

Blackwood's mind reeled. "What do you mean, the stalker is missing? Did it catch the girl?"

"No."

Shock gave way to indignation. "Why not? The target is *a little girl!*" exclaimed Blackwood. "Supposedly you're the best handler in the business. But not only do you fail, you dare to trespass here and demand answers from *me?*"

Hulder unfolded a piece of parchment and showed it to him. It was a map. "As you can see, the stalker tracked your *little girl* to here." He pointed to where a line of red dashes ended. It was, to Blackwood's surprise, near the southern edge of the Hornwood. The marks on the parchment were clearly wayfarer's ink linked to the stalker, so there was no doubt that the creature had tracked Cora there. "And then my stalker disappeared. Someone took its collar off. And trust me, *no one* takes its collar off. *I* don't even take its collar off. So who is this girl? What did you not tell me?"

"I told you everything!"

Hulder shook his head. "You didn't. And now I'm out a stalker."

Blackwood waved his hand contemptuously. "I withheld nothing from you. Now what are you going to do to make up for your failure? I paid you a handsome sum and I want results."

Blackwood found himself on the floor, his ear ringing. He hadn't even seen Hulder move, let alone strike him. The handler stood looking down at him.

"Let me be perfectly clear, Thaddeus Blackwood. You failed to divulge critical information to me, which resulted in the loss of one of my stalkers. I don't lose my stalkers. What you paid me for the job is but a tiny fraction of what you now owe me."

"And that is?" asked Blackwood.

"3,000 gold pieces."

Blackwood pulled himself into a sitting position. *In your dreams,* he thought. But he had underestimated this man. He looked up at him warily and said, with what he hoped would be taken for meekness, "I'll arrange for payment. It will take some time, I'm afraid. Close to a week for a sum so large."

"You have three days."

By the time Blackwood had gotten to his feet, the man was gone. The Overseer tentatively touched his ear, and moving toward an oil lamp, examined his shaking fingers. No blood. There was that, at least.

As the minutes passed, the fear that had coursed through him dissipated and Blackwood's heartbeat returned to normal. All that remained was a seething anger. If the man thought he could strike a member of the Council and attempt to extort him, he was gravely mistaken. If the man thought he could do those things and not suffer the consequences, he did not know Blackwood. Hulder's reputation, fearsome though it was, would not protect him. Blackwood was owed favors by several individuals who were more than capable of disposing of the handler, regardless of his reputation. Blackwood would ensure that justice prevailed.

The Overseer was less certain about what to do regarding the news that Hulder had brought. The fact that Cora was still at large bothered him. That she had been making her way north was enormously troubling.

Could she, in fact, have been following the Sand Coin to Agendor? Blackwood hated not knowing almost as much as he hated loose ends . . .

Still, he thought, *what could she do?* Even if Cora did manage to retrieve the Sand Coin—which was exceedingly unlikely—Imago would pursue her, retake it, and that would be the end of it. Maybe there was nothing to worry about after all.

Blackwood pulled on his pipe and let the smoke escape the corner of his mouth. No, there was nothing to worry about. He would never see Cora or the Sand Coin again.

III

CHAPTER TWENTY-FIVE

AGENDOR

CORA AND THE OTHERS stood panting in the center of a walled courtyard on a square of rust-colored flagstones. Behind them, the Door looked much as it had in the forest: a doorway made of iron and wood, unattached to any wall. Beyond the flagstones were fountains and manicured fruit trees and meticulously trimmed grass. The sky above was bright and cloudless and the palest of blues. The air no longer prickled, which felt jarring after being so long in the Hornwood.

"Is everyone alright?" asked Victoria. Somehow, even after the Spindle, her voice was steady. They all looked at one another. Each of them was a mess. Cora didn't know how they were all still on their feet.

"Why wouldn't we be?" asked Will, but his smile seemed forced.

Victoria ignored him and turned to Anders. "I know you weren't planning on coming back here after what I told you in the signal tower," she whispered, "but please act normal. If he suspects you know the truth . . . I don't think it'll go well for any of us."

Anders glanced at the serpent scales on the back of Victoria's hands and he bit his lip. But he gave a slight nod.

Two guards appeared through an archway across the courtyard and walked toward them. They carried spears and wore green and black tabards.

"Rogga! Trinn!" called Anders. "We're injured. Can you send for Vaga?"

The guards exchanged a few words and then one of them turned and walked briskly back through the archway.

"Where are the rest of you?" asked the remaining guard. "And Lord Arburry?"

"Arburry?" Anders looked confused. "What do you mean, Rogga?"

"Never mind," said Rogga. "Can you walk?" Anders nodded and the guard led them out of the courtyard and into a sprawling manor house. "Tell me what happened," he said.

"We were attacked by . . . outlaws," said Anders. "We got separated from the rest of the circus a while back. They should be along in a few days, I think."

The dimly lit house reminded Cora of a museum. The flickering light from the candle stands and oil lamps that lined the wide halls revealed sculptures and paintings and ornate rugs. Cora caught glimpses of rooms stuffed with old books and maps and objects that she couldn't identify. It seemed a pleasant enough place, but knowing whose house this was . . . everything took on a mysterious and sinister and foreboding look.

As they went up a flight of broad steps, Rogga looked over his shoulder and eyed Hart and Will and Cora. "Looks like the circus has some new blood, eh?"

Anders grunted but didn't answer.

Rogga guided them down a paneled hall and opened one of the doors. He caught up a lamp from a tall stand just outside and handed it to Anders. "The healer should be along shortly. And I'll have the kitchen bring the evening meal here. You all look famished." He turned on his heel and left them.

Anders set the lamp on a table in the middle of the room. By its light Cora could see bunks arranged in rows along the walls. The room was easily large enough to house everyone in the circus. It reminded Cora of the barracks in the Water Works building and she was suddenly struck with a longing to be home.

They sat or lay on the beds and looked at one another. Will cleared his throat dramatically and said, "Well, this was unexpected. What do we do now?"

"Are you all in league with Imago?" asked Hart. He ran his finger down the blade of his knife. How he knew about Imago, Cora couldn't imagine; no one had spoken of the magician in Hart's hearing as far as she could remember.

"No," said Anders, scowling. "We've worked for *Lord Arburry* for years, but only just discovered who he really is in the last few days."

"How'd you find out?" asked Hart.

"I told them," said Victoria.

Hart raised an eyebrow.

"He's been forcing me to work for him since the Storm. He has my brother."

"I'm sorry," said Hart.

"Hart, how did you know about Imago?" asked Cora.

"There have been whisperings in the Hornwood for some time about his coming and going. The trees see everything, and they talk, in their own way. But he was only ever seen in the east of the wood. When I discovered the Door last year, I put it together and knew it was his." Hart laughed bitterly. "My whole reason for coming to this side of the wood—well, the eastern side of the wood, I guess I should say now— was to destroy the Door. I didn't suspect that it was your destination or I wouldn't have brought you through Augrind's dream. The last thing I expected was to go through the Door myself."

"The Door wasn't my destination," said Anders. "All I wanted to do was meet up with Felix and the Youngers and then disappear. Tesh and Dane were with me. I don't know about Cora and Will. We only stayed with Victoria because she could guide us through the wood. By the way, Victoria, where exactly are we? I've always wondered where this place is."

"Agendor," said Victoria. "Imago's island between the mainland and the Bones."

Dane whistled. "Never would have guessed—"

Victoria raised a finger to her lips and pointed to the door. A moment later it opened and three women in green and black livery swept in. They carried covered trays that they placed on the table beside the lamp. One stayed to lay a fire and then, like the others, left without a word.

The door had barely closed when it swung open again and an ancient, spidery woman appeared, an old, leather bag clutched to her chest. Her eyes darted back and forth, taking in their injuries.

With a disapproving shake of her head, the healer skittered across the room and stood before Anders. "What have you gotten the circus into now, boy?" She stooped and examined the splinters protruding from his leg and side. "What could do this to a shagbark I don't know, but shagbark it is." She poked at one of the splinters. "Hard as stone, this is, hmm."

"It's a long story, Vaga," said Anders.

The healer rummaged in her bag and withdrew a narrow glass bottle. Her hands, despite being wrinkled and gnarled, were steady as she unstoppered the bottle and poured some of its contents onto a rag. The muddy looking substance smelled foul. She dabbed it on Anders' skin around one of the splinters and with a pair of pincers quickly and deftly pulled the thin sliver out and dropped it onto the floor. She repeated the process until all the splinters were removed.

"And your face, boy? You take off your token and let the animals have a go at you?" Vaga cackled and applied more of the medicine to the scratches across his forehead.

When she discovered the arrow wound in his shoulder, she clucked and shook her head. "What *have* you gotten the circus into?" she said again. "At least this seems to be healing well."

Without waiting for an answer, she moved on to the others, whispering to herself as she poked at them, looking intently at their cuts and scrapes and bruises. Her movements were jerky, yet precise, as though she had made them an untold number of times and didn't even have to think about what she was doing.

When she came to Hart, Vaga squinted at his face and said, "Now this is odd. You've walked under a different moon for some time now and you are . . . unchanged. Yet very much changed." She reached up and traced Hart's jawline with a bony finger, then peered into his eyes. "Been sleeping in the Hornwood?" Vaga clucked her tongue. "The world will pass you by if you're not careful."

"What's that supposed to mean?" asked Hart.

"Time moves slower there," Vaga said with a shrug. She twisted around and looked at each of them in turn. "A day there, three days here. Or four or five. Or two. Who can ever say? But I can see that you've all been sleeping in the Hornwood, though none as long as this one." She patted Hart's face. "If not for him, I wouldn't have noticed the signs on the rest of you . . . Now then, we should do something about your arm. Broken if I'm not mistaken."

"Wait, what day is it?" asked Cora. If time in the Hornwood moved slower than the rest of the world, it might already be . . . "Is it autumn yet?"

"Hmm?" asked the healer. She pulled violently on Hart's arm and he gasped in pain. She hastily and roughly put the arm in a sling. "There now, all set." Vaga caught up her bag and made for the door. "Might want to clean these up." She kicked one of the splinters across the floor and barked a laugh that turned into a hacking cough.

"Is it autumn yet?" Cora repeated in a louder voice.

"Autumn?" Vaga looked over her shoulder. "No, child, the Turn is in two days. Now then, everyone eat and rest up! I'll check on you again tomorrow." With that, she scurried out of the room and slammed the door behind her.

Two days until the Turn! Talk about cutting it close. Cora almost reached inside her coat for the vault, but then stopped herself. Before she sent the Sand Coin, she needed to take care of something.

She got to her feet and made her way over to Victoria as the others crowded around the table and started to eat. It was hard to look her friend in the face but Cora did and said, "Can I talk to you?"

Victoria nodded, but her face was a mask. Together they walked to the far end of the room.

Cora cleared her throat. "I wanted to . . . tell you that I'm sorry." It was difficult to even know what to say, but she forged ahead anyway. "For not defending you in the signal tower. For holding it against you that you work for Imago and that you're a shifter. That wasn't fair of me."

"Why *didn't* you stand up for me? I thought we were friends." Victoria's voice was raw and it cracked with emotion.

Cora looked down at the floor. "Honestly, I think I wanted someone to be angry with. I miss my parents, I miss Hildi *so much*, and it felt wrong to *not* be angry with you. Like if I defended you or excused you, I was somehow betraying my family. Like I said, it wasn't fair of me at all."

"What changed?"

"When we lost you in Augrind's dream, I realized how selfish I was being. You've been nothing but a friend to me, and I've treated you so badly. For the first time I saw things really clearly. So I went back for you."

There was a pause then Victoria said, "Are you sure it wasn't for the Sand Coin?"

Anger flared in Cora. "This has nothing to do with the Sand Coin! I went back for *you*. Didn't you hear everything I just said?"

Victoria's expression was guarded. Wounded. "I want to believe you. It's just . . . hard, you know?"

The words stung, but it's what Cora had expected. She swallowed her hurt and said, "You *can* believe me, Victoria. Because I've had the Sand Coin since we retrieved it from the outlaws." She reached into her coat and pulled out the vault. She popped it open and removed the white disc. "I went back for you because you're my friend, not because of this. I apologized because I really am sorry." Cora hesitated and then surprised herself by handing the Sand Coin to Victoria.

"How did you get this? How . . . ?" The girl stared down at the Sand Coin. "But why? Why are you giving this back to me?"

"So that you'll know I'm telling you the truth. And so you'll know that, as much as I care about the Sand Coin and what it means for Tarian, I care about our friendship just as much, if not more."

"That's nice and all," said Victoria, "and it means a lot, but I don't understand. Are you just giving up? Either I get the Sand Coin and give it to Imago, or you get it and leave. It's one or the other, it can't be both."

"We both need it," Cora agreed, "but I'm not giving up." She looked over at the others gathered around the table. "It might not seem like it," she mused, "but we really do want the same thing. We *all* want the same thing." She pushed a strand of hair out of her eyes and thought for a moment. "Maybe, just maybe, we can work together to get it . . . What do you think?"

"I'm not sure what you're getting at," said Victoria, "but I'm willing to listen."

Cora's mind began to race.

As they finished eating, Cora stood and looked around the table. "I want to talk about what's next."

Anders glanced at the clock on the wall and pushed back his chair.

"What's next for me is leaving. Anyone besides Tesh and Dane coming with me?"

"Where are you going?" asked Cora.

"To meet the circus. You think I'm staying here?"

"You'd be walking right into Imago," Victoria said. "He's with the circus."

Anders snorted. "That's absurd."

"You're forgetting Rascha," said Victoria. "Imago saw through Rascha's eyes. He saw the outlaws attack, watched as they got away with the Sand Coin. And then Rascha was killed. Imago was suddenly blind. He would have gone to the circus immediately, to ensure that the Sand Coin had been recovered."

"That explains why Rogga assumed Imago was with us!" said Will.

Victoria nodded.

"Makes sense," Anders muttered grudgingly.

"So you're staying," said Cora. "Good. I want to propose something."

Anders rolled his eyes but remained in his seat.

"It seems like we all want different things," began Cora. "Anders, you want to meet up with the circus and disappear. Hart, you want to destroy the Door. Will and I want the Sand Coin to protect Tarian. And Victoria wants to give it to Imago to keep her brother safe.

"Imago has hurt all of us. He's torn apart our lives and killed people we cared about. He's been using the circus, using Victoria, to do bad things. His plan with the tokens is already working and if he keeps going, Hibaria will be forever changed. I don't know if he's doing anything specifically to the Hornwood, but—"

"You don't have to convince me," said Hart. "He's bad. And what he's done has touched us all, I agree."

"That's right. That's my point," said Cora. "Imago is our common enemy. We want different things, but really, don't we want the *same* thing? Don't we want to see him fail? Don't we want to see him lose?"

"I do," said Anders. "I want him crushed. But while Victoria might say she wants to see him fail, she's still going to give him the Sand Coin. And if what you say about the Sand Coin is true, that would make him stronger. So you can say we all want the same thing, but we don't."

"Victoria doesn't want to give the Sand Coin to Imago, not really, she just feels like she *has* to." Cora took a deep breath. "But she wouldn't have to if we all worked together to rescue her brother. Then we work together to destroy the Door. And save the circus. And get the Sand Coin back to Tarian."

Out of the corner of her eye Cora saw Will's face break into a grin. Victoria gave Cora a grateful look, though it was tinged with doubt. No one said anything. The silence stretched out. And then Anders burst out laughing.

"This is your proposal? Even if I wanted to help Victoria get her brother—and I don't—it would be impossible. Going up against a magician is stupid. It'll only get us killed."

"Maybe," said Cora. "But this is bigger than any of us, as big as Hibaria and all of the Islands. Imago is evil, we all know this, and whatever he's planning will make the Storm look small. It'll affect *everyone*! I think we all know that. Yes, there's a chance we fail. We may even die. But there's a chance we can stop Imago, here and now, if we work together. It'll be dangerous, but you know this is the right thing to do, Anders."

"I won't work with her." Anders eyed Victoria. "You say it's the right thing to do, to risk our lives to fight Imago because he's bad. But so is she. She's a shifter."

Hart tensed and tightened his grip on his knife. Cora sighed. "It's true, Victoria is a shifter," she said to Hart. "But it's something she was born into. She's not an assassin for Augrind. What she is, is the result of someone else's choice long before she was born. She can't help that. She's *not* the same as Imago."

The explanation seemed to satisfy Hart. "Go on," he said.

"There's nothing more to say. She's a shifter," repeated Anders.

"Who saved your life," said Cora. "Not once but twice. The first time is what led to us finding out that she's a shifter. You think she didn't know the risk when she allowed us to see her arms? And then, after you wanted to kill her—'put her down' is how I think you said it—she saved you again. I honestly don't know why. And it wasn't just you who she saved, Anders. It was all of us. She spurred the wolves on, she made sure no one was left behind. She could have just ridden off on her own at far less risk to herself. The way we treated her, she should have. But she didn't. She may be a shifter, but she's not evil."

"She's a monster—"

"Who has acted less like one than any of us. Except Will maybe. And Hart." Cora looked at Anders, but he seemed unmoved by her words. Her heart sank. "What about the rest of you?" she asked. "Will you help rescue Victoria's brother?"

"You know I'm game," said Will. A moment later Hart nodded as well.

And then to Cora's surprise, Tesh spoke up. "I'm in." Turning to Anders and Dane, she added, "What Imago took from us with the Storm, he'll take from others. And we have a chance to stop that. You don't have to like her," she gestured toward Victoria. "I certainly don't. If it makes it easier, don't think of it as helping Victoria, think of it as depriving Imago of his most dangerous weapon."

"Huh," said Dane. "That's a good point."

Anders grimaced as he ran a hand through his hair and stared at the floor. At last he said, "Alright. What's the plan?"

"Well, I don't have a plan, necessarily," Cora began, "but—"

"Unbelievable," muttered Anders.

"But if we're all willing to come together to take on Imago, I *know* we can come up with one." Cora looked around the table. "Think about what we do with the circus, the amount of coordination and planning that is required to put on a performance. If we can do that, we can do this. We just have to know what we're dealing with. So, Victoria, tell us exactly what we're dealing with. Where *is* your brother?"

Victoria slowly exhaled. "This won't be easy," she said, shaking her head. "In fact, I don't know if it's possible."

"Well, that's what we want, really." Will cracked his knuckles. "What fun is it if it's not a challenge?"

"My brother is being held below us," said Victoria. "There's a secret stair in the library. It leads under the house to his prison. I was there, once, when Imago first put him there.

"At the bottom of the stair are two soldiers. And beyond the soldiers is a room, and Ori is in the middle of the room. He's on a rock, and it's kind of like an island with a pit surrounding it. There's a bridge across to him . . ."

"That doesn't sound so hard," said Cora. "Is the bridge guarded too?"

"You could say that. Imago has placed a spell on the bridge. Whoever crosses it forgets why they're there. Forgets what they meant to do. We can't cross to Ori without triggering the spell." Victoria paused and her eyes seemed to look inward. "Imago made me try. It was . . . it was like my mind was swept clean. With fire. And instead of wanting to rescue my brother, I only wanted to . . . to kill. For Augrind."

Cora bit her lip. This was going to be more difficult than she thought. She cleared her throat and asked, "How did you get off the bridge?"

"Imago pulled me off, and when he did my memories came back and I stopped thinking about Augrind. As Imago told me what had happened, he saw the expression on my face and he laughed. He told me it was forgetting magic, but not just any memory syphon spell; it was ancient forgetting magic from the Fenwood. *The Fenwood!* He had paid dearly for it, he told me. 'You'll sooner find the Augur Tree than overcome that enchantment,' he said."

Will stirred and frowned at the mention of the Fenwood, and Cora recalled their conversation in the merchant house. *He knows the Fenwood's power better than any of us,* she thought. *And judging from his face, he thinks this is beyond us. And if Will thinks we can't do it . . . No. There* has *to be a way.*

"Why don't you just shift?" asked Dane. "You could become a dragon or something. You'd make quick work of the guards and you could fly over the bridge, avoid the spell, and get your brother that way."

"I would, in a heartbeat, even if I knew with absolute certainty that I would lose myself by shifting again. But Imago thought of that. He put an enchantment over the entire island: I can't shapeshift here. No magic works here but his own."

"So it sounds like rescue is impossible," said Anders.

"I wouldn't say that," said Will as he leaned back in his chair. Cora stared at him, surprised. He grinned at her. "Look. It *sounds* impossible, but maybe there's something we're not considering, something we're not seeing. Maybe there's another way across to Ori. Or there's a way to counter the spell. Or maybe the spell doesn't work on everyone, something like that."

"I don't think magicians are that stupid," said Anders. "Besides, you heard Victoria. It's *Fenwood* magic."

Will shrugged. "Doesn't mean we should give up. Like Cora said, all of Hibaria is in danger because of Imago. We *have* to try. Besides, I think it'll be easy."

"I don't know about easy, but I agree that we have to try," Cora said. "And soon. Our window to act is pretty narrow. Imago is gone, but for how long?"

"We need a plan," said Anders stubbornly. "I'm not doing this without one." Tesh and Dane muttered agreement.

"Anders," said Victoria, "if you provide a distraction and draw the guards away, I'll try to rescue my brother with Cora's help. Maybe we can save him, maybe we can't, but we'll take the risk. You don't have to."

"I'm helping too," chimed in Will.

"How about this," said Cora. The pieces were falling into place. "Anders, Tesh, Dane, and Hart will create a diversion. You'll start a fire. The library makes the most sense, since the books will burn pretty quickly and easily, and it's near the entrance to the staircase that leads to the prison. The fire will have to be big enough to draw the guards from the prison, as well as the rest of the guards in the house, including any that might be near the Door. When the guards from below come up, Victoria and Will and I can sneak into the prison and try to free Ori. In the meantime, the Door will be unguarded, so Anders and the rest can slip through it and destroy the Door in the Hornwood. I'm guessing the Spindle will be gone by now. Then you find a place nearby to hide and wait for the circus. When Imago shows up with the circus and sees the Door gone, he'll be alarmed and leave immediately for Agendor. The circus would only slow him down, so he'll abandon them. Then you can come out of hiding, grab the circus, and go wherever you want.

"Meanwhile, once Will and Victoria and I have rescued Ori, we'll find a boat—there are boats here, right?" Victoria nodded. "The four of us can sail to Tarian. That is, if you want to. If you don't, that's fine—"

"I'd love to," said Victoria.

Cora beamed and looked around the table. "Well, what do you think?"

"I'd make a small change," said Will. "Anders and Hart go through the Door like you suggested. But have Tesh and Dane remain in the courtyard and destroy the Door here. Taking out both will be a real blow to Imago. After that, Tesh and Dane can get the boats ready to sail, including one for them. That way, once we've rescued Vic's brother, we can all just jump in the boats and go. Tesh and Dane can sail to the coast and meet up with Anders and the circus."

"Sounds good to me," said Cora. "Anders, what do you think? Are you in?"

Anders looked at the ceiling and thought for a minute, then shrugged.

"As long as the Spindle is gone, I think the plan's solid enough. Our part anyway," he gestured to Hart and Tesh and Dane. "I just hope for your sake that you succeed in your part. Seems pretty dicey. But that's your deal."

Cora didn't want to admit it, but she agreed with him. What she said, though, was, "Leave that to us, Anders. You do your job, we'll do ours."

"Alright then," he said. "When do we start?"

"As soon as possible."

CHAPTER TWENTY-SIX

THE RESCUE

THE CLOCK ON THE MANTEL chimed eleven times. They stood and looked at one another.

"Anders, Hart, Tesh, Dane," said Cora, "are you ready?" The four of them nodded.

"Anders, Hart, I guess this is goodbye then," said Will. "Good luck. We'll see you when we see you."

Anders grunted and started for the door. He along with the others carried shuttered lanterns.

"Remember, Tesh, the docks are through the door just past the guards' quarters. So be careful," said Victoria.

Tesh rubbed her nose. "We'll be fine. I just hope I remember to leave you a boat. We'll be burning the others to prevent pursuit, you know." She flashed them a smile that seemed anything but sincere. "Good luck."

After they had gone, Will put on his coat and slung his sword onto his back.

"Do you trust them?" asked Cora.

"I do," he said. "Hart for sure. And Tesh comes across as hard, but I think she's with us."

"What about you, Victoria? Do you trust them?"

Victoria was staring at the fire and didn't seem to hear. When she finally spoke, she asked, "Why are you doing this? We have no chance of rescuing my brother. None. So why? You *had* the Sand Coin. You could have taken it to save Tarian."

Cora wasn't sure how to reply. "It's . . . right. You're my friend, Victoria. I couldn't just leave you. Just like you can't leave Ori. Besides, it's not *no* chance. We'll figure it out. And when we do, we'll both get what we want."

"It's pretty close to no chance," muttered Victoria.

"Vic. You're forgetting something in all this." Will's face was serious. He paused and then spread his hands. "You have me. This is as good as done."

Victoria gave him a flat stare, but after a moment a hint of a smile formed around the edges of her mouth. "I certainly hope our success doesn't depend on your humility. Nevertheless, thank you for helping, Will."

"You're very, very welcome. Now then. Shall we be off?"

They crept along the hall, keeping to the shadows. At this late hour the house was silent as a tomb.

"The library is just ahead," whispered Victoria. She craned her neck to see around the corner. "It's clear." They scurried forward and slipped through a tall rosewood-colored doorway.

They were in a large room with vaulted ceilings. In the dimness, the dark beams that spanned the ceiling appeared to be woven together, forming a canopy above them. Before them was a wide aisle flanked by towering shelves. The shelves were stuffed with thick, leather-bound books. Cora had never seen so many. Burning them had been her idea, but it seemed a shame nevertheless.

As if reading her mind, Victoria said, "It's a good idea. They're important to him. And the guards know that, so they'll come. Besides, losing the books will hurt him, even if we . . . don't succeed in getting my brother."

Will pointed down the aisle. A ladder leaned against the shelves built into the far wall. Three-quarters of the way up was a figure, barely discernible in the shadows. It was descending slowly. From its movements, Cora guessed it was Dane.

"The entrance to the lower level is over there," said Victoria in a quiet voice. She waved off to her left. "Follow me." She ghosted away, her feet silent on the carpet. Cora and Will hurried to keep up. As they crept along, a soft chirp sounded from the far side of the library. It was Tesh's signal. Then came the others' signals in quick succession.

A tendril of smoke drifted down and across their path, and Cora held her arm over her nose and mouth. As the smoke thickened, Victoria held up a hand and they came to a halt in front of a bookshelf.

Under Victoria's direction they grabbed hold of the bookshelf and pulled. It swung silently away from the wall, revealing an open doorway. A stone stairway curved down into the floor.

"Hide here," whispered Victoria. When they had crowded behind a low shelf, she added, "Wait just a bit."

The smoke billowed and twisted across the ceiling like a creature blindly reaching out to grasp hold of them. Cora thought she could hear a crackle.

"Now," said Victoria.

Will stood and faced the stairway. He shouted, "Fire! Fire!" before ducking down again beside them in a fit of coughs.

They waited, and the crackle of flames grew and seemed to fill the room. Will started to stand again, but Victoria jerked him down as first one figure, then another, emerged from the passageway.

"Ring the bell!" shouted the first soldier. "I'll go for water!" They both dashed into the roiling smoke. As soon as they were gone, Victoria, Cora, and Will leapt from their hiding place and made their way down the curving stair.

The room they found themselves in was small and empty, apart from a table and two chairs. Behind the table was a single archway in a stone wall, flanked by two torches that hung in brackets. As they crossed the damp flagstones, Cora peered into the shadows of the archway and whispered, "Are you sure there are only two guards?"

"Imago doesn't need more. He doesn't even really need two," said Victoria.

They went through the archway and started down a tunnel. After a few steps the torchlight faded behind them. "Hold my hand," said Victoria. Cora found it and when Will had grasped hold of her other hand, Victoria led them forward. "I might not be able to shift here, but I can still see in the dark," she muttered. Then she added, "It's not far."

The air smelled of mold and dampness, and in the silence, Cora could hear the dripping and trickling of water. Ahead, a small gray rectangle appeared. It grew larger as they advanced, and presently, they came to the end of the passage and stopped.

They stood looking out on a wide, round room. A narrow walkway followed the wall around the entirety of the dimly lit chamber. The walkway had no railing, and it skirted a central well that fell away into blackness. In the middle of the well, level with Cora, was a column of rock upon which sat a boy. He looked to be about ten years old. A thin, stone bridge stretched from the rock to the walkway on the far side of the chamber.

"Ori," whispered Victoria, and Cora could hear love and pity and anger wrapped up in that single word.

Victoria moved forward and Cora and Will followed. Carefully they made their way along the stone walkway. Cora risked a glance down into the well and almost stumbled—she couldn't see the bottom. She quickly looked up and focused instead on the path. After a few moments she asked, "Can't Ori see us?" They had almost circled him completely, but the boy had barely stirred.

"No," said Victoria. "Just what Imago allows him to see." She gestured above her brother. "Those, pretty much." Cora looked up.

Thirteen stars filled the darkness over the rock, and it was their silver light that illuminated the room. But after a moment Cora realized they *weren't* stars—they merely looked like stars, and the more she stared at them, the less real they appeared.

"Are they supposed to be a Constellation?" she asked. She tilted her head. If it was, the constellation wasn't one of the twelve.

"Looks like a creature with a crown," said Will. "Or a ship. Or maybe it's a sheaf of wheat."

"Seems like you've really narrowed it down," Cora said drily.

"I don't know what it is," said Victoria.

They continued on the narrow path, hugging the wall to their left until they reached the bridge.

"I hope you have a plan," said Victoria. "Like I told you, when Imago made me try to walk across before, I forgot everything." She shuddered and left the part about Augrind unsaid.

Cora peered into the darkness all around. She had hoped for something, *anything*, to present itself that would make the rescue possible. But what had she expected? That Imago would leave a rope hanging from the ceiling that they could use to swing across the void? That he would build another bridge, one that Victoria somehow hadn't seen, that didn't have a spell cast on it? Cora felt embarrassed that she had been so foolish and so naïve.

She put a hand on Victoria's arm and drew an unsteady breath. "I suppose what Will said might be true. Maybe the spell only works on you." Cora fought down the fear that was rising within her, and managed to say, "I . . . I'll try to cross."

Will patted her on the shoulder as he edged around her. "Wouldn't work," he said as he turned to face the bridge. "You'd forget too."

"And you wouldn't?"

In answer, Will gave them a small smile, cracked his knuckles, and stepped onto the bridge.

He began walking. By the time he was halfway across, it was clear from his gait and posture that he was afraid. Cora couldn't see his face, but still she knew that Will was walking into the teeth of fear itself. And yet he did not slow. His feet did not stumble.

Cora and Victoria watched, open-mouthed, as Will, step by step, crossed the remaining length of the bridge until he reached the island.

Ori leapt to his feet, startled, apparently suddenly able to see Will. They exchanged words, and Will pointed back at them, but Cora couldn't hear what they were saying.

"He did it!" said Victoria. "He did it." There was wonder on her face, awe in her voice, and then she started to cry.

Will leaned down and lifted Ori. Then he started back across the bridge.

Watching Will return was harder than watching him go. It was the expression on his face. Fear filled his eyes and reshaped his mouth, making him all but unrecognizable. But resolve was there too, like a spark in the midst of the darkness.

But whatever hope Will could see, Ori could not. The boy first cowered in Will's arms, hiding from something unseen, and then writhed, trying to escape it. It took all of Will's strength to hold him and to keep them from plunging over the edge of the narrow bridge.

It was terrible to watch, to know the inner anguish they were both experiencing, and to see the danger they were in because of it. But Will's jaw was set, and his determination never wavered.

Will stopped and adjusted his hold on Ori. He whispered something in the boy's ear, and his words seemed to calm the child. And then Will was walking again, step after step, dragging himself and the boy forward. The whole way he fought to keep his footing.

They spilled onto the walkway, and Will collapsed to his knees. Victoria lifted Ori and clung to her brother and wept.

Cora knelt down beside Will. "That was really something," she said, shaking her head. "How did you know you could do that?"

Will frowned as he wiped sweat from his face. "I told you I'd been to the Fenwood. But I didn't mention the part where the Bear found me there and broke the spell."

"The Bear. The Constellation. You're serious?"

"Yes."

Cora was speechless. Questions flooded her mind, but she couldn't shape them into words.

Will continued. "My memories came back and the Bear gave me a lantern and this." He touched the sword on his back. "I was able to escape the Fenwood then. So when Vic mentioned that Imago used Fenwood magic on the bridge . . . I guessed it wouldn't work on me. And it didn't—I didn't forget a thing. But Imago must have woven another spell onto the bridge as well. A fear spell of some sort." He shrugged and looked uncomfortable. "We need to get out of here." He stood and brushed himself off. "Hope everything upstairs is clear."

"I can't thank you enough," said Victoria, touching Will's arm. "I'm sorry I doubted you." She pulled the Sand Coin from her bag and handed it to Cora. "And thank you, Cora. For even being willing to try this."

Cora hugged her. "Of course." Then, reaching into her coat, she brought out the vault. "This will only take a moment," she said. She placed the Sand Coin inside and closed the lid with a snap and pressed the brass buttons.

"If that's a vault, it won't work here," said Victoria, shaking her head. "Remember? Nothing but Imago's magic works here. You'll have to wait till we're off the island."

"Vaults seem to be more trouble than they're worth," said Will. "But no matter. We'll be on a boat soon enough."

Cora sighed, and tucked the vault back into her pocket.

They carefully made their way along the stone walkway in single file. This time Cora didn't look down into the abyss. When they reached the passage, Victoria led them into the darkness. Their footsteps echoed on the damp stones. Far ahead, they could just see the torchlight from guardroom. They crept forward as quietly as they could.

"Have the soldiers returned?" whispered Cora when they were close. "Can you hear them?"

Victoria listened a moment. "No, there's nothing."

As they emerged from the passage and crossed the room to the stair, Cora grew uneasy. Something wasn't right. She couldn't put her finger on it, but she knew something was amiss. Her eyes met Will's and he drew his sword. Victoria looked over her shoulder at Cora; she sensed it too.

Still, there was nothing to be done but go up. And so they ascended the stair.

When they stepped into the library, Cora suddenly realized the source of her alarm. There was no smoke. Not a trace. How had the guards already put out the fire? But then it struck her that even if the guards *had* managed to extinguish the fire, the smell of smoke would have remained. Which meant . . .

"What have we here?" said a voice. The air shimmered and a man appeared before them. Behind him were a dozen guards. The man's gaze locked onto Victoria and his lips curled up into a half-formed smile. "Wherever could you be going, child?"

CHAPTER TWENTY-SEVEN

IMAGO

IMAGO. ALL WAS LOST. AFTER everything they had gone through, after everything they had achieved, they had failed. Cora felt hollow.

"I asked you a question, Victoria," said Imago. "And it wasn't an unreasonable one. Wherever could you be going?" His gaze moved to Ori, then to Will, then to Cora. "Your reluctance to speak is disappointing."

As Cora stared at the magician, she realized that he was not what she had expected. He appeared . . . normal. Like a merchant or a low-level noble, perhaps. His clothes were fine, but not ornate, and there were ink stains on one of his fingers. And his voice . . . it was conversational, not overpowering, not demanding, not cruel. His eyes were even kind.

"I regret this," Imago said, making a vague gesture toward the stairway that led down to the prison, and Cora found that she regretted it too. They really shouldn't have tried to free Ori. "It pains me to have to take such extreme measures, but I'm afraid I'll have to lock all of you up. It's for your own good, you see. I *am* sorry it's come to this." Cora nodded.

Imago waved his hand, and without any hesitation Will slid his sword into its sheath.

"You lie," spat Victoria. "You've never regretted anything you've done. Not once."

When Victoria spoke, Cora seemed to awaken. The magician's words had sounded true, had been nothing if not reasonable. Her eyes widened as she realized how easy it had been for Imago to sway her. Cora had been, ever so briefly, completely taken in. She wanted to vomit.

The magician tilted his head and smiled as he cupped Victoria's face with his hand. "I *do* regret trusting you, child. I almost didn't believe Tesh when she told me what you were attempting. And yet here you are." He withdrew his hand and made a show of wiping it on his sleeve. "Now then, you will come with me."

At the mention of Tesh's name Cora went numb. It wasn't by chance, then, that they had been caught. She should have known Tesh would betray them.

One of the guards shoved Cora, and she staggered after the others. Imago led them out of the library. As they passed into the hall, to their left stood Anders and Tesh and Dane. Behind them were Felix and the Youngers. Hart was there too, and a guard stood beside him holding a knife to his throat. The guard pushed him forward and Will caught Hart before he could fall.

"Anders, the circus needs rest," said Imago. "Despite this unfortunate development with Victoria and these four, you'll still need to perform. Labryn Waite in a few days, unless I'm mistaken, no?" When Anders nodded, the magician said, "Very good. Get the animals settled and get some sleep. We'll talk in the morning."

Without waiting for a reply, Imago continued on. Cora gave Tesh a venomous look, but the curly-haired girl had already turned away.

"Are you alright? What happened?" Will asked Hart.

"Silence!" thundered Imago.

The guards pushed them forward and they stumbled along the shadowy hall after the magician. After several minutes of brisk walking, he turned and led them up a twisting, lamp-lit stair. The guards marched behind, their hard boots echoing on the stone.

As they ascended, Cora ran her hand over the vault in her coat pocket. *So close to succeeding,* she thought, *and yet so far.* Sadness and anger flooded through her. The magician would take the Sand Coin, and everything she had worked for would be for nothing. It wasn't fair.

They came to the top of the stair and were unceremoniously pushed into a spacious, round room. It was filled with curiosities. The magician walked past small tables covered in delicate metal instruments, the likes of which Cora had never seen. Many of the devices had knobs and dials the color of bone and pearl, and adjustable lenses that caught the orange, flickering lamplight and multiplied it. Imago lowered himself into a chair beside the fireplace and flicked a finger casually toward the hearth. As he turned to look at them, blue and green flames sprang up from the grate. Cora could feel the heat from across the room.

"Give it to me," he said, looking at Victoria.

Her eyes flashed defiantly. "I don't have it. We weren't able to find the outlaws."

"You wouldn't have returned here without the Sand Coin," said Imago. "I'll only say this once more: Give it to me."

Victoria threw her bag at the magician's feet. "See for yourself."

Imago didn't so much as glance at the bag. Instead, he rose from his chair and made a fist. Victoria began to scream in pain.

"Stop!" shouted Cora. She pulled the vault from her pocket and held it up. "Leave her alone! I have it."

Imago smiled and extended his hand. Victoria collapsed, sobbing. Cora hesitated and then walked forward and handed the vault to the magician.

"Do you see how easy that was?" asked Imago. When he glanced down at the vault, his expression hardened. "Trying to send it away, I see. I was right to take precautions." He twisted open the lid and removed the Sand Coin with care, then tossed the vault aside.

As he looked down at what he held, his face changed. The magician's bored impassivity fell away and his eyes shone with unbridled greed and lust. With a low laugh, he lifted the white disc and slipped its leather cord over his head.

His triumphant expression was immediately replaced by one of confusion, then fear. Imago crashed to his knees, and his head slowly bent forward until it almost touched the floor. It was as though a great weight, like an anchor, was pulling him down. His fingers frantically tore at the leather cord.

"Master!" Several of the guards ran to the magician, but before they could reach him, Imago, with a shriek, managed to slip the Sand Coin from around his neck. He staggered to his feet and roughly pushed the guards away.

He swayed, taking ragged breaths, his wild eyes fixed on the Sand Coin. Within moments, though, the magician had regained his composure. He stooped, and using a metal rod, he carefully lifted the white disc by its cord. Imago placed it on a table and examined it. He murmured a few words that Cora didn't understand and prodded the Sand Coin with the rod. Nothing happened. He spoke again, using different words, and waited expectantly. The result was the same. With increased impatience the magician uttered phrase after unknown phrase. Finally, he said something that included the word 'Tarian.' The Sand Coin, for a brief moment, shimmered.

"Rooted!" Imago snarled. He swore and hurled the metal rod across the room. "After all this, the Sand Coin is rooted to the city of Tarian! Cursed old magic!" He upended one of his tables. A glass sphere hit the floor and shattered, broken shards scattering everywhere. "But I need to use it *here!*"

The magician started to pace, flexing his fingers, his eyes wild. Then he stopped. "Anything rooted can be unrooted," he mused, "if one is willing to go far enough." He bent down and gingerly picked up the Sand Coin by its leather cord. "I *will* have your power." He carefully lowered it into a pocket of his robes. As he stood, he shouted, "Prepare the ships! We have a city to destroy!"

He turned and his eyes narrowed when he saw Cora and the others. It was as though he had forgotten they were there.

Without a word he strode to the wall. He placed his hand on the stone and suddenly there was a door where there had been none. Imago pulled a ring of keys from his robes and inserted one of them into the lock. "I'll deal with you when I return," he said, looking at Victoria as he opened the door. Then, to a guard he said, "Throw them in."

CHAPTER TWENTY-EIGHT

DEPARTURE

THE DARKNESS IN THE CELL was complete and the silence was heavy. Finally, Cora found her voice. "He's going to wipe out Tarian. Just because the stupid Sand Coin won't work for him!"

There was a flicker and a soft, yellow light sprang to life. Will leaned forward and placed a lit candle in the middle of the floor. It illuminated a small, square room made of black stone.

"I don't think Imago wants to destroy Tarian out of spite," Will said. "He wants the Sand Coin's power and it seems the only way he can get it is to take out the city."

"Maybe," Cora muttered. "Either way, the result is the same."

"We need to get out of here if we're to stop him," said Will. "Any thoughts, Vic?"

"We're not leaving this place." Victoria looked behind them. "That's another one of Imago's Doors. I didn't even know about this one. But even if we had the key, there's no keyhole on this side. This room is sealed."

Will whistled. "That's that, then."

With nothing else to do, the five of them sat on the floor. Cora leaned back against the wall. After a few minutes she said, "Tell us what happened, Hart."

Hart cradled his injured arm in his lap and shrugged. "There's not a whole lot to tell. Anders and Tesh and Dane and I started the fires in the library, then hid in the hall like we planned. When the guards from the courtyard came running in, we slipped past them and went to the Door. Anders and I were about to unlock it when it opened. And there was Imago and your circus. Immediately Tesh told him how relieved she was to see him, and that you," Hart nodded to Victoria, "were up to something in the library. Anders and Dane didn't say a word, but I wasn't having it. I tried to stab Imago with my knife."

"And?" asked Cora.

"And he's a magician so it didn't go well."

"Where's your horn?" asked Will.

"He took it."

"I hate to say it, but I'm not surprised by Tesh. Or Anders, for that matter." Cora glanced at Will. He had trusted them. *I guess he can't be right all the time,* she thought. "So what do we do?"

"Nothing we can do," said Victoria. Her voice was empty. "Like I said, that's a Door. And I guarantee you Imago is the only one with a key. We sit and wait until he comes back."

"If he's going to Tarian that could be days. Maybe weeks!" said Cora. "We'll be dead by then."

Victoria shook her head. "He won't let us die. Not after what we did to him." She eyed each of them in turn. "And besides . . . I'm more valuable to him alive." She looked down at the markings on the backs of her hands and made a face. "I'm sorry you're all a part of this now."

"We chose to be a part of this, Victoria," said Cora. "You didn't choose for us." She reached over and squeezed her friend's hand. "Whatever's next, we face it together."

Hart nodded in agreement and Will said, "That's right." Ori leaned over and put his head on his sister's shoulder. And then, because there was nothing else to do, they all closed their eyes and drifted off to sleep.

At first, Cora wasn't sure whether she was awake. She blinked her eyes. Nothing. Complete darkness. She stifled a yawn and stretched, and she felt the circus token shift against the skin of her neck. A thread of guilt wormed through her, but she pushed it down. It was a small price to pay for dreamless sleep.

It took a moment before she remembered where she was. Cora felt around on the ground in front of her until she found a pool of hardened wax. It was all that remained of Will's candle. Around her she could hear the slow, even breathing of the others. Then beside her Victoria stirred, whimpered in her sleep, and cried out.

Suddenly, there was a click and the Door opened. Its hinges squeaked painfully in Cora's ears as light flooded the cell. She covered her eyes with one hand as she gripped her knife with the other.

"Thinking about stabbing me?" said a girl's voice. "I wouldn't advise it."

The others were awake now and they all scrambled to their feet. As Cora's eyes adjusted to the light, a figure appeared in the doorway. It was Tesh.

"You traitor!" Cora lunged forward, but Will caught her arm.

"She's rescuing us, Cor."

Tesh twirled a set of keys in her hand. "Will's always been the sharper of you two," she said. "Now are you coming, or what?"

"But you turned us over to Imago!" said Cora.

"You're so dense. It was the only logical thing to do. I betrayed you to get his trust. Even Anders and Dane picked up on that. As soon as Imago came through that Door, he was going to find you and Victoria and Will. No way around it," said Tesh. "If I hadn't done it, we'd all be in here together. And that wouldn't leave anyone to steal these." She held up the keys. "Is it starting to make sense now? I tried to use small words."

Cora made a face and brushed past her into Imago's study. "You just happened to know about this Door? Victoria didn't even know it was here. And you stole Imago's keys?"

Tesh bared her teeth, but it looked more like a snarl than a smile. "I followed you up to Imago's study. I hid in the doorway and watched Imago unmask the Door. And yes, I stole his keys, just like I stole your bracelet: effortlessly. I would have gotten the Sand Coin too, but he didn't have it with him. But hey, if you really don't trust me, then by all means, stay here. I'd be more than happy to lock you up again."

"Take it easy," said Will. "How many guards are still here? When did Imago leave?"

"Oh, he hasn't left yet. It takes longer to get a fleet of ships ready to sail than you might think. Especially if several of them have unexpected leaks."

At these words, hope flared within Cora. There was still time! And if Imago hadn't destroyed the vault . . . She stooped, searching among the fragments of broken glass on the floor. And there it was! Cora snatched it up, closed the lid, and slipped the box into her pocket.

Will laughed. "'Unexpected leaks,' huh? That was pretty risky, Tesh. I'm impressed."

"Wasn't just me. It was the whole circus," the girl said. Then, turning to Cora she added, "You need to know something. I may not like you, and you may not like me, but we made a deal. I do what I say I'm going to do. It looks like you all freed Victoria's brother, but we still have some Doors to destroy, and unless I'm mistaken, you'll want to get your Sand Coin back from Imago. Now you have a chance to do that."

Cora flushed. It was twice now she had been wrong about Tesh. "I'm sorry," she muttered. Tesh merely arched an eyebrow.

"How much time do we have before Imago sails?" asked Victoria.

"Not much, but I think we can work with it. We delayed him as best we could without raising his suspicions—which took some doing—but I was only able to get the keys just now. We maybe have an hour."

They stood in the shadows beside the doorway that opened onto the wharf. The smell of tar and salt swirled in the air, and the cry of a gull drifted down from somewhere high above.

"Keep down," whispered Tesh. She ducked through the doorway, and one by one, on hands and knees, they followed her.

Tesh led them behind a row of barrels and across the cold paving stones until they were opposite the first pier. Anders and Dane were there, crouched in the shadows.

"Take a look," Anders said in a low voice. They peeked over the barrels. Dozens of ships, each packed with soldiers, floated in the harbor. Only a few remained at dock.

"That one is Imago's." Anders pointed to a large vessel with three masts still moored to the pier nearest them. *Blade of the Deep* was emblazoned on its bow. A steady stream of servants carrying boxes and crates of food snaked along the pier and up the gangplank.

"You think the Sand Coin is on board?" asked Cora.

"I do," said Tesh. "He didn't have it with him earlier, so it's probably in his cabin."

"Imago has been on the ship a few times, but right now he's in there." Anders nodded toward a building at the other end of the wharf. It was made of timber and plaster and it commanded a view of the entire harbor. "I heard him tell the captain to be ready to sail in thirty minutes. That was about five minutes ago."

"Now's the time then," said Tesh.

"To what, just go aboard and grab it?" asked Cora.

"Pretty much. You all should probably put these on first, though." Anders picked up a bundle of clothes and tossed it to her. It was green and black livery. "I took three sets from the servants' quarters. I figured you and Will and Victoria would do this."

Cora glanced at Victoria, then Will. "Are you with me?"

Will barked a laugh. "Of course I'm with you. Vic?"

Victoria caught up one of the servants' shirts and slipped it over her head. "Whatever's next, we face it together," she said.

After they were dressed, Anders handed them some crates. "These'll help you blend in. Be quick. We'll wait for you here."

Victoria squatted down and looked her brother in the eye. "I'll be right back, Ori," she said. "But if anything does happen, stick with Hart, alright?" The boy nodded. "And Hart, we'll look for the horn too."

"Thanks," said Hart.

Cora, together with Will and Victoria, rose and walked across the wharf to the pier. They joined the end of a line of servants that was slowly boarding Imago's ship.

"Follow me," murmured Victoria. "I know where to go. And Cora, the vault should work out here on the water. So as soon as we find the Sand Coin . . ."

They shuffled forward, their heads down. All they had to do was find Imago's cabin, locate the Sand Coin, and send it to Mr. Blackwood. Then get off the ship before they were caught.

As they moved up the gangplank, Cora kept expecting fear to well up inside her. This was a boat, after all, and this was the sea. But the fear never came. Cora only felt a dull calm. The token was working.

They stepped onto the deck and Victoria led them aft, past scurrying servants and shouting sailors. She was about to enter a door below the quarterdeck when a horn blasted.

"Make ready to cast off! Our Lord and Master approaches!"

Cora whipped around and craned her neck, looking back toward the wharf. She didn't have to search long. There, halfway down the pier was Imago, his white cloak billowing behind him as he marched toward the ship. Cora grasped Victoria's sleeve, but her friend had already seen the magician.

"This way!" Victoria hissed, and pulled them toward an open hatch. As the servants scurried for the gangplank, Cora and Will followed Victoria down the ladder. They found themselves in the darkened belly of the ship, surrounded by piles of supplies and soldiers' hammocks hanging from the rafters.

"Perfect," muttered Cora.

"Certainly not what we planned," Will said. "But then again, that's kind of how things have been going."

"First we hide," said Victoria. "Then we figure out what to do."

Muffled shouts sounded above them as the sailors readied the ship to cast off. As Cora and Victoria and Will crawled beneath a canvas tarp, the ship creaked as it came away from the pier. Then slowly, ever so slowly, it began to move forward through the water. They were heading for open sea.

CHAPTER TWENTY-NINE

RETRIEVAL

THE THREE OF THEM SAT beneath the tarp, listening to the groaning of the ship. After a few minutes Will said, "I didn't even think about this till now, but are you doing alright, Cora? I know it can't be easy to be on a boat again."

Cora felt the token against her skin. The token took away the difficulty of being on the boat, but she couldn't exactly tell that to Will. She felt guilty lying, but what else could she do? "It's hard," she said. "But we don't really have another option."

More silence. Then Will said, "So what's our play now? Vic, do you have any ideas?"

"Imago will call up the winds," said Victoria. "He's impatient and will call up the winds to hasten the voyage. He'll be on deck for that. When that happens, we'll slip into his cabin and get the Sand Coin."

"How do we know he'll leave it in his cabin?" asked Cora.

"We don't. But he can't wear it, and you saw how much it unnerved him to even pick it up, so hopefully that's what he's done."

"He could be calling up the winds right now," Will whispered. "Maybe we're missing our chance."

"I've sailed this way with him before," said Victoria. "Imago will want to clear the strait first. The water between the mainland and Marddir, the larger island to the south and east, is full of sand bars and shallows, and is treacherous in high winds. We'll be in deeper waters well after nightfall. That's when he'll do it."

It had been several hours since they had set sail, and it was unbearably hot and stuffy under the tarp. A handful of soldiers had come below and a chorus of soft snores now filled the belly of the ship. The deck above was quiet.

"Are you ready?" Victoria's voice was barely audible.

Neither Cora nor Will answered, but they quietly pushed away the canvas and stood. Soft starlight filtered into the hold from an open hatch. The sleeping soldiers were gilded in silver and swayed gently in their hammocks.

Victoria led them through the maze of supplies to the foot of the ladder. "There are dozens of sailors on a ship this size," whispered Victoria. "If we're seen, most will assume we belong here if we don't act suspiciously. Just move with purpose." She flashed them a rare smile and scrambled up the ladder.

The cool breeze tugged at Cora's hair and made her eyes water. Above, the stars were just beginning to appear. To the west, the dark contours of the mainland stood out against the fading sunset. Dozens of ships, like so many black insects, filled the waters around them.

Victoria touched Cora's arm and nodded toward the forecastle. Three figures stood there, facing the opposite direction. The shadows made it difficult to see, but one of them wore a long cloak. A gust of wind caught it and it unfurled like a flag.

"White," said Will in a low voice. "That's him. Let's go."

Cora and Will followed Victoria across the deck, past the mainmast and the lifeboat, then aft. Victoria ducked through a low door below the quarterdeck. The narrow hall they found themselves in was lit with oil lamps.

"These are the officers' quarters," Victoria whispered as they passed two doors. "And this cabin is Imago's."

Cora's heart thumped in her chest. She glanced behind them along the hallway. "It's clear," she said. Victoria opened the door and they crowded inside.

Three glowing glass spheres floated near the ceiling and cast the cabin in a harsh, white light. Despite it being Imago's cabin, it was a cramped space with a single chair and a small round table crowded in the middle of the room. A number of odds and ends—mostly papers and books and quills and inkwells—were spread across the table. Paper weights secured the scattered documents. Hart's horn was among them, but there was no sign of the Sand Coin. Will retrieved the horn and slung it across his body.

Victoria bent down and rummaged through a set of cabinets built into the wall beneath the windows. After a few moments she straightened and shook her head. Cora had similar luck with a set of drawers.

"He's a magician," said Will. "Think about how he hid the Door in his study. It was there, but it was masked. He probably did the same thing with the Sand Coin. It's probably here, just invisible to us."

"If it's invisible, we can't—" Cora began.

"There!" Will exclaimed. He edged around the table and stood looking down at a spot on the narrow sill beneath the windows. "Do you see that?" he asked. He crouched and tilted his head. "It's a faint shadow."

Cora didn't see anything. Victoria gave no indication that she did either.

Will reached out and his hand stopped a few inches from the sill. With a visible effort he closed his fingers around *something*. And then, suddenly, the Sand Coin was in his hand.

"I don't believe it," whispered Cora.

"Quick, write Mr. Blackwood a note," said Will. "He needs to know Imago's coming."

Cora snatched up a quill and pulled the stopper from a bottle of ink. She scribbled a few lines and then reached in her coat for the vault.

At that moment, the ship heaved and surged forward, as though pushed from behind by an enormous hand. Cora lost her balance, tumbled first into Victoria, and then slammed into the table. There was a splintering crunch.

"Oh no," she moaned.

"Are you hurt?" Will scrambled to his feet.

Cora withdrew her hand from her coat and held up the broken fragments of the vault. It had been completely shattered.

They looked at one another, eyes wide.

"That's it then," said Cora. Her voice was hollow.

The ship lurched again and its timbers creaked and popped as it gained speed.

"He's called the winds," said Victoria. "We need to get off the ship." She grabbed Cora's wrist and pulled her from the room. They were halfway down the hallway when one of the doorways opened and an officer stepped out.

"You there!" he shouted, but Victoria barreled into him, punching him hard in the stomach. He tumbled back into his room with a grunt.

They burst onto the deck. The wind had risen to a howl, and the sails were so full it looked as though they might tear under the strain.

"The lifeboat!" shouted Victoria. They staggered forward, gripping the rail, until they were next to the small boat. Will thrust the Sand Coin into Cora's hands and drew his sword and slashed the ropes that secured the lifeboat to the deck. As the ropes fell away, a streak of blue fire tore through the air just above their heads. Cora turned and there, not twenty paces away, was Imago, his hands upraised.

"You have nowhere to go," he said, and though the howling of the wind was deafening, his voice cut through it like a jagged knife. "Drop the Sand Coin, girl, or suffer unimaginable pain." Lightning danced on the magician's fingertips.

Victoria looked over her shoulder at Cora and Will, and her blue-green eyes flashed fiercely. But there was sadness there too. The scales on the backs of her hands glittered. "Boat," she said, and as she turned to face Imago she had already started to shift.

It happened quickly, quicker than the lightning that flickered in Imago's hands. Victoria was a sea serpent, a massive thing armored in emerald, and the deck of the *Blade of the Deep* gave way beneath the snake with a splintering groan. Black water roared in and the ship began to come apart. As Cora and Will grabbed hold of the starboard rail, the lifeboat slid over the side. It spun in the air and its hull hit the water with a slap. A moment later, Cora and Will jumped.

Somehow, despite the heaving sea and the howling wind, they landed in the boat. The small craft bobbed in the swirling waters that were made more turbulent by broken pieces of the sinking ship that crashed down all around them.

The sea serpent that was Victoria rose up, until it was higher than the mast. Its scaled body swayed in the raging wind, and then dropped like a thunderbolt toward where Imago still stood on the broken ship. But as the serpent came down, lightning streaked up. The crackling ribbon of white struck the snake just below its head, searing into the scales and soft flesh of its neck.

"No!" screamed Cora, but then the snake hit the water and the ensuing wave nearly engulfed the boat. They were spun away like a leaf and it was all Cora could do to not fall overboard. When she regained her feet, she strained to see if she could catch a glimpse of Victoria. But there was no sign of her friend.

Will grabbed hold of a coil of rope that was tied to a ring in the bow of their boat. "We need to get out of here!" he shouted.

"We can't just leave her!"

"We're not!" Will flung the rope toward a patch of open water.

"Where's—?" Cora began, but then the sea serpent rose from the inky waves beside them. When Cora saw the raw wound on the snake's neck, she gasped. "Oh Victoria!" But the snake did not acknowledge her, at least not in a way that Cora could see. Instead, it swam past them and caught up the rope in its mouth. A moment later the rope went taut and the lifeboat sped away.

It wasn't long before Imago's fleet disappeared behind them. The sea serpent that was Victoria set an unflagging pace, and pulled them south across the starlit water.

Cora and Will sat on the bottom of the boat, facing one another.

"Can't say I saw that coming," said Will.

"Do you think Imago drowned?"

Will's face was skeptical. "I wouldn't count on it. But we can hope. Vic *did* destroy his ship, and *maybe* in the chaos he drowned."

Cora looked at the ripples of the water caused by the sea serpent and shook her head. "That burn on her neck looked bad. I hope she's alright." Then she added, "Do you . . . do you think Victoria will be herself? When she changes back, I mean?"

"I don't know," said Will. "She was scared that if she shifted again, it would really change her."

"But she did it anyway. She didn't even hesitate."

"And now she's bringing us back to Tarian." Will glanced at the Sand Coin in Cora's lap. "We still won't be in time, though, will we?"

"I don't think so," said Cora with a sigh. "The tidal surge happens at moonset." To the east, the moon was rising, a hair-thin, golden crescent. "She'll be setting around three tomorrow afternoon and there's no way we'll be back by then."

Will was quiet for a time. Then, "You really are handling this well," he said. "Being on a boat again."

Cora met his eye and then looked away. "It helps if you don't remind me."

"Cora." Will cleared his throat and then said, "Your . . . your circus token probably helps, doesn't it?"

Cora looked down before she could stop herself. The silver token hung outside her coat. It must have slipped out when she jumped from the ship.

"I, uh, I," she stammered. But what could she say? He had caught her. Shame and guilt washed over her. Anger too. "It's not your concern!" she snapped.

Will's face was unreadable. Eventually he said, "I get it, you know."

The words caught her off guard. "What do you mean?"

"The token makes you forget your nightmares. And yours are terrible. It dulls your bad memories, and you have a lot of them. For you, the token is . . . like a gift. Who wouldn't want that?"

Cora felt like he was laying a trap for her, but she didn't care. So she just nodded. It was, after all, exactly how she felt.

"And as far as Augrind goes . . . one token only helps him a little, right?"

Cora listened for the sarcasm, but it didn't seem to be there. So again, she nodded.

"So I get it," said Will. "I get why you kept it. If the tokens worked on me in the same way, I would probably be tempted to keep it too."

"Aren't you going to tell me to get rid of it?"

"Would you listen if I did?"

"No," she said.

They sat for a long time, looking up at the stars as they slowly coursed across the sky, at the sickle of the moon as it cut through the night.

"The truth," said Cora as she stared at the moon, "is that I hate it.

I hate that I need it." She squeezed the silver disc between her thumb and finger, and felt the images of the birds press painfully into her skin. "I'm so ashamed. I hate that because I choose to wear it, I'm choosing to help Imago and Augrind, even if it is only a little bit. Imago killed my family, and he'd do it again, and I'm helping him! It's absolutely the last thing I want to do. But it's been seven years and I still can't be near a boat without falling apart. And those nightmares . . . I can't bear the thought of having them again. When I wake up from a dream of the Storm, it's like it's happened all over again, like they're dying all over again. It's so fresh and raw and terrible. So I kept it. I hate it, but I'm keeping it." She fell silent. Will watched her, unblinking.

"How do you do it?" Cora asked. "You have plenty of bad memories. And I know you have nightmares. How do you numb yourself to them? How do you turn off those memories?"

"Turn them off?" Will ran a hand through his hair and laughed. "I can't turn them off. They're there. Always. Fighting the snow beast in the Fenwood is always there, and it's terrifying. Memories of my father, they're always there. I . . . wrestle with them, maybe, but I've had to accept that they are mine, and they're with me. They're a part of my story, and somehow that gives me a kind of peace."

"I don't think I could be strong enough to do that," muttered Cora.

"I'd help you," said Will. "If you'd let me. And I know Vic would too."

"And what would you do? What *could* either of you do?"

Will shrugged. "Be your friend. We'd be there for you when you need it. Share your burden."

"And that would make these dreams, these memories easier to live with?" Her tone was harsh, but Cora didn't care.

"I think so," said Will. "The nightmares would still be horrible, the memories would still be bad, *but you wouldn't be alone,* and that *would* make things easier. And you'd be fighting back without surrendering anything to the enemy. I know that's something you want, Cora."

She *did* want that, and she wanted it badly. The cost, though, was so high . . .

Cora turned and looked along the rope that stretched away and disappeared into the water a stone's throw in front of the boat. Just below the surface she could see the body of the sea serpent that was Victoria, its scales shimmering in the moonlight. The snake's pace did not slow, its course did not waver.

Victoria had shifted, despite what it might cost her. She had been willing to do it in order to save Cora and Will, in order to fight Imago, even if doing so stripped away who she was. *Victoria* had not considered the cost too high. And if her friend had lost a part of herself in the shifting . . . Cora would still be there for her, even then. And Cora suspected Victoria knew that.

With that realization, the tightness in Cora's chest, a tightness she hadn't even realized was there, began to loosen. It was like a thread had been pulled, and an unraveling had begun. Yes, to get rid of the token would be enormously difficult, but she *could* do it. Her friends would be by her side, and that was worth more than she ever would have guessed.

"If . . . if I were to get rid of it," said Cora, "right now, I would be a mess. The memories would overwhelm me. You know that, right?"

"I know," said Will.

"I could wait till we get to Tarian. It would probably be better . . . but I don't want to. I want to get rid of it now."

Will edged closer and took her hand.

Cora reached up with the other and pulled the token from around her neck. And then, before she could stop herself, she threw it into the sea.

C H A P T E R   T H I R T Y

DECISION

WHEN CORA RELEASED THE CIRCUS token, the smell of the sea, the rocking of the boat, the feel of the breeze on her face, stirred memories that had, in her waking hours, lain dormant for years. She had relived the Storm in her nightmares, but those dreams, as powerful as they had been, seemed pale and weak when compared with what now raged inside her mind. Cora huddled against the side of the boat. Her jaw was clenched and she squeezed her eyes shut.

Sorrow and fear, guilt and anger assailed her as the Storm once again unfolded in her mind's eye. Sorrow for the loss of her parents and Hildi, fear of the enormous and pitiless power of the sea, guilt for her own survival. And anger that it had happened at all. Cora was now forced to face what she had so long sought to avoid.

"I can't do this," she whimpered. She squeezed Will's hand as hard as she could.

"I know," said Will. "I know it feels that way. Just breathe, Cor. One breath at a time."

She inhaled through her nose, breathed out through her mouth. "It's so bad, Will. It's so terrible. They didn't deserve to die, not like that."

"No, they didn't."

The salt stung her nose and she coughed. Why had she thrown the token away? This was all too much to bear. She tried to push the memories down, but could not.

"Tell me about your family," said Will.

"Not the best time for that."

"No, really."

Cora didn't want to, but anything was better than silence. She breathed in, breathed out. "My father was kind," she said. "He had brown eyes. He squinted when he laughed. He laughed a lot."

"What made him laugh?"

Cora pushed against the images of the Storm, pushed them aside and thought back, sifting through her memories. "Hildi made him laugh. I don't know how she did it, but she always knew how to make him laugh. They used to tease each other, but not in a way that was hurtful. There was just something about how they related to each other. It was comfortable to be around, to watch, to listen to."

Cora paused as she let her mind drift. "He brought out a different side of Hildi too. Made her more . . . thoughtful. Compassionate maybe." Cora tugged at the beads of her bracelet and looked down at it. "You asked me once why this was so important. It was a gift from my sister. I think my father put the idea in her head to give it to me. She and I had fought, which was rare, and I was in the wrong, but I didn't want to admit it. Hildi shouldn't have been the one to ask for forgiveness, but she did anyway. And she gave me this. She called it a peace offering. She said it didn't matter who had been wrong. To be whole was better than to be broken. That was right before the Storm. I've always regretted not going to her first."

They sat quietly for a long time, listening to the boat and the waves and the wind.

Eventually Will asked, "And your mother?"

"She was strong. Not that my father wasn't, but I remember thinking of Mother as a rock, as someone who was always there, and that was a comfort. When I was small, I was scared of the dark. I remember once I couldn't sleep because of the shapes of the shadows on the wall, and I climbed out of bed and found her beside the fire, mending the nets. She hardly said a word, but she held me and I felt so safe." Cora rubbed her eyes. She hadn't thought about that night in years. It stung to remember, but there was warmth there too.

"They didn't deserve to die," she said again. The words tasted bitter in her mouth. "And it wasn't just them. Thousands died in the Storm, and none of them deserved it."

"I imagine that makes you angry at Imago," said Will.

Cora looked up. "Imago, yes. But also the Constellations. They could have done something."

Will nodded. "Maybe."

"Maybe? The Bear saved you. The Badger saved Hart. There's no 'maybe' about it. They could have, but they didn't." She looked up at the stars. They were so close, so bright, and yet so, so far away.

"I suppose you're right," said Will. "I hadn't thought about it like that before."

To the east, the sky showed a hint of gray. The moon was now almost directly overhead, between the red star and the Badger.

"What was it like?" asked Cora. "Talking to the Bear?"

Will pursed his lips and his eyes grew distant. "It was comforting, I guess. The Bear didn't say much, but it gave me the sword and a lantern to fight the snow beast. It gave me courage. It gave me what I needed. Does that answer your question?"

Cora shrugged. "I don't know. I just want to know how to think of them. The Sky Lords, I mean."

As the night retreated before the dawn, the serpent that was Victoria began to slow. Will noticed it first. "She must be exhausted," he said.

"And we still have a ways to go." He peered at the coastline. "Do you recognize anything, Cora?"

A gust of wind cut through her coat, and Cora looked over her shoulder. She gasped. Arrayed across the northern horizon was Imago's fleet. Though the ships were distant, Cora could see that their sails were full. Imago *had* survived, had rallied his ships, and had called the winds once more. Even as she watched, the gusts gained strength and the waves began to grow.

"Victoria!" she shouted. She scrambled to the rope and yanked at it. When nothing happened, she leaned over the gunwale and slapped the water. "Victoria!" she called again.

The head of the sea serpent rose above the waves and fixed her with its blue-green eye.

"They're coming!" Cora pointed to the north. "Imago is coming!"

The snake responded instantly. It dove beneath the waves and the boat suddenly shot forward with renewed speed.

Cora had thought they had been making good time before. But now the little boat fairly flew over the water. As the sun rose, Cora spied Whitewall, perched atop a stretch of chalky cliffs. She and Will exchanged glances, amazed that they had come so far so quickly. The village slid past and was soon lost to sight behind them.

The morning stretched on, the coastline slipped by, and slowly, ever so slowly, Imago's fleet began to gain on them. Cora couldn't tell if it was because Victoria's strength was flagging, or Imago's winds were growing stronger, but the ships were closing the distance.

"If he catches us," said Cora, "I'm throwing this overboard." She held up the Sand Coin. "I'm not letting him have it."

"Hold onto it for now," Will said with excitement. He pointed. "Look!"

"What? I don't see anything!"

"It's the Eye! I can't believe it, but we're almost to Tarian! And if you squint, I *think* that's the top of the Iron Spire! Vic's done it! We're going to make it!"

Cora's breath caught. There, on the horizon was the city's island watchtower. She looked over her shoulder at the fleet, and then forward to the Eye. They *would* make it. All they needed now was the new Master of Tides.

Suddenly Cora had an idea. She scrambled to the front of the boat, leaned over the side, and slapped the water. Moments later the sea serpent's head emerged from the waves. Its eyes were bloodshot, clouded with pain, and beyond weary. The journey had taken a larger toll on her friend than Cora could have imagined. She choked back a sob, but managed to say, "If you can, take us right past the watchtower, Victoria. And then on to Tarian. We're almost there!"

The sea serpent adjusted course.

"Flags?" asked Will.

"Flags," said Cora. "Mr. Blackwood won't let us down."

They were still some distance from the thick tower of green stone when its fire sprang to life. The fire was red, signaling a coming attack to Tarian. The watchmen had spotted Imago's fleet. A few moments later, the faint blast of a horn echoed across the water. Tarian had seen the signal and had sounded the alarm.

As their boat neared the Eye, Cora waved her arms and shouted. Moments later, a watchman appeared on the battlements. Before he could speak, Cora called out, "Use the flags to tell Overseer Blackwood that the ships are Imago's. But tell him we are bringing the Sand Coin and to be on the docks with the new Master!" The watchman's mouth fell open. "Do you understand?" demanded Cora. The man nodded, and disappeared into the tower.

Cora couldn't remember the last time the Eye's flags *had* been used, but as Works Leader she had insisted those employed by the Water Works watch for them anyway. If all went well, Finn or one of the others would see the flags, and relay the message to Mr. Blackwood, and he would be ready for them.

Suddenly the boat heaved to the side and almost capsized. A twisting coil of the sea serpent had brushed the hull. Beneath the surface, its scaled body thrashed furiously against the water.

"Her strength is starting to go," said Will.

Cora looked behind them. "Imago is closing, but I think we're too far ahead." Under her breath she whispered, "Hold on, Victoria. We're almost there!"

With painful slowness the Iron Spire came into view, then all the rest of Tarian. At first, the sprawling city was an indistinct mass of blocks and shapes piled atop one another, but they slowly resolved into individual buildings. At the highest point was the grand Council Chamber with its lofty dome. There, atop the hill of the Middle Ward was the library, and set behind it, the solid, reddish stone of the Water Works building. The blackened scar of what remained of the Pike stretched away from the harbor and merged with the glittering windows of the merchant houses of the Glass District.

"It really is something," breathed Will. He glanced over his shoulder and his eyes widened. "I don't know if we're going to make it, though. Look, Cor!"

Somehow Imago had halved the distance between them. The fleet was now passing the Eye.

"He's almost on us, Vic!" Will shouted.

Cora joined in. "Please, Victoria, Imago is catching up! Just a little farther!"

The sea serpent heard and the boat shot forward.

As they entered the relatively calmer waters of the harbor, Cora could see that the docks and wharf were empty of fisherfolk and merchants and sailors, empty of everyone, in fact, except for two figures that stood at the end of the south pier. One of them wore a bright red coat.

"It's Mr. Blackwood!" Cora cried out, "And the new Master of Tides! He got the message!"

Victoria was spent; the snake's sides heaved with exertion. With one last effort, it jerked its massive head and sent the boat toward the pier.

"Cora!" Mr. Blackwood's voice boomed across the water. "As I live and breathe, you've done it! Quickly now, girl! We haven't any time to spare!"

The boat approached the dock at a glide, and Will tossed the rope to Mr. Blackwood as it slid in beside the pier.

"The Sand Coin, Cora, pass me the Sand Coin!" said Mr. Blackwood as he secured the boat. Cora scrambled up the ladder, the gritty, white disc clutched in her hand.

Mr. Blackwood and the new Master of Tides stood side by side. The new Master was a tall, thin man, and his seafoam-colored robes flapped in the wind.

"Tarian thanks you, child," he said as he held out his hand.

Cora gave the new Master the Sand Coin, but to her surprise he didn't put it on. Instead, he handed it to Mr. Blackwood.

"What are you doing?" she demanded.

"You really have made a mess of things, Cora," said Mr. Blackwood. "I tried to keep you out of this, I really did." His eyes were filled with sadness, regret, but there was resolve there too. "I wish you hadn't involved yourself."

"What are you doing?" Cora repeated.

"I'm returning the Sand Coin to its rightful owner: Imago."

"*What?*" shouted Cora and Will together. He had joined her on the pier and they now stood together, facing Mr. Blackwood and his companion.

"You wouldn't understand. Now step aside, children."

Mr. Blackwood, a traitor. Cora's knees almost gave out.

"You're the one who doesn't understand," said Will. "You may have promised the Sand Coin to Imago, but the Sand Coin is rooted here. Imago is coming to Tarian to destroy the city. Apparently, that's the only way he can use the Sand Coin's power. If you give it to him, we all die."

"Nonsense," said Mr. Blackwood. "I'll only say this one more time: Step aside."

When neither Cora nor Will moved, the man beside Mr. Blackwood—the man Cora had thought was the new Master of Tides—flicked his wrists and thin, curved blades appeared in his hands.

"Mr. Fallow, no!" shouted Mr. Blackwood, but the man ignored him and lunged at Cora and Will with a snarl. Without thinking, Cora ducked under the man's knives, darted forward, and snatched the Sand Coin from Mr. Blackwood. As Will crashed into Mr. Fallow, Cora backed away, but she was at the end of the pier. She was trapped.

"It has to be you, Cor!" shouted Will as he grappled with the man. "It's the only way!"

Mr. Blackwood leapt forward, his hands outstretched toward the Sand Coin. With nowhere else to go, Cora stepped off the pier and plunged into the swirling sea.

The icy, foam-flecked waters closed over her and she sank like a stone. The dappled light above dimmed as she was swallowed by the vastness of the deep. Cora clung to the Sand Coin, and tried to kick, but despite her struggles she sank deeper and deeper into darkness. *All this was for nothing.* The thought skittered across her mind. *Tarian is lost.*

There was nothing she could do to slow her descent. The pressure on her ears moved quickly from uncomfortable to painful. Her lungs began to burn. Cora knew she wouldn't be able to hold her breath long enough to get back to the surface.

And then her feet hit the bottom of the harbor. She tried to launch herself upward, but she could not command her legs. It was as if she were shackled to the spot.

Panic gripped Cora, and she tasted bile in her throat, and all the sounds of the entirety of the sea roared in her ears.

And then the Sand Coin began to glow. Its pale light illuminated the darkness around her and its leather cord twisted like a tendril of smoke before her, and in that moment, Will's words echoed in her mind: *It has to be you, Cor!*

With shock, she realized he had meant that she could be the Master of Tides, no, that she *had to be* the Master of Tides. *But I don't want to be,* she thought. *I can't be. I wouldn't know what to do.* She stared at the Sand Coin, floating before her, and the all-too-familiar fear of the sea gripped her heart. *I'd rather die.*

Her lungs were on fire. She had only to take a breath and it would all be over.

But if not me, what then? Cora looked up, half expecting to see the bellies of Imago's ships, far above, sail into the harbor, but the darkness of the deep covered her like a shroud. *If not me, Imago wins. If not me, Imago captures Victoria again. And probably Will too. And he'll destroy Tarian.*

The roar of the sea thundered through her. Cora reached for the Sand Coin and pulled the looped leather cord over her head.

CHAPTER THIRTY-ONE

THE MASTER OF TIDES

IN AN INSTANT, THE LIGHT from the Sand Coin went
out and all became silent. Deep within Cora there was a sudden
twisting, a writhing, a tearing. She felt her insides shift as every
fiber of her being was unraveled like the strands of a rope. Stars, white
hot and blinding, filled her vision as she was torn apart thread by thread,
and the pain of it was almost too much to bear. Cora clenched her teeth
and her fists, and was unmade.

And then, after an eternity, or perhaps after only a moment, she
felt herself being woven together again in a new way. She could feel the
currents of the sea inside her, flowing around her muscles and ligaments,
just below the skin. She could feel water, thick with salt and seaweed,
coursing through her veins. She could feel the pull of the moon in her
mind, and the enormous power of the tides at the edge of thought. And
the need to take a breath was suddenly gone.

Cora opened her eyes and she could now see through the darkness.
Enormous stones littered the harbor floor around her and the broken
remnants of a shipwreck were half-buried in the mud beside her. Silver
fish darted among bunches of pitch-black seaweed that waved slowly in

the current. Cora turned and saw the posts of the pier rising like giant trees into the emerald light above.

Immediately, her only thoughts were for her friends and the threat they faced from Imago. No longer anchored to the sea floor, Cora shot upward toward the light. She rose through the swirling waters, and when she broke the surface, Imago's ships were almost upon her.

She braced herself, her feet supported by the waves, and without really knowing how, she pulled in the tides. She pulled, and a mountain of water formed beside her in the harbor, a monstrosity that reminded Cora of what she had seen in the Storm. Higher and higher she pushed it. And then she released it on the foremost ship.

It fell with astonishing speed, with enough force to crush a city, but it never reached the ship. Instead, it struck something above the vessel and sluiced harmlessly away on either side.

Through the spray Cora saw Imago standing in the forecastle, one hand held above him. He twisted his other hand, and a blue ball of fire appeared. An instant later it arced through the air toward her.

Reflexively, she pulled the tides to herself like a shield, like a cloak, like a second skin, and the fireball was swallowed with a hiss.

It worked, but it had been a mistake. Suddenly she felt weak. The weight of the water pulled at her, dragged at her like chains, threatened to overwhelm her. Cora released the tides and staggered, gasping.

Imago smiled. He formed another fireball and hurled it at her.

She dropped below the surface of the harbor, her mind racing. Cora did not know how to wield this power effectively. She was no magician, but Imago was, and he would make short work of her if they continued to fight toe-to-toe.

On the edge of her perception, something stirred. It was like a great creature, somewhere distant in the vastness of the sea, rousing from its slumber. What it could be, Cora couldn't possibly imagine, but the power she sensed, even over so great a distance, made her tremble.

She pushed the awareness aside with desperation. This was all so new, so unfamiliar, and she couldn't allow herself to be overwhelmed by whatever it was. No, she had to deal with the matter at hand, and that was Imago.

Tentatively, Cora reached inside herself and assessed her strength. It was not gone, but what she had done to defend herself from the magician's attack had caused her power to lessen dramatically. Which meant that when she struck next, it would have to be a decisive blow that Imago wasn't expecting.

She breathed in the brine and slowly, agonizingly, drew in the power of the tides once more. She reached out, through the waves, and found Imago's ships, floating in formation behind him. She felt the sea lapping at their hulls, and an idea came to her.

Cora took hold of the currents at the bottom of the harbor and redirected them into a circular path on the harbor floor beneath the fleet. She guided the waters, and as she fed them, they swirled around faster and faster, their pull growing in strength with each revolution. The result was a maelstrom, a whirlpool of churning mud and spinning bubbles that sucked the water from above down into a vortex. But she needed the water to go *somewhere* for this to work. Could she . . . ? *Yes.* Cora directed the spinning water into Harbor 1, sending it into the network of pipes of the Water Works.

Cora, still below the waves, made her way to the pier and held onto a post and waited. The waters continued to swirl on their own, and they continued to pull in more and more of the sea. In minutes, all the water in the entire harbor had moved toward the rotating spiral.

She could see the bottoms of Imago's ships that were nearest to her, as they were caught in the whirlpool. Two collided, and a deep splintering sound reverberated through the water. Another collision. Then another as the whirlpool gained speed.

Finally, Cora surfaced again. The fleet was in disarray, spinning toward the center of the vortex. Imago's ship spun with the others, and the magician, his hands raised, was looking down and seemed to be casting a spell to counter what she had done. This was her chance. Cora gathered herself and gathered the tides. She pulled them in, slowly, hand over hand like her father used to pull in his nets, and began to give the water shape.

Behind and above her, the bell in the clocktower in the Great Square rang out one, two, three times. And suddenly Cora remembered: Today was the Turn.

In a panic, she opened her mind and cast it out over the waves. The unknown thing, the giant creature that she had sensed awakening from its sleep somewhere in the distant deep, was no longer distant. It had come. With terrifying speed and power, the tidal surge had come.

CHAPTER THIRTY-TWO

AFTER

THE MASTER OF TIDES LOOKED out over the Eastern Deep from her tower beside the wharf of Tarian. The sea was calm and sparkled in the late afternoon light. Below her gulls wheeled, their thin cries drifting up on the wind. The harbor bustled with activity as ships docked and unloaded and set sail. It was difficult to believe that it had looked so different just a few days before.

Cora's battle with the tidal surge had almost proved to be too much for her. And yet, somehow, she had stood and grappled with the waters for three days, wrestling with whatever mind controlled them, despite barely understanding her own power. She had simply acted on her instincts. Cora knew, though, that she had also been very lucky.

She glanced down at her hands, half-expecting them to look different—she could feel the waves in them, the ebbing of the tides—but they appeared as they always had.

Three ships near the middle of the harbor drew her attention. They were, by her order, searching the harbor floor for any sign of Imago. Wreckage from his fleet was plentiful, but Cora had hoped to find something that showed definitively that the magician was dead. Imago's ships had been swallowed during her fight with the tidal surge, she had been told, and their broken pieces were still being pulled from the water, but there had been no sign of the magician himself. Even as she watched, Cora knew—she wasn't sure how—that the divers had been unsuccessful again today. She sighed. Perhaps they would find something tomorrow.

There was a whisper in the air. Cora shivered and rubbed her arms, then turned and composed herself. She straightened her robes and touched the Sand Coin lightly with one hand. The walkway that ringed the top of the Iron Spire curved away to her left until it disappeared from view around the edge of the tower. After a moment she heard a door open, then footsteps.

When Will appeared, Cora sighed with relief.

"Has it been that bad?" asked Will. He now openly wore his sword at his side and had dispensed with his cloak. "That you'd actually rather see me than someone else?" He grinned. "Does that mean we're friends? After all this time?"

Cora rolled her eyes but ignored his questions. Instead she asked, "How's Victoria?"

It had been Will who had found their friend on the rocks south of the harbor while Cora had struggled with the surge. Victoria had transformed from a sea snake into a girl once more, and had been unconscious and barely alive.

"Getting better. She . . . woke this morning."

"And? Is she still . . ." Cora couldn't bring herself to ask the question.

"Human?" finished Will. "Yes. There's a change in her, but she's still human, despite her shift. She asked for you, Cora. Can you go visit her? She's too weak to come up here."

Cora's stomach twisted. She wished she could explain it to Will, but she wasn't sure she understood it herself. She was compelled to be here at the top of the tower, compelled to guard the city from this spot. After the tidal surge had retreated, she had been exhausted, but despite her desire for rest, she had felt a stronger desire to come here first. The pull, the gravity of the Spire, was impossible to resist for long—it was too strong. Most alarming, though, was that the desire to be here crowded out everything else. Victoria, Will, they were secondary now. It bewildered her. It frightened her. All she could manage to say was, "I want to go see her, more than anything, Will. But I can't. I just . . . can't."

Will cocked his head and after a moment he nodded. It looked like he wanted to ask more about it, but instead he said, "There are a couple more things I need to tell you. The first is about Mr. Blackwood. We still can't find him. He and Mr. Fallow were seen leaving the wharf and going into the Glass District. Someone did claim to have seen two men being dragged into an alley near the edge of the Glass District, but it was just one report. I looked into it, but couldn't find anything. They're just gone."

Cora chewed her lip. "Will the Council keep looking?" she asked.

"I think so," said Will. He hesitated, and then said, "But maybe you should issue an order or something. Don't forget, you're in charge now."

She sighed. The truth was, Cora didn't know *how* to be in charge of a city, let alone how to be the Master of Tides. It was all so much to take in, too much to understand and navigate. But they did need to find Mr. Blackwood. He had to be held accountable for what he had done. "I'll do it," she said.

"Cor." She looked up to see Will was staring at her. "I know this is new and you don't feel like you know what you're doing. It's probably really scary for you. But you *can* do this. And, if you'll let me, I'd like to help you. I meant what I said on the boat about being your friend and being there for you. That goes for nightmares as well as being the Master of Tides. I mean, I don't know what I'd do—"

"Yes," said Cora, interrupting him.

"Yes?" Will looked surprised.

Cora knew she couldn't do this alone. And Will *was* a friend, she had to admit. After days of struggling to adjust to this new reality, Will's words were sure things, steady things in the storm that Cora now found herself sailing in. "Somehow I'm the new Master of Tides," she said. "I think Imago escaped and I'll probably have to face him again. But whether he's alive or dead, Will, I don't know what I'm doing. Really, I haven't known what I'm doing since this whole thing began. But through it all you've been there with me. So yes, you can help me. I'd be honored."

Will let out a low whistle. "Cor, I'll be honest, I never thought—"

"It's 'Cora'," she said, but she spoiled it by smiling.

He made a mocking bow.

"Don't make me regret this, Will. Now what was the second thing you were going to tell me?"

Will's face became serious. "I know you have a lot going on, but . . . have you noticed that the Sky Lords haven't changed over?"

"What do you mean?"

"The Mountain Cat and the Firefly and the Rabbit haven't emerged from the Rift. They should have come out at the Turn. The autumn Constellations are gone too. The other six are still in the sky, or they were last night, anyway."

Cora rubbed her forehead. "I hadn't noticed. Has this ever happened before?"

"I went to the university and asked around. This is the first time anything like this has ever happened. And the scholars, they're worried."

"Because of Augrind."

Will nodded. "The Sky Lords are guarding him. Or they're supposed to be. And when six of them are suddenly unaccounted for, well, it's not a good sign."

A wordless whisper drifted through the Iron Spire, a whisper only Cora could hear. She glanced past Will along the walkway. "Someone's coming," she murmured. Will looked at her curiously, but moved around to stand beside her.

She heard the door open. The six remaining members of the Council strode into view. They were imposing figures, with stern faces and long gray robes. The foremost, Chief Councilor Wickett, said, "Forgive us for the interruption, Master, but there is someone here who insists on speaking with you. She says she was sent by one of the Constellations."

Cora barely nodded and the members of the Council stepped aside to reveal a young woman. She wore a travel-stained cloak the color of the forest, and her red hair hung in two braids over her shoulders. Cora's breath caught.

It was Hildi.

MEETING

IMAGO RAISED HIS HAND AND pressed his palm against the carved letter on the stone. He trembled as he stepped into the shadow.

The forest shifted, twisted, transformed. It was like he had stepped into a black fog. The magician cleared his throat and glanced around nervously before he could stop himself. He hated allowing his unease to show, even if no one was around to see it.

The darkness that permeated this place was heavy, uncomfortable even for him. But it had to be borne. He looked up at the red-tinged sky and began to speak.

"Astoria. Principa. Dimus. Cervi. Limbus." The magician continued on through the list, until he had spoken all thirteen names. Then he gathered his cloak tightly in one hand and waited.

He felt it first. A slight shaking of the ground. Then a low rumble, like a distant avalanche, or thunder just over the horizon. And then came the wind.

Imago stood firm as the trees around him bent in the gale, as the crimson sky above him flickered black. The muddy earth heaved and the magician staggered and almost fell. Above, the clouds roiled. They looked like dull embers. And then the howling of the wind ceased.

Augrind stood before him. The smell of rotting death mingled with white-hot fire was all but overpowering.

Imago leaned back as he looked up. The Emperor of the Night, wrapped in a robe of decaying leaves and ragged dreams, gazed down at him. His was a terrifying face to behold. Piercing blue eyes peered at Imago out of what looked like a mask but was not. Augrind's face resembled the broken skull of a deer, its pieces sewn together with leather and bark and vines. Broad, twisted antlers spread from the top of his head and appeared to reach like claws into the sky above him. He lifted a hand, or what might pass for a hand, and said, "Greetings, small one. Are my captors captive?"

"They are, Master. The Firefly and the Mountain Cat and the Rabbit are contained, as are the Fox and the Fish and the Raven. They are imprisoned beside you in the Rift. The chains that bind you work equally well on them."

Augrind's laughter shook the ground and echoed through the dream. "And you have the Sand Coin? Its power, combined with the power of the tokens should be more than enough to break my bonds and awaken me."

Imago worked moisture into his mouth. "Master, I was unable to secure the Sand Coin."

Augrind stared at him for several moments and the magician forced himself to meet his gaze. Then Augrind tilted his head and his eyes narrowed into slits of blue fire. "My patience is growing thin. Your failures multiply."

"My failures? I captured six of the Sky Lords! I created and distributed the tokens that have given you strength! I've—"

"You failed me at Dragon Rock. You failed to take Sidyn. You failed to control the Storm I showed you how to summon. It was to destroy Tarian and it did not even come close to the city. And now you have failed to acquire the Sand Coin."

Imago knew he was in dangerous waters. He spoke carefully, his tone neutral. "There is still a way forward, Master. We still have your nightmares."

"The strength they harvest is not enough," growled Augrind.

The magician held up his hands. "Not yet, but it is *almost* enough. Thousands of tokens are now being used. And if you make a concerted effort to sow the seeds of nightmares throughout the Islands, those people that have the tokens but are not using them, they will change their minds. They will put on the tokens, adding to your power. And those that do not . . . well, you will still get *something*, some small scrap of strength from their dreams. And every little bit helps, does it not?"

Augrind's glittering eyes did not blink. Then he said, "I will rain down nightmares like fire. They will cover Hibaria and the Islands, and for your sake I hope they are enough."

Imago gave a deep bow. "They will be enough, Master."

"And the remaining Sky Lords? Can you withstand their efforts to free those you've managed to imprison?"

"I can," said Imago.

"We will see. Until next time, small one."

The wind rose, almost tearing Imago's cloak from his shoulders. The trees in front of him creaked and groaned, then broke in half like brittle bones and were swept away in the gale. The air crackled and hummed with power. There was a blinding flash of darkness and the magician reeled and fell to the ground.

The silence was sudden. Imago got to his feet and when his vision returned, he was alone in the dark forest of the dream. The trees around him were whole again, black and twisted and tortured, reaching toward the blood-red sky.

It was almost as if Augrind had not been there at all. Almost.

As he turned to go, the magician grimaced and covered his nose and mouth with his cloak, but it could not mask the smell of death and burning that lingered in the air.

Thank You

Thank you to all who walked with me during the writing of this story. Writing is lonely and difficult and a great way to become intimately acquainted with discouragement. Writing is also wonderful and something I can't not do. So I'm grateful for the people who have journeyed beside me during the long and arduous shaping of this novel. You have repeatedly told me to keep after it, and for that I am forever in your debt. I'm even more grateful for those of you who managed to do this without rolling your eyes.

About the Author

Jamin Still, the accomplished artist and storyteller, found recognition and success with his book *Tales of Hibaria: The Awakening*. From his early days as a prolific young artist and writer to his circuitous journey through education and ministry, Jamin's path has been marked by creativity and dedication. Today, he continues to breathe life into the captivating world of Hibaria, leaving a lasting impact on readers and art enthusiasts alike.

jaminstill.com
facebook.com/jaminstillart
instagram.com/jaminstill